PRESSING PROBLEMS

PRESSING PROBLEMS

*

VERONICA BIRD

THE
COMPANION BOOK CLUB
LONDON AND SYDNEY

THE COMPANION BOOK CLUB

The Club is not a library; all books are the property
of members. There is no entrance fee or any pay-
ment beyond the low Club price of each book.
Details of membership will gladly be sent on
request.

Write to:
The Companion Book Club,
Odhams Books, Rushden, Northants.

Or, in Australia, write to:
The Companion Book Club,
C/O Rigby House Books, P.O. Box 252
Dee Why, N.S.W. 2099

*Made and printed in Great Britain
for the Companion Book Club
at The Pitman Press, Bath*
600 872904
383/389

Chapter One

LAST NIGHT I dreamed of a village called Piscop, where once I was happy. It is a few miles north west of Paris, and there is a hotel there, the Robin des Bois – Robin Hood, I suppose. The hotel is a small château, turreted, like a fairy-tale castle illustration from a child's story book. It is set beside a lake, and there is a bridge over the lake, and swans glide white on the water.

In my dream I was trying to find my way back to the château before the darkness came. I wasn't sure that it was there any more. It might have been closed up or knocked down. Last time I drove through that part of France the bulldozers had been busy, and the fields had given way to skyscrapers.

It was dusk, and I was carrying a child, a little boy. He was heavy, and I was tired and desperate. The ground was rough and perilous, and I was afraid to put him down because there were snakes which came out to copulate in the night. I hurried, faster and faster, my feet scarcely touching the ground. It was June, and in the hedgerows the poppies were like splashes of blood in the twilight.

It was June when it all began. The night had been stiflingly hot, and I had tossed and turned under the duvet, unable to sleep. At about two a.m. I had got up, removed the duvet, taken a tepid shower, flung open the windows and managed to fall asleep. I awoke to the noise of London traffic, and sunlight streaming into the bedroom. I put my hand across the bed beside me, and it was empty, and I felt the sense of desolation and loneliness that I always knew when I woke alone, with no-one beside me.

Tired after the fitful night, I dozed again; but another buzz, apart from the traffic, awakened me. Toby stood in the doorway between the bedroom and the bathroom, shaving with his battery razor.

'I thought you'd gone to work,' I said. 'I was feeling sad, because you hadn't said goodbye.'

Toby smiled at me. He was wearing only a small white towel tucked round his waist. He was exactly on the brink of middle age, and it fascinated me. At some angles he still looked like the outstandingly handsome young man he must once have been. At others, there was a glimpse of the fleshy degeneration to come, when expense account lunches and too much alcohol had taken their toll. Most times I only saw the younger version, particularly when he smiled with that attractive, lazy radiance, as he did now.

'I wouldn't go to work without kissing you,' he said.

I held out my arms, and he came to me.

'Are you going to be late tonight?' I asked.

'No, I should be back at the usual time. Would you like to go out to dinner? The heat is obviously going to be unbearable again. We might drive out along the river somewhere, and find a country pub to eat at.'

'That sounds appealing,' I said, 'but I've already got some veal in the fridge, and it'll be wasted. The forecast is that the hot weather is going to last some days. Maybe we could do it tomorrow?'

'We can do it any time you like,' Toby said, 'but right

6

this moment I've got to get off to a meeting. Any chance of some breakfast?'

I got out of bed and, while he dressed, I made scrambled eggs and coffee, and watched him while he ate them. When he had disappeared through the front door, I poured myself another cup of coffee, had a shower, and considered my wardrobe. I took out a cotton suit in a brilliant peacock blue, and a white silk blouse, got dressed, and looked at myself in the full-length mirror. The colour went well with my short, dark hair, and the effect was striking, but not particularly feminine. I took off the jacket and blouse again, and removed my bra. The thin silk of the blouse clung to my breasts. Give the gentlemen something to think about in those boring meetings they kept on arranging, I thought.

I cleared the kitchen clutter into the dishwasher, locked up the flat and collected my car from its reserved space behind the block. I joined the long crawl up the Cromwell Road to work. Although it was still only nine o'clock the heat was already building up, and overheated cars clogged the road, making the journey into the office take twice as long as usual.

The offices of the United Magazine Company were housed in a new block in West London, only a couple of miles from where I lived. It was sheer idleness to take my car, but I hated the dirt and crowds of the Underground. I drove into the basement car park, and took the lift up to my fifth floor office. The door was labelled HILARY TOOGOOD. It's my real name. I used to be teased about it at school: 'Hilary Toogood, too good to be true,' they used to mick, and of course they were proved to be right. It was a good name for my present job, anyway, I couldn't have done better if I'd invented a pen name. It was easily remembered, and sensible sounding.

The chill of the air conditioning was a welcome relief after the stuffy car. Ruth, my secretary, had obviously

7

been in for some time, and there was the inviting smell and sound of freshly percolated coffee bubbling away in the electric coffee maker.

Ruth said: 'There's been a call from the telly to ask if you'll take part in a discussion programme this afternoon on the new best-seller about women and sex. I've put cuttings of the reviews of the book the programme is to be based on on your desk. And God's on the rampage already – he's had an idea in his bath.'

I said, 'Which telly? Beeb or ITV? And I'm glad to hear that God's had a bath. He was suffering from B.O. last week, in spite of the air conditioning.'

Ruth said, 'ITV. Shall I tell them yes or no? And d'you want God to know you're here yet, or not?'

'Tell the telly yes,' I said. 'And I'll have my coffee and deal with the post before I face God.'

God was our illustrious and illiterate Editor, Gerry O'Dwyer. Gerry was an ebullient Irishman who had clawed his way up from the gutters of Liverpool to become editor of one of the most powerful women's magazines in the country. His parents were literally illiterate, which is how they came, unknowingly, to give him the initials of G. O'D. Gerry learned to read and write, though not to spell, and became an office boy on the *Liverpool Post*, from where he progressed to being a telephone reporter – an important title for the not-so-important copy-typist who sits with earphones receiving dictated stories from reporters out of the office. Eventually he became a reporter himself, moved to Fleet Street, and became Features Editor of a Sunday newspaper. He met our Managing Director at a press reception, and sold himself to her – he's a superb salesman. When the last Editor of *Herself* flew out of the building in a menopausal tantrum, God was invited to occupy the vacant editorial chair.

I wanted to unwind slowly from the rushed start to the

8

day before dealing with God's exhausting enthusiasm. I went through to my office, which was dark and cool. The blinds were partly drawn to keep out the brilliant sunshine, and Ruth had filled the vase on my desk with early sweet peas, white ones; she knew my predilection for white flowers. The room was quiet and fragrant. On my desk were all the day's papers, some cuttings of the reviews of the book on women and sex, and a pile of letters from readers. These had been opened, and were stapled to their envelopes in a neat pile.

I read the reviews first, to prepare myself for the afternoon's discussion programme, and then I started dealing with the letters. Being Family Affairs Editor encompassed a multitude of assorted tasks. I dealt with the health section, the problems page, the cookery department and the horoscopes. The first three I suppose did come roughly under the heading of family affairs, but for the life of me I couldn't see why horoscopes came into my province. God had ordained it so, and brooked no argument. I suspected that the real reason was that he didn't hit it off with the astrologer, a domineering elderly lady who swept into the office from time to time, and from whom God wanted to be protected.

My first task each day was to decide who should deal with the readers' problem letters, and mark them accordingly. For example, did the reader who complained of painful intercourse have a physical problem, to be dealt with by the retired nurse who answered our health letters (mostly by encouraging the writers to consult their own doctors) or was it an emotional problem, to be dealt with by our agony auntie, a social worker/counsellor? Whoever actually replied, those replies which were selected for publication always appeared under my name.

'Dear Hilary Toogood, Should I move into my boyfriend's flat? I am twenty and have always lived

at home but I met a young man at a disco six months ago, and we have been going steady ever since. Now he wants me to go and live with him, but I don't know how to break it to my parents and . . .
Hilary Toogood says: This is a move you should consider very carefully . . .'

The postbag was always heavy on a Tuesday: problems which women had worried about over the weekend, and on which they were too embarrassed or fearful to consult their doctors, or about which they didn't know whom to turn to. Parents, money, sex, teenagers, in-laws. Anxieties about cancer, babies, rashes, discharges, lumps, warts, deformities, abnormalities. Am I normal? What should I do? What do you think? I don't know whom to turn to . . .

I worked steadily through the pile of post, marking each letter with the initials of the expert who was to deal with it, and then there was one which made me stop, and read it again, and then again, and then sit, with thudding heart, unable to think of anything at all.

It was typed on cheap, white paper, and when I turned it over and looked at the envelope it was postmarked London, Friday. The address at the top was 15, Overstrand Mansions, London SW6. Like all the others, it began, 'Dear Hilary Toogood,' Then it went on:

I am a career girl, working for a large company in London. My husband's work keeps him out of town, and so from Mondays to Thursdays I live in a rented flat on my own.

'About a year ago, I met a man to whom I was very much attracted, and we began having an affair. My lover is married too, and neither his wife nor my husband knows about the affair.

10

'My lover is a Member of Parliament, and marriage between us is out of the question. It would be damaging to his Parliamentary career if our affair became public knowledge, and his wife would never give him a divorce. It would be damaging to my career, too. My problem is: should I give up my lover, and try to make a fresh start with my husband? Should I tell my husband about the affair? Don't ask me to give up my job, it means too much to me, and I could never do that. I have been happy up until now, but if someone found out about our affair, my whole world could collapse. I could lose everything.

Yours sincerely, Helen Turner.'

I felt cold, and shivered. I got up briskly and went to the door.

'Ruth, this air conditioning is altogether too much of a good thing. I feel quite chilled. Could I have some more hot coffee? And I need to make a private phone call. Please don't let anyone in, not even God, for the next few minutes.'

Ruth brought in more coffee, and then went out, closing the door carefully behind her. I picked up the red telephone, my private line, and dialled the public relations agency at which Toby was usually to be found in the mornings.

'Hilary?' he sounded cheerful. 'Is everything all right?'

'Toby . . . I've had a shock. I'm feeling worried. I've just had the most extraordinary letter. It sounds . . . it sounds just like us.'

'What d'you mean, it sounds like us?'

'The situation the writer describes – she says she's a career girl living in London, her husband's in the country, and she's having an affair with someone . . .'

11

'That must apply to hundreds of people. Well, dozens, anyway.'

'Yes, but she says that the man she's having an affair with . . . he's a Member of Parliament.'

'Oh.' Toby paused. 'Well, we're not unique, you know, darling. There are more than six hundred MPs, and though I don't suppose that *many* of them are as lucky as I am, I guess that there must be dozens having affairs, and some with career ladies with out-of-town husbands. It's just a coincidence.'

I shivered again. 'It's a funny coincidence, though, isn't it?'

'What are you going to do about it? The letter, I mean?' Toby asked.

I considered. 'I think I'll reply to it myself.'

'I'd love to know what you're going to say,' Toby said.

'I'll take the usual fence-sitting line, with conventional moral overtones,' I said. 'You have to be careful, these days. You never know when it isn't some other journalist sending made-up letters to a number of agony aunties, and publishing a selection of the replies in *Over 21*, or the *Daily Mail* Femail page.'

'Don't work too hard, darling,' Toby said. 'And don't worry. I'm due in a meeting in a moment. We'll talk about it tonight. I'll be home about seven.' He rang off.

Having told him about it, I felt better. Of course he was right, and it was a coincidence. No-one could possibly know anything about Toby and me.

I had met Toby at a dinner party about eighteen months ago, and he'd telephoned me the next day, ostensibly to discuss the work of a committee he was interested in, which was investigating adoption. We were both ripe for an affair, but it had taken several months for us actually to get into bed. Toby had never deceived his wife before, he said, and although I wasn't sure if it was true, I felt instinctively that if it was, he now had to make

12

the decision to do so alone, without any pressure from me. When we had finally made it, he had been an ardent and insatiable lover, making up for months of deprivation by a frigid and unloving wife. And as for me . . . well, that was another story.

The buzzer went. It was Ruth.

'Hilary, God's called again. I said that you were in, but tied up with the telly. I don't know how much longer I can hold him at bay.'

'Okay, Ruth, will you tell him that I'm on my way to his office?'

I swept the post into the out tray, with the exception of the letter from Helen Turner, which I put into the top right-hand drawer of my desk.

And that was the beginning of it all. But then, I had no inkling that from that day onward, my life was destined to be different.

Chapter Two

GERRY O'DWYER'S office was furnished in an extraordinary mixture of styles which gave an assortment of clues to his personality. He had photographs of himself everywhere: shaking hands with Royalty, speaking at dinners, boarding Concorde, presenting wheelchairs to handicapped children, judging a Miss World competition. There was a wall of covers of *Herself* magazine, and a vast modern cocktail cabinet which lit up inside when opened. His desk was huge, antique, with a cold, marbled top – like a mortuary slab, the staff joked – but he rarely sat behind it. He usually occupied one of the leather sofas in front of it, patting the seat beside him invitingly when female staff came in. They were usually wary, and sat on the sofa opposite.

Personally, I always thought that Gerry *talked* like a womanizer, but didn't act like one. I'd never heard of him jumping on anyone, and I believed that he would really have been quite alarmed if anyone had taken his sexual banter seriously.

He was sitting on the sofa scribbling when I went in, and when he patted the seat beside him, I took it.

'Darling girl,' God greeted me (he called all female members of staff 'darling girl' or 'sweetie,' all male members 'darling boy' or 'mate'), 'I had an absolute inspiration in my bath this morning.'

14

I managed to summon up an alert and interested expression. He needed no more than this for encouragement.

'Did you know,' God digressed, 'that Basil wears swimming trunks in his bath?'

Basil was our Advertising Manager. Compared with Gerry, he was rather prim. But then compared with Gerry, *anyone* was rather prim.

'Basil wears swimming trunks in the bath because he doesn't like looking down on the unemployed,' God said, falling about with laughter at his own joke while I waited patiently for him to come to the point.

'I had this flash of inspiration – we'll invite our readers to adoptagranny.'

I looked at God in a rather fazed way.

'To do what?'

'To adopt a granny,' he enunciated more distinctly. 'It's to be called the 'Adopt a Granny for *Herself*' scheme. You know how much our readers enjoy doing Good Works, and espousing Good Causes. What could be better than doing something for the Old Folks? I can just see it – pictures of sweet little old ladies in shawls, with *Herself* readers taking them home-baked cakes. *Herself* readers knitting bed-socks for grannies, perhaps – we'll have a knitting competition. Grannies playing with readers kids. Maybe readers taking grannies on seaside outings . . . Isn't it terrific? Do try and show a little enthusiasm, sweetie.'

'Where are we going to find the grannies?' I asked.

'That's where you come in, darling girl. Ring up an Old Folks' Home, and ask them if they'd like to be adopted.'

'And what about the grandpas, and the Sex Discrimination Act and all that?'

God pondered on this briefly.

'Well, they can be adopted too. White-haired old men, and sweet-faced old ladies – it's a sure-fire winner.

Look – here's some notes I made. Take them away and ponder on them, will you?

I gathered them up obediently.

'Everything else all right is it, darling girl?' God asked.

Was I looking pale, I wondered?

'It is now, though I had an altercation with the Art Department on Friday,' I said. 'They made nonsense of the diagrams for the stuffed mice, but fortunately I noticed before they went to the printers.'

'Stuffed *mice?*' God said.

'Yes, you know – they were part of the 'Toys to Make' section for the special pull-out.'

'Oh, toys,' God said. 'When you said stuffed mice, my thoughts turned to the cookery department.'

I laughed.

'I can think of more interesting things to stuff than mice,' God said, his eyes flickering over my breasts. 'On the subject of which – are you still living on your own in that flat, Hilary darling? When are you going to invite me to come up and see you sometime?'

'Come come, Gerry, what would Marjorie say?' I asked him.

'Ah, my lady wife.' He sighed on being reminded of her. 'But she'd never know, would she, sweetie? Any more than your old man knows what shenanigans you get up to while you're in the wicked city, and he's stuck out in the sticks.'

I was reminded of the letter, and that I had to deal with it, as well as with God's 'Adopt a Granny' notes, and sundry other matters, before going off to the television studios.

'I've got to go, Gerry. I'm on the mid-afternoon chat show.' I told him.

'Have it VTR'ed, won't you, then we can see the recording later? Okay sweetie, I won't keep you. Let

16

me see something from you on the 'Adopt a Granny' scheme this week, will you?'

I was in the bath that evening when Toby arrived home. I heard him let himself in and pause in the hall to call out, 'Hallo! Are you there?'

'I'm in the bath,' I shouted, and he came in with a bottle of wine in one hand, and a bunch of white roses in the other.

He bent down to kiss me, and then brushed aside the bath foam to look at me.

'Are we going to eat first, or afterwards?' he asked.

'Whenever you like. Thank you for the lovely roses,' I said.

'Are you tired?' he asked. 'Would you like to change your mind about going to dinner?'

'I'm paralytically tired – too tired to eat out. I was going to stick the veal in the oven, and I hoped that you might settle for that, with salad and cheese,' I said.

'What have you been doing?'

'God has an unbelievably awful scheme for adopting grannies . . . and I did a chat show this afternoon, on which I was attacked by a shrewish and strident women's liberationist with the unlikely name of Flora Cutting, who took the opportunity to launch an attack on *Herself* as being wholly and solely responsible for all the ills that beset women today. We were helping to keep women chained to the kitchen sink, she said, and reinforcing their domestic role instead of helping them to break out, break loose, break away, break up . . . We saw them as their husbands' chattels, so this was how they saw themselves, and they swapped sexual inter-course for life in semis instead of being free and open and natural and . . .'

'I thought women's liberationists were an extinct breed,' Toby said, clearly bored. 'What did you say?'

'Oh, well, I pursued the usual *Herself* policy of dignified, slightly amused rising-above-it-all, and said that many women were happy in a home-making role, found satisfaction in being wives and mothers, enjoyed their traditional work of caring for husband and children. You know.'

'Do *you* find satisfaction in your traditional role?' Toby asked. He was sitting on the bathroom stool, watching me. I let the bathwater out.

'Lots of satisfaction,' I said, and he enveloped me in a towel and his arms, and kissed me, and murmured that he couldn't wait. And we went through to the bedroom, and he was urgent and preoccupied. I cried out when he penetrated me, but he couldn't wait to rouse me fully, and I lay quietly enjoying his urgency.

He came quickly, and apologized and kissed my breasts and stomach, which were still damp from the bath.

Toby said: 'You're most aptly titled Affairs Editor'

I automatically corrected: '*Family* Affairs Editor', and he got up, and went, whistling, to the bathroom to wash. I got up and put on a kaftan and sandals, and went to the kitchen and lit the oven.

Toby came into the kitchen and opened the wine, and watched me arranging the delicate white roses in the tall black vase.

'You've already got roses in the sitting-room, I've just noticed,' he said. 'They must be the ones you brought back from Sussex at the weekend.'

I carried the white arrangement through to the sitting-room, and placed them on the bureau, and he followed me.

'Yours are quite different,' I said. 'These are sophisticated city ladies. The others are full-blown country peasants,' and indeed it was quite true. The garden

18

roses sat in a squat white jug on the low white table, a riot of mixed colours and full-blown vulgarity.

They were the only splash of colour in the black and white room. I had furnished the whole flat entirely in black and white. I hadn't intended it like that, it had just happened. It had begun, I suppose, when I had bought a lot of white units, and then low seating covered in black corduroy, and I had gone on from there. The carpets were black with white rugs, the pictures black and white etchings, and I even had a collection of black and white games – the infuriating kind where you have to get silver balls into tiny holes – in a big white basket on the coffee table.

'It's schizophrenic,' a psychiatrist friend had once said, laughing, on first seeing it, but I hadn't understood. It wasn't until many years later that I discovered that seeing things wholly in black and white is a symptom of some forms of schizophrenia.

Only on the balcony, which overlooks the playing fields, is there a riot of green. I have trees, shrubs, plants and trailing creepers hanging from macramé baskets, and throwing interesting dappled shadows in the evenings.

Now, Toby stood on the balcony, drink in hand, while I made the salad and put out cheese on the cheese board and called him to the dining-table.

After dinner, Toby said: 'I forgot. I've got something simply *amazing* to show you.'

And I laughed and said 'What, again? So soon?

And he said 'Patience, woman! No, it's something else, first,' and he went to get his briefcase from the hall. He produced from it a copy of *Penthouse* magazine, and opening it gave it to me.

And there, before my astonished gaze, was Ruth, my secretary, as I had never seen her before. Her dark hair, which she normally wore pinned into an attractive geisha style, was loose over her shoulders, and there were four pages of provocative poses of her, totally nude, with her legs spread wide. They were completely unretouched photographs.

'Wait till you read the captions,' Toby said, laughing at my expression. The caption story was indeed almost more unbelievable than the pictures it illustrated.

'Ruth is just a home body (and who wouldn't like to have a body like hers at home?)' one caption read. 'She's an old-fashioned girl with old-fashioned tastes – cooking, sewing, knitting and country walks.

'Ruth knows the way to a man's heart, and she knows how to keep a man happy.

'"I love doing things for a man. I can't get enough of it," she says. She is a girl of great taste, with a taste for all that's good!' (this below a picture of Ruth with her tongue out suggestively, and her eyes closed ecstatically.)

'Ruth is a talented designer with a novel line in knitting patterns – she makes extra special little gifts for the men in her life – willie warmers.'

I read this last line unbelievingly but, sure enough, the last picture showed Ruth, her legs enormously widely spread, with a pair of knitting needles and multi-coloured wool, knitting an unmistakable cylindrical shape.

'For special friends, Ruth makes snugly-fitting triple partitioned warmers, but never *too* snugly fitting – there's always room for expansion, she says,' the caption story went on.

It concluded: 'Ruth works as a secretary by day, and at night she is employed by an escort agency. She can escort us any day.'

Toby let out a hoot of laughter at my expression. When I had finished laughing, I said

'But how *could* she, Toby? Do you think it's true that

she moonlights for an escort agency? Oh, my Lord. What if the Snow Queen, our own dear Managing Director, sees this? Willie warmers and an escort agency . . . the Snow Queen will never stand for it. I shall lose an extremely good secretary.'

'Don't be silly,' Toby said. 'Knitting willie warmers and working for an escort agency aren't grounds for dismissal.'

'Working for an escort agency means screwing Arabs at London hotels,' I said. 'And that activity isn't compatible with working for *Herself*, a magazine of high moral tone which upholds the traditions of family life etcetera, etcetera. Just flashing her fanny in *Penthouse* is enough to get her thrown out, in my opinion.'

'Well, the Snow Queen probably doesn't read *Penthouse*,' Toby said.

'No, but I bet God does. And I wouldn't put it past him to show it to her.'

'Oh, no,' Toby said positively. 'Even if he does read it, I doubt that he would admit to it. And anyway, Ruth hasn't involved *Herself* magazine. What she does in her free time is up to her, isn't it? So I don't see why you should lose her at all.'

I picked up *Penthouse* again, and he peered at it over my shoulder.

'Her tits aren't as good as yours, and that enormous black bush is a bit off-putting,' Toby said, studying objectively the more intimate areas of my secretary's anatomy.

'Why do you suppose that she did it?' I asked.

'Money?' Toby suggested. 'Or a suppressed tendency towards exhibitionism?'

'I shall never look at her in quite the same way again,' I said.

'Nor will a lot of people, I guess', Toby said.

'What are you doing reading *Penthouse*, anyway?' I asked him.

'Well, I have to do something when you're away,' Toby said. 'Jean is so cold and rejecting I have given up trying as far as sex is concerned. I don't think you could ever have called it making love. So anyway, I don't bother her, and I have to do something. Perhaps you should knit me a willie warmer,' he mused 'capable of expanding of course.'

'As a kind of chastity belt?' I asked.

'Maybe not.' Toby kissed me. 'I'm awfully sorry, Hil darling, but I've got to go back to Battersea tonight.'

'Oh.' Something tightened inside me. That was why he'd brought me the roses. And why he'd made love to me earlier on. I swallowed the anger.

'D'you want to go to bed again before I go?' he asked.

'No thanks,' I said distantly.

'Hilary – you're not angry, are you?'

'You've got to go back because Jean's going to ring, haven't you?' I asked. It was against the rules by which we played, but I couldn't help myself asking.

'I'm sorry, Hilary,' Toby said. 'She called last night, and the other chaps in the flat covered for me. I tried to ring her from the office earlier today to forestall her, but she was out. Her mother's ill, you know.'

Privately, I wished her mother dead, and Jean with her. However, I said, 'I see,' and it only sounded a little cold.

Toby kissed me again.

'It should be okay for tomorrow,' he said, and I managed to smile.

I went to my lonely bed, and cried myself to sleep.

Chapter Three

THERE WAS AN unprecedented number of visitors to my office during the next week or so. By the following Wednesday, I calculated that every member of our Board of Directors had 'just popped down to see me' on one pretext or another instead of asking me to go up and see them, as they usually did. To a man, they paused to ogle Ruth, and exchange a little light banter with her.

The male members of the Art Department also found an exceptional number of queries that needed discussing with me. When I went into their room on the Thursday morning, I saw the copy of *Penthouse* on the Art Editor's desk, and wondered just how many more were circulating in the building.

By the Thursday afternoon, God had seen – or had been shown – one of them. He invited me up to his office for a drink, and asked if I knew. I said that I did.

'We must just hope that Shirley doesn't know,' God said. Shirley was the Snow Queen, our Managing Director.

I said firmly that I thought Ruth's private life was Ruth's private business.

'Not if it damages the magazine, it isn't,' Gerry said aggressively. 'Can you imagine what a good story it would make for *Private Eye* – that someone on this highly respectable magazine is a high-class call girl?

23

Particularly since she works in the Family Affairs Department. They'd have a field day. You'll have to speak to her, Hilary.'

'What d'you want me to say?' I asked.

'Well, tell her – tell her to be more bloody discreet, for a start.'

'She didn't mention *Herself*,' I pointed out.

Gerry let forth a strangled cry, and poured himself a large vodka and tonic.

'I should bloody well hope not,' he said. 'Anyway tell her to keep her private parts rather more private.'

So I did, more or less. I thought that it would be difficult, but in fact it was quite easy. Ruth said yes, she knew that pictures of her had appeared in *Penthouse*, and, yes, it was true that she worked for an escort agency some evenings. Not every evening, she said. If ever I wanted her to work late, there was no problem. I told her what God had said about *Private Eye*, and, being an intelligent girl, Ruth saw the point. No problem, she said. It's Ruth's favourite – and most comforting – expression. She utters it regularly and tranquilly, as crises come thick and fast, and she says it with such conviction that everyone believes her. She said that if *Private Eye* telephoned her, she would simply deny that it was she.

After all, Ruth said, one cunt looked much like another from that angle, didn't it? I gulped, and suggested that she omitted that last remark from any discussion with *Private Eye*, as it might get quoted. Ruth said that she'd been paid a lot for the pictures, but had had to kick the photographer in the balls afterwards, it hadn't been worth it, and she didn't think that she'd do it again anyway. I said thank you very much, and she said would I like some more coffee?

I didn't go home that weekend. We had ten readers and their children up in London for our 'Supermum Herself' competition, and I had to look after them. It was a full time job. Each lady had been nominated by her child for the title, which carried a prize of ten thousand pounds and a trip to Disneyland. The entrants, who numbered sixty thousand, had been whittled down to ten by the tie-breaker: '*My Mum's a Supermum because . . .*' in not more than ten words.

It was, I decided when I met the ten finalists at dinner at their hotel on the Friday night, a very ill-thought-out competition. To start with, we should have insisted on photographs. One supermum lacked front teeth, one was cross-eyed, and one was eight months pregnant. Most of them looked so eminently unattractive that it was difficult to imagine how they had become mothers at all. As the weekend wore on and we got to know them better, our trepidation increased. The one and only presentable one, for whom the photographers made a bee-line, confided in me that she was not actually married to Superdad. One of them was stoned out of her mind by breakfast time. And yet another was related to the Sales Director of Supermarge, which had donated the prizes.

This last competitor, I thought, might get us into considerable trouble if she won. The rules precluded the families of the sponsors from entering. I summoned the company lawyer, a barrister named Harry Bacup, who was known throughout the company as Harry Ballsup.

Harry, who had had a large liquid lunch, said that the competitor, a Mrs Withers, should be disqualified. Mrs Withers refused to accept disqualification. She had got the bit between her teeth, so to speak, and her eye on the ten thousand pound prize. She contended that she was not a blood relation of the Supermarge Sales Director. She just happened to be his father's second wife.

Harry argued that a stepmother was a relation, but he was no match for Mrs Withers. She threatened to call in her lawyers on the spot. After much wrangling, she finally agreed to withdraw from the competition on being promised a large, secret ex gratia settlement.

So I herded the remaining competitors, minus Mrs Withers, to the television studios, where the judges asked them their views on education, nutrition, corporal punishment, family size and other taxing subjects. Finally a winner emerged – the cross-eyed reader who, although thoroughly unphotogenic, was at least legally married, of sober habits and had the appearance of being unlikely to let down *Herself* by featuring in a child battering prosecution immediately on receiving the title. The photographers concentrated on Supermum's son and nominator, a pleasant seven-year-old tearaway who smiled gappily for them and said that his slogan had been '*My Mum's a Supermum because she's Superlative in every way*'. I found it difficult to believe that he had known the word 'superlative' and hatched the slogan unaided, but I decided to keep my suspicions to myself.

I took all the competitors and their offspring to a musical on the Saturday night, gave them Sunday lunch at a rooftop restaurant, and bade them goodbye on the Sunday evening with heartfelt relief and weariness. Toby had gone home to Jean, who lived in his constituency, for the weekend. I hadn't even had time to miss him.

It was on the Wednesday that the shock came. It was a routine day, with a lunchtime conference at the NSPCC, and a visiting foreign journalist in the afternoon. I was dealing with my post rapidly in the morning, therefore, when I found the letter halfway down the pile.

It was *my* letter to Helen Turner. It had been returned to me by the Post Office marked NO SUCH ADDRESS.

I looked at the address again – 15, Overstrand Mansions, London SW6. I checked with the original letter. It was correct. I checked with the A to Z. Overstrand Mansions was not listed.

So Helen Turner had given a false address. Well,

people sometimes did, and sometimes they gave no address at all. They had no idea that we received hundreds of letters, and they expected to see their own particular problems answered on the page instantly. They didn't know, either, that the magazine was printed six weeks before it reached the book-stalls, and rapid replies weren't possible.

Nevertheless, it made me uneasy. It was strange seeing my own advice returned to me – coming home to roost, you might almost say.

'Dear Helen Turner, (I had written)

'I am so sorry to learn of your unhappy situation. Perhaps you might ask yourself why it has arisen? What is lacking in your relationship with your husband which you find in that with your lover? Are you expressing some angry feelings towards your husband through this other relationship?

'Of course, from a practical point of view, it must be lonely for you without your husband, and I wonder if it is from choice or necessity that you live such separate lives?

'You say that you yourself stand to lose everything if your secret is discovered. Perhaps it would be a good idea to sort out your priorities and to decide if your career is really more important than your marriage. Do you love your lover enough to give him up? And why do you feel that you want to tell your husband?

'Obviously there is much more to your problem than you have been able to fit into one short letter. A marriage guidance counsellor would be able to help you to sort out your feelings and confusion. Please do write to me again if you feel that I can help you in the future.

Yours sincerely, Hilary Toogood.'

I extracted a few well-chosen sentences from the original letter I had received and from my reply, and typed them as copy for the next issue of *Herself*. I then put it all out of my mind, and went out to the press reception.

That evening, Toby took me out to dinner at Mon Plaisir, and I told him about it. As a mystery it was interesting as well as disturbing, but Toby thought that I made too much of it, or said that he did.

'So she gave a false address,' he said. 'She just didn't dare to give the true one. What if the letter fell into unscrupulous hands, and she was blackmailed?'

'But why give an address at all?' I asked. 'In fact, why write, since it's not possible for me to reply to her?'

'I expect that, like lots of your readers, she wanted a reply published on the page,' Toby said. 'And perhaps she's read one of those innumerable articles about agony aunties where they say that anonymous letters are thrown away. So she tried to make it seem as genuine as possible. Put it out of your mind, and let's talk about something more interesting. I'm going to a conference in Paris in October. Would you like to come?'

'I'd *love* to come,' I said. 'But what about Jean? Not to mention Martin. Isn't it a risk?'

'I don't think so,' Toby said. 'I'll book you in as a delegate, but of course you won't go to the sessions, you can go shopping or something instead. After the daytime work is over I'll cut the official dinners, and we'll eat *à deux* in small restaurants, and of course we'll have the nights together.'

'I see,' I said. I tried to look expressionless, but it hurt inside. I was not to be acknowledged, but kept hidden, and taken out secretly. We should not share a room, but I should go to Toby's, or he to mine, and creep back in the morning.

'What's the matter?' Toby said.

'Nothing,' I said, crumbling my bread and avoiding his eyes.

'Yes, there is,' he persisted.

'Oh, well . . . I suppose that I get fed up with the secrecy, sometimes.' I knew as I said it that this wasn't how the game was played. Never complain, never demand. Take what was offered and be grateful and cheerful.

Toby said: 'I know, darling. But that's how it has to be. Would you rather not come?' And although his voice sounded sympathetic, I heard the warning in it.

I shook away my mood and said instantly and cheerfully, 'Of course I understand, and I want to come *very* much. It'll be marvellous. How long is it for?'

'It starts on a Wednesday, and finishes on a Friday,' Toby said. 'It thought if you could manage it, we might stay on a day or so and come back on the Sunday.'

I felt heartened.

'That would be fun. Would we be able to stay in another hotel, move out of the conference one, I mean, and be Mr and Mrs Abbott?'

I knew that it was another mistake the minute I'd said it. Toby looked at me warily.

'Darling, you knew when this started . . .' he began, and I said hastily:

'I only meant metaphorically, of course. I mean, you have to give your real names in French hotels, anyway. I just thought that it would be good to share a double room with you, rather than scurrying down corridors and one of us have to go back to a cold bed. Making love is more exciting in a hotel bedroom, isn't it?'

Reassured, Toby took my hand.

'Yes, of course we can move to another hotel,' he said. 'The conference is being held in one of those Hiltonesque ones, and it would be more fun to be in a small, really French one in the centre, near l'Opera, perhaps.'

'With a mirror on the ceiling,' I suggested.

'Do you know one?'

'I'm afraid not, it was only an idea.'

But I had not headed him off by changing the subject.

'Hilary darling,' he said, stroking my hand, 'you're not getting too deeply involved, are you? I don't want you to be hurt. When we began this, it was just for fun, and we weren't going to allow it to become too serious for either of us. We agreed. You understood that I couldn't leave Jean because of my job, and because of the children, and you accepted that. If you're becoming too deeply involved now, perhaps we ought to reconsider.'

'I'm not,' I said, lying as countless millions of women have lied before me. 'I understand perfectly. It's quite all right, really it is. I don't expect anything at all of you that you don't want to give. I understand about the job and the children. It's fun to be together, and make love, and Paris should be terrific, really great. I know that it's just an affair, and has to end sometime. Let's make the most of it.'

I'm a convincing liar, because Toby was satisfied. Inside, I was hurting at denying my real feelings. Because I knew that I really loved Toby. It was no good pretending to myself that I didn't. It was all very well trying to apply the discipline which I had learned all those years ago, trying to pretend that it was all in the head, and that my heart did no more than pump blood round my body to keep me alive. Because this time I couldn't deceive myself. It became more and more difficult to behave like the copybook mistress and be always cheerful, welcoming, witty, sexually responsive, undemanding, unpossessive, unjealous, understanding, interested and interesting. I loved this man, really loved him. I wanted to have him, to marry him, to bear his children, to be passionate, to scream at him, to be jealous, possessive, angry, depressed, elated, tired and *natural*. To be able to be honest, unguarded, relaxed, *myself*, was a luxury denied to me. Whereas before, with other men, I hadn't cared, with Toby I did. I wanted to relate to him outside of the roles we had cast ourselves in, to strip ourselves of these roles, maybe, and confront each other naked.

And I knew that if I did, I would lose him.

I had to go on playing the game, and because I loved Toby, I was beginning to hate the game.

I felt as though it were a trap. What made it worse was that I had carefully and deliberately constructed the trap myself.

Toby was talking, and I hadn't heard anything he'd said.

'. . . So she was nagging about buying a house in London,' he said.

'What?' I said stupidly.

'Jean. She says she's fed up with being stuck out in the country, and she wants us to buy a house in London.'

'Oh, no,' I said, involuntarily, and he looked at me sharply.

'I mean,' I said quickly, 'we shouldn't be able to be together nearly so much, should we? You'd never be able to spend the night with me as you do now.'

'No, well, I'm fighting it,' Toby said.' But as I said, I wonder if it's significant? I mean, does she suspect something? Anyway, as I was saying, I think that I'll win over it, because the children are well settled in the local primary school, and it would mean taking them away, and a primary school in London might not be nearly so good. Particularly in the sort of area where we'd be able to afford a house, property costing what it does just now. And we could never afford private education. So I don't think it's really on the cards.'

31

'Oh Toby,' I said, resting my head on his shoulder, 'I'm tired. Let's go home to bed.'

Toby paid the bill, and drove me home in his Daimler. Later that night, under my black and white duvet cover, he said suddenly:

'It is all right, isn't it, Hil darling? I mean, you are happy as we are?'

'Of course I am,' I reassured him. 'I suppose it was just that my letter came home to roost from Helen Turner, and I had told her to think about her priorities. Maybe I started brooding on mine.'

'But everything *is* all right as it is?' Toby persisted.

'Everything is absolutely fine,' I said.

But two days later, on the Friday morning, everything was not fine at all.

Chapter Four

IT WAS THE first Friday of July, and Mrs Carstairs was due to make her quarterly visit to the office. Mrs Carstairs lived in a mansion flat in Battersea. Every three months or so, she emerged from the darkness of this rather cavernous dwelling to bring in her star forecasts for the next quarter. She did not trust her copy to Her Majesty's Post Office. She was probably better informed than we were about the possibility of mail strikes and hold-ups. Anyway, she always brought it in person, mid-morning, and took a glass of sherry with me and made a few portentous predictions before returning to her lair.

I was trying to clear my desk at top speed so that I could give Mrs Carstairs (who wrote 'Gipsy Rose Lee sees all') my full attention, when I was brought up short by the letter.

I knew even before I got as far as the signature that it was Helen Turner again. I read it twice, and then I got up and found the first letter, and compared the notepaper and the typing. They were identical. The typing looked familiar in a way I couldn't quite place.

Then I sat down, and read the new letter again, and felt frightened and sick and shaky and cold. I reached for the phone, and rang Toby.

Toby was in a meeting with a client, and it was obviously difficult for him to talk.

33

'I've had another letter,' I told him. 'I really want to talk to you about it.'

'Can we meet this evening?' Toby asked, clearly trying to sound as if it were a business matter.

'It's not possible. I've got to go back to Sussex for the weekend. I didn't go last weekend because of the Supermum competition, and I really have to. Are you free at lunchtime, by any chance?'

'I've got a business lunch, I'm afraid. Perhaps we could have a brief meeting before lunch? Say about twelve thirty, for half an hour or so?'

'Okay,' I said.

'Your correspondence . . . it's from the same people who contacted you previously, is it?' Toby asked.

'Yes, Helen Turner.'

'On the same subject?'

'No, not the same . . . but she knows something else. It's terrible, Toby, I'm so worried.'

'Oh, I don't think that you should worry about it,' Toby said, trying to sound businesslike and cheerful. 'We'll discuss it at twelve thirty, then, but I'm sure that we can cope with it for you. I'll just make a note in my diary. Where did you say?'

'I didn't,' I said. 'Can you make the wine bar?'

'Yes, that's fine,' he said heartily. 'See you then. No problem.' And he rang off.

I sat looking miserably at the hateful letter. My intercom buzzed.

'Mrs Carstairs is here,' Ruth said. 'Shall I show her in?'

I slipped the letter into the top right-hand drawer of my desk.

'Yes, okay,' I said, and even before I had hung up Mrs Carstairs, wearing a large, blood-red hat, swept into my office.

'Here we are again, Hilary darling,' she cried, bearing

34

down on me and kissing me with difficulty, because of the hat. 'My dear child, you do look pale. Are you well?'

I mumbled incoherently, looking shiftily away from her.

Mrs Carstairs was no mean psychologist.

'What is it, my darling?' she demanded. 'Something is the matter, I can see. Tell Mother all.'

I had a strong urge to do so, but I suppressed it.

'I'm feeling a bit off colour,' I said, smiling wanly. 'And how are you?'

'Now what has caused that, I wonder?' Mrs Carstairs said. 'You're Libra, aren't you, dear? Of course Uranus isn't very well aspected, and your Moon is in Pluto . . .'

At least I *think* that's what she said, anyway. I wasn't attending properly, I had a wild desire to giggle at her remarks about Uranus, but I often had an inclination to giggle when Mrs Carstairs was around, and I always managed not to. Like all astrologers, she took herself and her subject with deathly seriousness.

'It's a difficult time for you at the moment, isn't it, dear? Mrs Carstairs said. 'All Librans are finding the same thing. And I'm afraid that it's going to go on for quite a long while. But eventually, there's a silver lining, you know dear, if only you look for it.'

'What do you mean by eventually?' I asked, drawn into it in spite of myself.

Mrs Carstairs looked at me intently.

'Why don't you drop by my flat sometime, dear, and I'll give you a personal reading?' she invited. 'I can see that something is troubling you, and I think I know about it. You Librans always achieve the balance you are striving for eventually. Do come, and we will look at the cards together.'

I tried to shake off my feelings of apprehension and anxiety.

'Would you like a glass of sherry?' I asked her. 'How are things with you?'

'Thank you dear, I will partake,' Mrs Carstairs said. 'I must have a teensy word with you about those naughty sub-editors. They are supposed to send me a page proof each week, you know, and they haven't been doing it. What's more, they've been *butchering* my copy. Really hacking it about. If it doesn't fit, they simply chop a sentence off the end, and sometimes that alters the meaning of the entire forecast.'

'Oh, dear,' I said, weakly, 'I'm so sorry, I'll speak to them. Here's your sherry.'

'I'm off to the States soon, to advise on that company merger I was telling you about, so I've brought you some extra copy, to tide you over till I get back,' Mrs Carstairs said, handing me a large envelope. 'Now I wonder if you could speak to God about my fee, Hilary dear? It hasn't been increased for a year now, and with the cost of living going up as it is, I really can hardly make ends meet.'

'I did speak to him a few weeks ago,' I told her. 'And he said that you are our most highly-paid contributor anyway, and he really couldn't do anything until the new editorial budget at the beginning of the next financial year.'

Mrs Carstairs sighed. 'Parsimonious, isn't he, dear? Typical Scorpio, of course. But ask him again, anyway. Scorpios are in a benevolent mood at the moment.'

'Mrs C, dear, I really would have thought that you could perfectly well forecast what he's going to say – and it's going to be 'no' again,' I said with some asperity. 'When God says no, he means no. Perhaps that's a Scorpion trait too. If indeed he is Scorpio.'

Mrs Carstairs studied me intently for a few minutes. Then she leaned forward and said confidentially

'It's your hubby, isn't it, dear?'

'What do you mean?' I said.

'You're not yourself at all, Hilary, it's not like you to be sharp,' she said. 'It's a teeny problem to do with hubby, isn't it? I can see that it is.'

I didn't know what to say. I looked at her dumbly. She sipped her sherry and continued to regard me shrewdly.

'Well dear, I don't intend to pry,' Mrs Carstairs said. 'Any time that I can be of help, though, don't hesitate to drop by my flat. If you know your exact time of birth, I can cast your horoscope properly, and tell you exactly when the troublesome times will end. Well almost exactly. Timing is the most difficult thing of all for us, of course. We can see what is on the horizon, but not exactly how far away it is. It's all to do with the change in the calendar . . .'

I drank my sherry and thought my own thoughts. Her voice rose and fell in the background, but the words seemed a meaningless jumble. I refilled her sherry glass mechanically and she maundered on. She seemed to be talking about numerology. Eventually she finished her sherry, rose, and, rather flushed, patted her hat back into place.

'Well I mustn't detain you, dear,' Mrs Carstairs said. 'Busy busy busy, I expect. But don't overdo it, will you? You need to look after yourself these next few months. I shan't be very long in the States, so don't forget what I said, do come and see me if you'd like to, won't you darling?'

She kissed me, knocking her hat askew in the process, and made for the door. When she reached it she stopped and turned and said, 'And don't worry about the letters, will you dear?'

I felt as though my heart had given a lurch. How *could* she know? I said in a choked voice, 'What do you mean?'

'They're obviously worrying you,' Mrs Carstairs said.

'Yes, they are,' I said, sitting down suddenly.

'Well, don't let them,' Mrs Carstairs said.

'How did you know?' I asked.

'How did I know what, dear? That you got letters, or that you worried about them? Well, everybody knows what a big postbag Hilary Toogood gets. And I know Hilary Toogood, and you're a dear conscientious person and take it all *much* too seriously. Try not to. Try not to worry."

'Oh,' I said foolishly. 'I thought you meant Helen Turner.'

'Who?' said Mrs Carstairs.

'Never mind,' I said, making a Herculean effort to pull myself together. I stood up and managed to walk steadily towards her. I opened the door, and smiled. Mrs Carstairs saw the anxiety behind it.

'The darkest hour is just before the dawn, darling,' she reassured me. 'It'll all be right as rain soon, you mark my words. Now come and have a nice chat one day soon, and meanwhile, don't *worry*. Never trouble trouble till trouble troubles you, as my grandmother used to say. It'll all come out in the wash, won't it?'

She sailed out on a sea of platitudes. As the door shut behind her, I refilled my sherry glass, and took a large gulp. Was it my imagination, or had her first remark about the letters been significant? Had she passed it over lightly later, and pretended to be talking about the general correspondence? How could she have known? I looked to see if my desk drawer was shut. It was. I opened it, took both letters out, and put them in my handbag. I picked up my umbrella, and set out to meet Toby.

The wine bar which Toby and I used regularly was one of those trendy places with all the furniture painted green, and straw mats on the floor. Toby was sitting at one of the tables with two glasses and a half bottle of red wine in front of him when I arrived, and I slid in beside him and he took my hand.

'What is it, love?' Toby asked. 'Your hands are so cold.' He rubbed them between his. I didn't say anything.

'Drink some wine,' he ordered.

'I've already drunk quite a lot of sherry,' I told him, picking up the full glass of wine and sipping it.

'It's another letter, is it?' Toby asked. 'Have you brought it?'

I opened my bag and produced the two letters. He read the first one in silence, then he picked up the one which I had received in the morning. He read it twice, then put it down on the table and looked at me.

'Well,' he said. 'Well. Is it true?'

I nodded.

'You never told me,' Toby said.

'No, I didn't.'

He picked it up again.

'How do you know?'

'I caught him once. Accidentally. In the act, more or less.'

'But how could you let it continue?'

'Oh, Toby,' I said. 'Don't. Please don't. I suppose that's why I never told you. What could I do?'

'I've got a son,' Toby said, cold and angry. 'A little boy of ten.'

I was weeping. My tears melted the iceberg of his anger.

'Don't, darling,' he said, putting his arm round me. 'But how *could* you let it go on?'

'What could I do?' I said again.

'Did you talk to him about it?'

'Of course I did.'

'You could have left him.'

'I have, more or less,' I said.

'You still go back at weekends.'

'It's not him, it's the house. I grew up there. It's my roots, my security.'

39

'Well, throw him out.'

'How can I? It would mean the school would close. Then the house would have to be sold.'

'You mean that you let this – all this – go on just to keep your family home?' Toby demanded, indicating the letter. Anger was rising in him again.

'Only partly,' I said, tears rolling down my cheeks. 'It's him as well, I suppose. He was kind to me, at the beginning. I don't love him, but I don't hate him either. I feel sort of bonded to him. And if I tried to turn him out, to take away from him his home, his livelihood, it would finish him. Besides, he would fight. He said he would. He said he wouldn't go. The only way that I could do it would be by making it all public. And then he'd go to prison. He said he'd kill himself.'

'You would probably lose your job, too, of course,' Toby said, as the complications of the situation began to dawn on him. 'It would destroy both of you.'

'All of us,' I said. 'There's his mother, too.'

'But the children . . .' Toby said.

'I know. But if I did . . . what you suggest, some of them would be involved, too. They'd have to give evidence.'

We sat in silence for a while.

'Is it still going on?' Toby asked.

'I don't think so. He promised that it wouldn't. I think he probably didn't, for a while. But now – I'm not sure.'

'How long ago did you catch him?'

'About the beginning of last year,' I said. 'It had probably been going on for quite a long time.'

'And what are you going to do now?'

'Show him the letter.'

'Not both!' Toby said.

'No, just this one.'

'Maybe it's quite a good thing,' Toby said. 'Maybe it'll stop him.'

40

'Yes, but don't you see – it means someone else knows. Helen Turner. Who is she? And is she going to do anything else? If so, what? I'm frightened, Toby. How does she know? She knows about us, too. What else does she know?'

'What else is there to know?' Toby said. 'But I see what you mean. Do you really have to go to Sussex tonight? Can't you stay in London, and we can discuss it again this evening?'

'I've got to go. There's a Governors' meeting. I'm a Governor. And I've got to talk to him about it.'

'And I've got this bloody lunch,' Toby said. 'Well, look, there's nothing that we can do immediately, anyway. I don't know if there's anything we can do at all. Hire a private detective to find Helen Turner, perhaps. Or go to the police.'

'No,' I said.

'No. Well, let's think about it over the weekend, and perhaps by Monday some sensible course of action will have evolved. I hope . . .'

'What do you hope?' I pressed him.

'I hope that it isn't the beginning of a blackmail compaign,' Toby said.

I shivered.

'Look, darling,' he said, 'it's no good worrying. Obviously you've got to talk to Martin, and then you and I will talk more on Monday. But there's no reason to think it's any more than a malicious person who has stumbled on this . . . information, and is saying with these letters, "See what I know about you!"'

'Toby, you do still love me, don't you?' I said. 'You don't think any less of me for not having done anything about Martin, do you?'

'I love you very much, and I'm beginning to understand the problem,' Toby said. 'Look, I'll get you another glass of wine. Sit here quietly and drink it, and

41

don't go back to your office till you're feeling better. I'm sorry I can't stop. Now don't worry, will you?'

'I'll try not to,' I said.

He kissed me briefly, and was gone.

Chapter Five

IT WAS LATE when I got back to my office, so an early departure was out of the question. By the time I had finished my work and cleared my desk, the weekend rush to get out of London had reached a peak. The heat was oppressive, and it felt as though a storm was building up. Along the main roads through the south London suburbs the traffic slowed to a crawl. I turned on the radio, and tried to quell rising feelings of impatience and frustration. The radio weather forecast reported that the heat wave would continue. Temperatures in the eighties were predicted.

Further south, at the borders of Surrey and Sussex, a magpie flew out of the hedgerow, and I remembered the old rhyme: 'One for sorrow, two for joy, three for a girl and four for a boy.' Was that magpies?

The queue of cars moved slowly, impeded by vehicles which had overheated and were blocking the nearside lane, reducing the traffic to a single file. It was the end of the rhododendron season, and the bushes at the side of the road were a riot of pinks, crimsons, scarlets and purples. Flowers incarnadine . . . no, it was the multitudinous seas incarnadine that Lady Macbeth had been on about, wasn't it?

It was at about this point in the journey that I felt I went through a kind of Jekyll and Hyde transformation. I left behind Hilary Toogood, and turned into Mrs Martin Shipton, wife of the Headmaster of Falconbridge Preparatory School. My two lives were separate, with different homes, friends and even clothes in each. I sloughed off my London identity and wardrobe like a snakeskin; but the simile was not quite appropriate because it was not discarded, but taken up again at the end of each weekend.

The long line of cars reached the cause of the hold-up, a bad accident involving three or four cars. Police and ambulance-men were dealing with the crash. The broken glass and crumpled metal had been pushed to the side of the road. On the grass at the kerbside lay what looked like a stretcher, covered with green tarpaulin. A corpse? It couldn't be, to be thus casually disregarded. But perhaps the living were the first priority, and the dead were not so urgent . . . It seemed to be accorded scant respect. Maybe it was a dog, dead under the covering. I averted my eyes and drove on. The traffic, suddenly free of the bottleneck, was moving swiftly at last.

I looked at my watch. The accident, combined with the late start from London, meant that the meeting would have started. Oh, well, too bad. I branched off on the narrow road across the Downs, noticing the patches of buttercups like pools of melted butter in the warm evening air.

As I swung the car in between the tall stone gateposts topped by lions, I felt again the surge of love which I always felt on returning to Falconbridge. The dear familiarity of the old house, hidden in a fold of the Downs, gave me a feeling of security which I experienced nowhere else on earth. There were several cars parked in the drive; they belonged to my fellow Governors. I parked mine alongside, but before I went into the meeting, I tiptoed through the hall and scuttled round the side corridor to the octagonal wing at the side of the house. I climbed the staircase to the tower room at the top, and threw myself into the white rocking-chair by the window looking out over the spinney.

This room had been my nursery and playroom, then my bedroom, then a nursery again, and now it was my bedroom when I was at Falconbridge.

It was my stronghold, my citadel. It had views to the south over the spinney now blazing with rhododendrons and azaleas; to the west over the lawns and beds of roses, and to the east over the lake. Through these windows I had watched many times the first snowdrops emerge, then clumps of crocuses, giving way to wild daffodils and bluebells, to be followed by primroses, dog daisies and finally the changing colours of autumn leaves, the bright-berried holly and the winter jasmine.

It wasn't a large room, but in addition to my divan bed I had a desk and typewriter, my rocking-chair, and an old Chesterfield settee covered in pale pink velvet. Some-one – probably Alice, the cleaning lady; it wasn't Mother Shipton's style – had put a huge bowl of honeysuckle and roses on my desk. By the telephone there were a couple of scribbled messages on the message pad:

'Colonel Grant has asked us to dinner tomorrow night. Said yes, if you're not too tired – hope that's okay. Martin.'

And:

'Drinks with the Carters Sunday a.m.???'

There was a knock on the door. I called, 'Come in.'

Mother Shipton came in. All the boys called her Mother Shipton, and of couse she knew, but didn't seem to mind. She was a brittle-looking woman in her late sixties. She dressed elegantly and unobtrusively, usually in grey. A Colonel's daughter, she had been widowed twenty years previously, before I met Martin, so I never knew Father Shipton. When Martin took the job of

45

English master at the school, she came with him as Matron, thereby solving two of my father's problems at once. Now we employed Matrons – when we could get them – but Mother Shipton supervised them, and the catering, and in fact did all the things that I might have done if I had been a full-time, dedicated Headmaster's wife, which I wasn't.

'Ah, Hilary dear, I thought I heard your car,' Mother Shipton said. 'The Governors' meeting has started, they didn't wait, they thought that you were very likely stuck in a traffic jam.'

I felt rebellious.

'I was. I was just recovering for a few minutes before going in,' I said.

'Of course, dear' Mother S had had too much experience of dealing with recalcitrant small boys to engage in a skirmish she couldn't win. 'I expect you're tired. Perhaps you'd like me to convey your apologies, and say you can't take this meeting?'

'No, I'm going down in a minute, thank you,' I said, feeling thoroughly contrary. Mother S had that effect on me, I didn't know why.

'Did you see the messages about the dinner tomorrow night, and the Sunday drinks?'

'Yes, thank you,' I said, deliberately offhand. I resented my mother-in-law's intrusion into this room, which I regarded as my private kingdom, and I particularly hated the thought of her being in it when I wasn't there. I suppose that really, I resented her in my home, but I new that she was necessary to Martin, and essential to the school, and I did usually manage to tolerate her presence more gracefully and graciously than I was doing at the moment.

'Well dear, I'll see you at supper, shall I?' Mother S asked placidly, seeing my resentment and withdrawing from it and from the room. I instantly felt

ashamed of myself for behaving so badly and childishly.

I did feel battered and weary though, and it was an
enormous physical effort to drag myself up from the
rocking-chair, comb my hair and prepare myself to
meet the other Governors.

The school had been started originally by my great
grandfather who, having invested his money unwisely
and lost it all, had to look for a way of earning some
more. He decided to turn the family home into a small
school for the sons of gentlemen. My grandfather had
kept it going, and under my father's headmastership it
had become a really thriving boys' preparatory school.
His only disappointment had been that he had no sons
to carry it on after him.

When I married one of the assistant masters, my
father was delighted, and Martin had been groomed to
become Headmaster in his turn. I had inherited the
school on my father's unexpected death five years
previously – he had been flying as a passenger in a light
plane piloted by one of his former pupils – and Martin
had been running it ever since.

I went reluctantly downstairs again towards
the meeting. As I entered the hall, however, I heard
the sound of voices, and realized that it was ending.

A small knot of men standing in the hall greeted me
with smiles and kisses. I murmured apologies, and saw
them to the front door. Colonel Grant, tall and
immaculately turned out as if fresh from the hands of
his batman still, said:

'Do hope you can manage tomorrow evening,
m'dear?' and I said, 'Yes, of course, I'm looking
forward to it,' and within a couple of minutes they
were all gone, and Martin and I were left alone,
confronting each other in the huge, beautiful hall, with

its carved wooden staircase and portraits of my father and grandfather in oils at the end.

'What kept you, Hilary?' Martin asked, the headmaster demanding an explanation from a miscreant pupil.

'Traffic,' I said, nettled again, deliberately offhand as I had been with his mother. Why did they have this effect on me, both of them?

'Well, it was a purely routine Governors' meeting, there was really nothing to discuss, except the insurance renewals.' Martin excused me.

'I have something I need to discuss, and I'm flattened with fatigue,' I said.

'D'you mean with the other Governors?'

'No, with you, It's private. Do you think that we might opt out of school supper, and have it by ourselves for once?' I asked.

Martin hesitated. I knew he hated asking his mother if we might have our supper privately in our sitting-room. She didn't like it, and it was a nuisance for the staff, too.

'I really need to,' I said.

'Okay, I'll ask Mother. What is it?' he said.

'I'll tell you in a minute. I could do with a drink first,' I said.

Martin went to find his mother to arrange about supper, and I went into the ground-floor room with French windows out onto the garden which we kept as a private sitting-room.

I helped myself to a whisky out of the cupboard, and poured one for Martin, too. I made it a stiff one. I handed it to him when he came into the room.

'You'd better sit down,' I said. 'It's going to be a shock.'

There were two chintz sofas facing each other. Martin sat down opposite me.

'It's not that . . .'

'Don't try to guess, Martin,' I said, for once feeling in charge of the situation. 'You won't be able to, not in a month of Sundays. It's not very good news, anyway, and I can't think of any gentle way of breaking it. You'd better read this.'

I fished around in my handbag, and pulled out the letter I'd received that morning. It seemed an eternity ago now. I handed the letter to Martin, and watched him in silence as he read it.

Martin was a large man, balding, who dressed customarily in hairy tweed suits which were baggy and shapeless but doubtless inspired confidence in the parents. He looked a bluff, hearty English gentleman, a good sport, no-nonsense, plenty of sensible discipline, just the person to whom to entrust a treasured son.

Now, however, there was not very much bluff heartiness about him. I saw him flinch as he read the letter, and when he had read it through twice, he set it on his knee and sat, head bent, not looking at me. I wondered if he were weeping.

'Martin?' I said.

'Who is Helen Turner?' he asked.

'I don't know. She doesn't exist. I – tried to trace her, and it's a fictitious address. It's a kind of anonymous letter.'

'How does she – the writer – know? Whom have you told?'

The pompously correct 'whom', even in this moment of stress, was characteristic of Martin.

'I haven't told anybody,' I said, remembering as I said it that I had in fact told Toby. But I had told him after the letter had arrived, I argued with myself, and Martin meant whom had I told who could have used the information to write the letter.

'Well, somebody obviously knows,' he said flatly.

'They don't know through *me*,' I said. And then it

occurred to me, 'Do they know through you? Does somebody else know?'

Martin shook his head. I remembered that, anyway, Helen Turner didn't only know about Martin, she also knew about me and Toby. So perhaps it wasn't another aspect of Martin's past or present.

I picked up the letter, and read it for the umpteenth time.

'Dear Hilary Toogood, (it read)
'My husband is a schoolmaster, and I don't know how to tell you what my problem is, but well, he prefers the boys he teaches to me. I don't know what to do about this, and I am at my wits end. I am scared that he will be found out, and that could mean the police and prosecution, and the end of his job, of course. I feel badly about the children, although I know he doesn't harm them, he really loves them, he only plays with them, and I think that some of them like it. Do you think it does them any harm? What would you advise me to do?
'Yours sincerely, Helen Turner.'

'Does it still go on, Martin?' I asked, watching him closely.

From his eyes, I knew that it did.

'Well, first of all it's got to stop, straight off,' I said, and he nodded dumbly, and I had never seen him look more like a whipped dog. 'I suppose we'll just have to wait for the blackmail demand, and work out what to do then,' I said.

Martin got up and helped himself to another whisky.

'Do you want one?' he asked, and I held out my glass.

'You've never touched Dominic, have you, Martin?' I asked suddenly. 'I want the truth.'

'I have never touched Dominic.' He looked me straight in the eye, and I was satisfied.

'Was that why you married me, though?'

'No, it had nothing to do with it.'

He sat down heavily, and buried his face in his hands.

'I feel so ashamed, Hilary.'

'You ought to get some psychiatric help. I told you at the time,' I said.

'But if I did, it would all come out,' he argued.

I shook my head. 'No, it wouldn't. The psychiatrist would never reveal it. You would simply go and see him once or twice a week, no-one need ever know where you're going, you could say it was the dentist, or meetings or something. You don't even need to go through the GP, I know lots of psychiatrists through the magazine. I'll pretend it's a reader, and make enquiries as to who is the top expert in this kind of thing, and then I can get you an appointment direct. They're not supposed to see you privately without a letter from your GP, but they always do.'

'All right, then.' He looked defeated.

'Well, apart from the benefit to you, I think it's a good thing to do for other reasons. If it all does come out in some way as the result of Helen Turner's malice, at least you can demonstrate that you are trying to fight it, and do something about it.'

'You're right, of course,' Martin said. 'You don't think it's possible, though, that it's a real letter, and just a co-incidence?'

'I'm sure its not possible,' I said. I didn't tell him why.

We didn't speak of it again during the weekend. On the Monday morning, I woke at five thirty in my tower room, and lay listening for a while to the birds under the eaves, scrabbling and squabbling noisily. When I was wide awake, I got up and flung open the windows. There was a

51

blackbird on the lawn, and the dew still glistened, but already the sun was rising in the sky, drying the ground and taking the chill off the early morning air.

I went downstairs in my dressing-gown, found a pair of scissors in the kitchen drawer, and went out to cut roses to take back to London with me. The grass was wet and cold under my bare feet, and droplets of water fell from the roses onto my skin. If Martin had been up and about, he would never have allowed me to cut the roses so heedlessly. He regarded them as his personal property.

'Don't cut the ones with buds,' he would always say sharply, watching carefully and suspiciously as I chose them.

When I had gathered a large, fragrant bunch, I took them upstairs and, as I dressed, I listened to the house awakening. Small boys in grey flannel suits clattered noisily on the stairs as the breakfast bell went, and stood rubbing the sleep from their eyes, waiting for their corn-flakes and milk. I heard the cleaning ladies arriving from the village, and the occasional roar of one of the young assistant masters, chasing up latecomers or chivvying minor wrongdoers into the early morning jankers, running round the grounds.

I made tea in my room, gathered up the roses and my suitcase, stuck my head round the dining-room door to say goodbye to Martin and Mother Shipton, and headed away from the Sussex coast back up the London road. There were no hold-ups, for once, and I arrived at the office before Ruth. I put the coffee on to percolate, and sat down peacefully with my address book to find a psychiatrist for Martin.

Three phone calls later, I had an appointment for Martin with an eminent psychiatrist who was a consultant at a big London teaching hospital. It was for the Thursday, and so I scribbled the name and the address of the Harley Street consulting rooms on a piece of paper, put it in an envelope addressed to Martin and labelled PERSONAL AND PRIVATE in case his secretary opened it, put a first class stamp on it, and put it in my out tray.

Then I rang Toby.

'Are you in a meeting?' I asked.

'No, I'm on my own. How are you? What news on the letter front? Are you feeling better than you did on Friday? Are you okay for this evening?'

'So many questions at once,' I said. 'I'm fine, thank you. Yes, I'm feeling better than I did on Friday, I've recovered from the shock, I think. It's okay for this evening. I'm looking forward to seeing you, and I'll tell you all the news on the letter front then.'

'It's okay, is it?' Toby asked anxiously.

'It seems to be okay for the moment,' I said guardedly.

Two days later, I knew that I was right to be guarded.

Chapter Six

THE THIRD LETTER arrived on the Wednesday morning, and Ruth brought it in on top of the pile.

'There's a letter from someone called Helen Turner,' she said, 'and the name rings a bell. I think we've heard from her before. Would you like me to check the files for you?'

She moved towards the filing cabinet in the corner of the room.

'Don't bother, Ruth, it's okay, I think I know who she is,' I said, sounding, I hoped, casual, by a supreme effort.

'Just leave it with me, will you? I'm rather tied up at the moment. I'll deal with it shortly.'

Ruth noticed and accepted the dismissal in my voice, put the letters down on my desk and asked, 'Would you like some coffee?'

'Please,' I said.

I did not touch the letters until she had brought the coffee and left the room. Then I picked them up and sure enough, there it was on top, the familiar paper and style of typing.

My hands were trembling as I read it, and when I'd finished, I went to the cupboard where I kept the sherry for Mrs Carstairs, and rooted round for the half-bottle of whisky I remembered putting there when I'd brought it back from a press trip a couple of months ago. I found a glass, and poured myself a generous measure. Then I picked up the phone.

'Ruth, I want to make a private call. Keep everyone out, will you?' I said. I often made private calls, to Toby. She wouldn't connect it with the letter.

I rang Toby's office. From his tone, I knew that he wasn't alone.

'Hello, what can I do for you?' he asked impersonally.

'I've had another letter. This time it's about Dominic,' I told him.

'Oh, no!' I heard the shock in his voice which he wasn't able to conceal. But almost immediately, he regained control of himself.

'That's not very good news. I'm so sorry,' he said, as if I were a client telling him that one of his publicity campaigns had fallen slightly short of its objectives.

'What does she want, Toby?' I asked desperately.

'It's difficult to say, isn't it,' Toby said. 'Look, it's a bit difficult at the moment, I'm in the middle of a meeting. I'm frightfully sorry to hear about it, but I was wondering if I could call you back?'

'It's not possible, I'm afraid. I've got appointments all through the day, starting in ten minutes,' I said. 'But Toby, I'll have to go and see Dominic, I think. I'll take a day off tomorrow, and do it. I'll have to cancel our lunch. What about dinner the following day, if you'd like to come round?'

'I'll do that,' Toby said, 'and don't worry about the lunch. But have you really thought through this course of action? I mean, as you've only just received the latest information, might it not be better to digest it for a while and see what the best course would be after due consideration?'

'Oh, Toby, I've got to tell him. I should have done it years ago,' I said. 'And I'd rather he heard it from me than from anyone else. I don't know who Helen Turner

55

is, or what she wants or intends, but I'd hate for her to tell him.'

'I know what you mean,' Toby said. 'I'm sure you know best. You know you can count on my support, of course.'

Tell me you love me, Toby, was what I wanted to say. I don't want you pretending I'm a client and proffering support, I want your openly declared love, care, protection, affection, demonstrated, obvious, free, for all the world to see. Not this subterfuge, deception, double-talk, cross-talk . . .

But I said politely, 'Thank you, Toby darling, it means a lot to me. See you tomorrow evening, think of me to-morrow.'

'Of course; hope it all goes well. Bye bye then,' Toby said, and was gone. I hung up the phone, and the tears came unbidden to my eyes and splashed onto my desk. Was I crying for myself and for the love I longed to express and feel expressed, or for Dominic, or for both of us? I didn't know.

Dominic had no telephone in his Oxford flat, so I wasn't able to ring him to tell him that I was coming. However, I was confident that he'd be there. I knew that he was due to go to Greece the following Saturday, and that he would be getting his things together and (possibly) clearing up the flat before he went.

Toby was at an official dinner that evening, so I went early to my solitary bed, and set the alarm for seven the next morning. I wanted to nip out to the supermarket before setting off for Oxford, and I intended to get there in time to take Dominic for an early lunch.

I washed my hair, but didn't bother to blow-dry it into shape. I scrambled into jeans and a loose cotton shirt, collected the shopping I needed, and set out for Oxford. How and where should I tell Dominic? Not at lunch, the

56

restaurant would not be private enough. Perhaps after lunch we could get a punt, moor up in a quiet backwater of the Cherwell, and I would find a way to tell him then.

Driving over Magdalen bridge, I tried to see if the river looked busy, or if we stood a chance of getting a punt. There seemed to be a lot of tourists around. Of course it was the vacation, so there weren't many students.

I drove out along the Woodstock road, and turned off down the quiet avenue where Dominic's flat was situated. The big red-brick house had been divided into four flats, and I had bought one for my son when he had come up to Oxford a year previously. Until that time, he had spent holidays from Winchester mostly with me in London. The long University vacations were obviously going to be more of a problem, and setting him up in his own apartment seemed to both of us a good idea. I didn't realise it at the time – or perhaps I did, subconsciously – but it coincided with the beginning of my affair with Toby, and having the London flat to myself left me at liberty to pursue this with a freedom which I hadn't experienced for years.

I rang Dominic's bell, and there were sounds of reluctant life. The lazy beggar probably wasn't up yet. I waited patiently. After what seemed at least five minutes the door creaked open, and I was just about to step forward and hug my son when I realized that the young man who confronted me, although wearing Dominic's bath-robe, wasn't Dominic.

'Oh!' I said. 'I was looking for Dominic.'

'This is his flat, but he isn't here.'

'I'm Dominic's mother,' I said. 'Where is he?'

'Come in, won't you?' the young man invited. He wrapped Dominic's bath-robe round him more securely. He didn't appear to be wearing anything else.

'I'm Chris,' he said.

I followed him into the living-room of the flat. It was a

57

shambles. There were dirty coffee mugs and empty beer cans everywhere, newspapers on the floor, and books piled high on most of the chairs.

'My God,' I said.

'If I'd known you were coming, I'd have cleared up.' Chris said. 'You're the famous Hilary Toogood, aren't you?'

'I'm Hilary Toogood,' I confirmed.

'Would you like some coffee?' he offered.

'Is there anything clean to drink it out of?'

'Probably not. I could wash a couple of mugs.'

I hesitated.

'Will Dominic be back soon?'

'He's in Cambridge. He'll probably be back this evening, but possibly not till tomorrow morning. He'll certainly be back then, to get his things together for Greece,' he said.

'What's he doing in Cambridge?' I asked, irrationally irritated with my son for having left Oxford when I had arrived to see him.

'Oh, the usual thing . . . it's a new girlfriend,' Chris said, picking up a couple of mugs off the floor.

'I'll make some coffee, I know where everything is,' I said.

'Okay, I'll go and have a shower and get dressed,' Chris said. 'There isn't any milk, but I think there's some Coffeemate.'

'Are you living here?'

'For the moment, but not permanently,' Chris said. 'I'm at Magdalen too, as you probably know. At the end of term I didn't want to go home, so Dom said I could stay with him for a bit.'

He disappeared into the bedroom, and I set to work clearing up the room. I found seventeen mugs under various chairs, some of them still with price stickers on. My son seemed to have found a novel way of avoiding washing up – he just bought new crockery. I took the mugs through to the kitchen, and put them to soak. I cleared up the newspapers and books, opened the windows and put the kettle on. I removed the top layer of dust from the more obvious surfaces with an old pair of socks I found in a corner. By the time that Chris emerged from the bathroom, the room looked quite presentable, and there was a tantalizing smell of coffee.

'That was quick!' he said, looking round in surprise.

'Turning disorder into order is quite creative and satisfying; I enjoy it,' I said.

He looked different in shirt and jeans. He was tall, with crisp curly hair, and startling blue eyes – a very good-looking young man, about the same age as my son, I guessed.

'Did Dominic know you were coming, and forget, the rotter?' he asked.

'No, I came on the off chance. I wanted to talk to him about something. I was going to take him out to lunch,' I said.

'Take me instead – I'm famished,' Chris said.

I felt mildly annoyed at his presumption.

'You can put it on your expenses, can't you?' he said.

'I certainly can't!'

'My father would.'

I let that pass.

'I'm just wondering whether to wait for Dominic or not,' I said, handing him a mug of coffee. 'I suppose having driven all this way, I might as well. And I suppose I need lunch, and should be glad of some company. Okay, I'll take you to lunch.'

'Hooray! I'll take you to tea at the Union in return. Toast and anchovy paste,' Chris said. 'How soon could we eat? I'm starving.'

'We could go now. The Eastgate is good value for hearty appetites, if that's all right with you,' I said. 'Did Dominic give any indication of what time he'd be back?'

'None at all. Whatever time she threw him out, I suppose. She seems to have let him stay last night, the lucky sod,' Chris said.

'Who is she?'

'A nurse at Addenbrooke's. A sister, actually.'

'Good Lord. How old is she?' I asked, feeling protective about my ewe lamb, and wondering what he had got himself into.

'Six or seven years older than Dom. But don't worry, he knows how to look after himself and avoid matrimony.'

'Does he, indeed!' I said. 'Well, come on, let's go and eat.'

We climbed into the car, and I headed back towards Carfax. The Eastgate Hotel was full of tourists, but the head waiter noticed that Chris was an undergraduate, assumed that I was his mother, I suppose, and found us a table. Chris ate heartily, and I appreciated the relish with which he did so. He was an entertaining companion, and told me anecdotes about the speakers at the Union, quoting some of the better points from the last term's debates. I sat back and enjoyed myself.

After lunch, Chris said, 'I feel marvellously replete, and guilty about having invited myself. Can I take you out in a punt to make amends a little?'

I hesitated. It was a magnificently warm afternoon, and a punt sounded idyllic.

'Is there any chance Dom will be back, d'you think?'

'Not a chance,' Chris said. 'You might as well relax and enjoy yourself.'

'All right, I'd love a couple of hours on the river.'

We took a punt from Magdalen bridge, and I lay back idly and watched Chris deftly propelling us up the river.

We soon pulled away from the tourists, who were shouting, and going round in circles, and crashing into each other, and found ourselves drifting under willows among meadows of buttercups.

'I'm hot, I wish I'd brought something to drink,' Chris said, peeling off his shirt.

'You're probably dehydrated after the wine at lunch. You'd better rest a bit,' I said.

So he moored the punt to an overhanging tree, and jumped ashore saying, 'I'm going for a pee.'

A couple of minutes later he returned, and I said, 'I've got cramp in one leg. I need to walk up and down a bit.'

He helped me out of the punt, and I hopped around on the bank. When my leg was better, I sat on the grassy bank, and he threw himself down beside me. With the wine I had drunk and the heat of the sun, I started dozing.

A minute or so later, I woke with a start. Chris's hand was on my breast. I sat bolt upright.

'What on earth are you doing?' I said.

He withdrew his hand at once, scarlet-faced.

'I'm sorry,' he said. 'I didn't mean to wake you.'

I felt sorry for his embarrassment. What on earth did it matter? Why was I behaving in such a prudish way?

'It's okay, it really doesn't matter,' I said. 'It just startled me, and I woke rather suddenly.'

'I'm so sorry, you won't – I mean – my father,' he muttered, still red-faced, and I said:

'Oh, for God's sake, Chris, don't take it to heart. It's all right, I like it; here, come here,' and I took his hand and replaced it on my breast, thinking, poor little sod, he'll be sexually crippled for life if I'm not careful.

Chris looked at me in amazement, as well he might. It turned rapidly to delight, and he ran his hand over my other breast, and before I knew what was happening he was kissing me passionately and pressing the length of him against me, and I could feel that he had the most enormous erection.

'Here, hang on a minute,' I said, struggling wildly, as I thought that any minute the act was going to be consummated.

He pulled away from me, and sat a little apart.

'I want you very badly,' he said.

'I know, I could feel it,' I said.

'Please, I'm desperate for you –' he reached for my breast again.

'Chris wait, not here,' I said, his urgency kindling an urgency in me.

'Where then? The flat? Will you?' he said, and I nodded in spite of myself.

I don't believe any punt has sped up the Cherwell so rapidly as the punt returned to Magdalen bridge that afternoon. It was like a speeded-up film. We raced up the steps, into the car, back to the flat, and stood panting in the sitting-room.

I said, 'What about Dominic?' and Chris said, 'It's all right, I've put the bolt on,' and pulled me into the bedroom, and we tore off our clothes, and he was onto me and into me and came.

I lay stroking the curls at the back of his neck, and he stirred and said, 'Oh! The softness of you. I've never felt anything like it. May I look at you?'

I laughed and spread my legs, and he sat beside me, fingering me, and I said, 'That wasn't the first time for you, by any chance, was it?'

And he said, 'Yes, it was,' and I said, 'You'll remember it all your life,' and he said, 'Yes, I will.'

A little later on, I said, 'I'm going to make some coffee,' and he said:

'No, wait, I want to try again,' and he did. This time

we both came, and he said, 'That little moan – I pleased you, didn't I?'

'Very much,' I said, and fell asleep.

When I awoke, I couldn't remember where I was. I looked round the unfamiliar room, and then I realized that I was lying on my son's bed, and my son's friend, whom I had just seduced, was sleeping naked beside me. I reached for my watch in something like panic, and saw it was just after five o'clock. I slipped out of bed, struggled into my jeans and shirt, made some coffee, brought two mugs to the bed, and wakened him with a kiss.

He struggled up from sleep, took the mug and lay sipping it drowsily, looking at me with wonder and pleasure. I sat on the bed beside him, drinking my coffee. He set aside his mug and slipped his hand under my shirt, and I said 'Oh, no, Chris! Not again. Suppose Dominic comes back!'

'He won't be back just yet. Anyway the door is bolted,' Chris said. 'Please! See how I want you,' and indeed his erection was obvious again. He pushed up my shirt, and his mouth was on my breasts, and somehow the fact that I was dressed and he was naked made it more exciting. He pulled off my jeans and pants and forced himself between my legs and this time, having come twice quite recently, he did not come so quickly, but thrust into me hard for about five minutes, and I came, and burst into tears.

He withdrew, still erect, and looked at me in consternation.

'What's the matter? What have I done? Hilary, don't cry, please,' and I said:

'It's all right, I'm crying because I'm happy. Go on, I want you to come.' And I put him back inside me, and with a couple of hard thrusts he came, and lay quietly beside me, tracing the course of my tears with his finger.

'Hilary, you were protected, weren't you?' he asked.

I said, 'Yes, I'm on the pill. But I must get myself together. Dominic might be back, you know,' and I picked up my discarded clothing and went into the bathroom, showered and dressed myself resolutely, made up my face and combed my tousled hair.

When I emerged, Chris was dressed and was tidying the bed. He came towards me and put his arms round me, and kissed me tenderly on the mouth.

'Thank you very much indeed,' Chris said. 'You're a lovely, generous, soft woman, and I'll never forget you, ever.'

'I'll never forget you either,' I said. 'But right now, I need a drink. You didn't buy me that tea you promised me at the Union, we were otherwise engaged. How about taking me to a pub, instead?'

'Certainly,' he said. 'We'll leave a note in case Dominic materializes,' and he kissed me again, and went to find pen and paper in the sitting-room.

We went to the Turl, and sat in the garden drinking ice-cold lager, which was wonderfully reviving after the exertions of the afternoon.

'Well, I'm one up on my father,' Chris said.

'What do you mean?'

'What I did, with your kind help, this afternoon, is something that he couldn't do.'

'Do you mean making love to a married lady?' I asked.

'I mean making love,' Chris said.

'Don't be silly,' I said. 'You're here, aren't you? Or were you a visitation from the Holy Ghost?'

'Something like that. I was the result of artificial insemination, actually,' Chris said.

I looked at him in amazement.

'You're joking.'

'No, I'm not.'

'But how do you know?'

'I've heard my father and my mother quarrelling

several times. She taunts him with it. Can't get it up, she says. I've always been afraid that I might be the same. Now I know I'm not, thanks to you. I'll always be grateful, Hilary.' He touched my hand.

'No wonder you don't want to go home for the vacation,' I said. 'That sounds like pretty nasty quarrelling.' And then, 'Does that mean that you don't know who your father really is?'

'Yes. It worried me a lot, at first. I had fantasies about growing up and marrying my sister by accident. The worries got worse when I came up here, and started getting seriously interested in girls. I went to see the student counsellor, and she helped me get it into perspective. It's a million to one chance that I might sleep with my sister – and anyway, it's a chance that everyone takes really, isn't it? I mean, few people can be absolutely positive about their paternity – or even maternity if you were born in hospital, the NHS being what it is.'

I struggled to grasp what he was saying.

'You mean that your father might be married with other children?

'Yes. My father was probably a medical student. They're often paid to be donors for artificial insemination. So he's likely to have been intelligent, single, of good family, etcetera etcetera. He probably married later, and had a family. I do tend to avoid chatting up doctors' daughters, even though it may be a million to one against them being my sisters. Maybe that's why I was successful with you – there's no chance whatever that we're related.'

Underneath it all, I heard the sexual insecurity.

'You were successful with me because you're a normally-sexed young man who can be successful with anyone,' I told him firmly. 'I don't know what's the matter with the man you call your father, but it's obviously impossible for you to have inherited it, and I can

65

tell you for sure that there's absolutely nothing the matter with you. Certainly not – you're very much all right.'

'I don't know why I've told you all this,' Chris said. 'I've never told anyone before, except the student counsellor, I mean. You won't tell anyone, anyone at all, will you?'

'Of course not,' I promised.

'Hello,' said a voice behind us. 'I see that you're already acquainted with the son of God.'

Chapter Seven

MY SON WAS standing by our table. So engrossed had we
been in our conversation that we hadn't noticed him
approach us across the garden.

'Hello, Dom. Can I get you a drink?' Chris asked.

'What d'you mean by that blasphemy?' I asked my son.

'I'd like cider,' Dom said to Chris. And to me: 'Well, I
mean you and Chris seem to have introduced
yourselves.'

We'd done a bit more than that, I thought to myself.
Aloud, I said, 'Yes, but why the son of God?'

'Because he is, of course. Chris, haven't you introduced yourself properly? Mother, may I introduce Chris
O'Dwyer. Chris, meet my mother.'

'Chris *O'Dwyer*,' I said. 'Not the son of Gerry
O'Dwyer? You mean you really are the son of God? Why
didn't you tell me?' I was absolutely amazed.

'But I thought you *knew*.' He was equally astonished.
'I said 'I'm Chris', and you didn't say 'Chris who,' or anything. I thought that Dom would have told you who was
staying with him.'

'Dom never tells me anything,' I complained, as
mothers have complained through the ages. 'But how
astonishing! I mean, God being your father.'

And then I realized that of course God wasn't really his
father, if what Chris had been telling me in the past ten

minutes were true, and I was sure that it was. Sexy old Gerry O'Dwyer couldn't actually get it up at all.

'When did you arrive, Ma? And to what do we owe this unexpected honour?' Dom was breaking into my confused thoughts.

'I'll go and get that cider for you, Dom,' Chris said. 'Would you like another drink, Hilary?'

'I'd like a whisky and water,' I said, fishing round in my handbag. 'Take this, will you Chris –' I proffered a fiver, as I would have done to my son.

Chris flushed.

'Please let me buy it for you,' he said.

Dominic looked at him curiously.

'Why not accept it?' he said. 'Ma can afford it more easily than you can.' But Chris shook his head, picked up our empty glasses and headed into the pub.

Dominic kissed me, and sat down.

'Is everything all right, Ma?' he asked, studying me. 'You look funny.'

'I'm just taken aback about Chris being the son of Gerry O'Dwyer.' I said. 'I knew that Gerry had a son up here, the same age as you, and at Magdalen, and I suppose that if I'd thought about it, I probably knew that his name was Chris. But I never connected it all up when I met Chris.'

'Doesn't matter, does it?' my son asked.

His scrutiny made me uncomfortable.

'Of course not,' I said.

'Sorry I wasn't here, anyway,' Dom said. 'You didn't tell me you were coming, though – did you?' he asked doubtfully.

'No, I didn't,' I reassured him. 'I came on the off-chance. When you weren't here, I took Chris out to lunch instead, then we took a punt on the river.'

Chris came back over the grass towards us, carrying a tray.

'Thank you for looking after my mama,' Dom said.

Chris gave me a happy smirk, which I hoped my son had not noticed. I glared at him.

'What did you want to talk to me about, anyway?' Dom asked me.

At that point I remembered Helen Turner's beastly letter, which I had put out of my mind for the afternoon.

'I need to talk to you privately,' I said. 'I don't feel much like eating dinner, since I ate lunch. Could we go back to the flat?'

'Yes, of course. We'll get a bottle of wine and some take-away food,' Dom said. 'Is it serious, Ma? Have you been fired or something?'

'It's quite serious, I suppose, but no, I haven't been fired,' I said. 'Don't bother about food for me, I'm quite happy with wine and a piece of cheese.'

'I think I'll go and invite myself to coffee with Peter,' Chris said. 'I say, I've just realized, Hilary – if you didn't know I was God's son, you must have thought I had a frightful cheek inviting myself to lunch with you.'

'I did a bit, but I'm glad you came, anyway,' I said, smiling at him, and realizing it was a *double entendre* the minute the words flew out of my mouth.

I felt I was still reeling. First from the unexpected events of the day, then from the discovery that the young man with whom I had made love was the son of my boss – or rather, he wasn't, but the world knew him as the son of my boss – and then from apprehension about the coming talk with my son. I was going to have to impart to him facts about his own paternity which up until now, he hadn't known.

I took a large swallow of whisky, and reminded myself firmly that in a couple of hours time I was going to have to drive back to London, so I mustn't drink too much. I would have to hold back on the wine at the flat. I also wanted to stay sober to pick my words carefully for

Dominic. I began to rehearse in my head what I would say, and how I would tell him.

'You're a long way away, Hilary,' Chris said. 'Where are you?'

Chapter Eight

I WAS SITTING at a table with a glass in front of me, but it was another age, another place.

I was many years back in time. It was a pavement café in Paris, and I was drinking Coca Cola.

A man stopped by my table, and said something in French. I looked at him blankly. My schoolgirl French was not equal to it.

'*Ah, vous êtes anglaise* ,' he said. 'Is this seat taken? Do you mind if I sit here?

'That's okay,' I said.

'Are you in Paris by yourself, Mademoiselle?'

'I'm with a school party,' I said.

He looked around.

'Where are they?'

'They're in the museum. I felt hot and tired, and Sister gave me permission to meet them back at the hotel.'

'Sister?'

'Sister Agnes, she's in charge of us.'

'So, it's a convent school?'

'That's right.'

'And what is the average age of your party?'

'I don't know, really. Seventeen, eighteen, I guess.'

'But you, Mademoiselle, you are younger than seventeen, I think.'

'No, I'm not!' I was furious. 'I was seventeen last Christmas.'

He smiled, and ordered a drink, and said 'Can I get you another of whatever you were drinking?'

I said rather doubtfully: 'It was Coca Cola,' and he sighed, and ordered from the waiter in French. As he did so, I looked at him. He was something like my father in age and appearance, with a grave, rather melancholy face which came to life when he smiled, an authoritative manner, and beautiful clothes.

I also noticed that there were quite a lot of empty tables. He had not needed to share mine.

'My name is Pierre,' he introduced himself. 'Do you know Paris well? If not, may I show you a little of it?'

And that was how it all began. Pierre abducted me – there is no other word for it – from the school party. Oh, he did it with such finesse and accomplishment that I can hardly believe that it was the first time he had done such a thing. He invited me to stay with him and his wife, and when I accepted, he said perhaps we had better tell Sister Agnes that he was my uncle, so that she would be completely happy about the arrangement. He came to the hotel with me, and told Sister that his sister, my mother, hadn't told him that I was coming to Paris, we had met by chance, and that of course my aunt wished to see me, and that he would take me home to her, and deliver me to the Gare St Lazare the following Saturday at ten sharp to join the party again. Sister Agnes was dazzled by his charm, and swallowed the story hook, line and sinker. She literally pushed me at him. I collected my suitcase containing my change of school knickers and climbed into the taxi with him, and was conveyed to the fourth-floor flat in the Rue Marguerite.

Of course, his wife wasn't there. He pretended surprise, at first, and said that she must have gone to her sister's. Well, he said, we would go out to dinner, and probably she would have returned by the time we got back.

He looked rather doubtfully at my regulation grey skirt and jumper, and asked if I hadn't anything else to wear. I apologized, and said that I hadn't. We went out to a small restaurant a couple of blocks away and had a delicious dinner, and I drank too much wine.

I knew perfectly well that when we returned the flat would still be empty. I didn't care. Like Sister Agnes, I was dazzled by Pierre, who had a marvellous accent, told amusing stories and treated me like an adult. That night, I lost my virginity. He was expert and kind and masterful. The next day I got up and examined my face in the mirror, and thought how odd it was that I didn't look any different. Pierre came up behind me and asked me what I was thinking, and I told him. And he said no, not after the first time, *ma petite*. But after a little while, if you let me continue to enjoy you, you will feel different and look different too.

Just about then, on that first morning, the phone rang. Pierre went to answer it, and a long conversation ensued in rapid French. He made a couple more phone calls, and then came back and kissed me.

'We are going to stay somewhere else for a couple of days,' he said. 'A small hotel north of Paris. You don't mind, do you?'

'No, I don't mind, but why?' I said.

'Well, my wife is coming back,' he said. 'She has been away on holiday, and she is returning early. I want to be with you, so we shall move. It is arranged.'

He made some coffee, and I washed up, and he made up the bed we had slept in with clean sheets, because those of the night before had my blood on them. And then we climbed into his Citroen and he drove out of Paris to the north, to Piscop, to the château called Robin des Bois, where we were the only guests.

73

'This house was built for a Scottish princess,' Pierre said. 'So it's appropriate for you, I think.' I was neither Scottish nor a princess, but I was enormously flattered, as he intended me to be.

We had a large four-poster bed, and we hardly left it for the next three days. Sometimes we went down to meals. One afternoon he drove me to visit the Château at Chantilly. The rest of the time he made love to me: passionately, tenderly, desperately, wearily.

On the last afternoon before we were due to part, it happened. At the end of our love-making an extraordinary feeling spread upwards through me, as though my whole being were melting uncontrollably. I wept, and he comforted me, and told me now I was a woman.

'And you are a very sensual woman,' he told me. 'You are a woman for men who recognize and appreciate rare instruments, and I have showed you how to play fine music so that you can give a man exceptional pleasure. Don't waste these gifts.'

When he took me to rejoin Sister Agnes and the others, she twittered about him flirtatiously. He kissed my cheek in an avuncular fashion, and bade me tell my mother that she owed him a letter.

'I have forgotten to tell her that my office has moved,' Pierre said. 'Please give her this new address in case she needs it.' He pressed a visiting card into my hand, and was gone.

I put the card, inappropriately, into my Bible, and forgot about it until a month later.

That was when I first suspected that I might be pregnant.

So I wrote to Pierre. I had wanted to write to him previously. In fact I had written, whole pages of 'My darling Pierre', but I knew instinctively that he would not like it, so I did not send them.

74

This time I composed a brief, stilted little note, which I sent to the office address on the visiting card.

'Dear Pierre, (it said)
'I'm sorry to trouble you but I think something may have gone wrong. I'm nearly three weeks late. I've never been late before. I don't know what to do.
'All my love, Hilary.'

For two weeks, I heard nothing. My anxiety hardened into fear. If he was going to write, it was nearly the end of term, and the letter would be held up–perhaps until next term? Or worse, it might be opened.
Two day before the end of term, a letter came.

'Dear Mademoiselle Toogood, (it said)
'Monsieur de la Tour is away at present, but I am his confidential secretary, and he has asked me to say that if you are still worried, you should contact Mr F S Jaure at 189A Harley Street, telephone WELbeck 4030. I have been in touch with Mr Jaure, who is expecting you to call him and make an appointment. Financial arrangements have been taken care of.
'Yours sincerely, David Todd.'

I was angry and disappointed. Furious that Pierre had not even written to me himself, but had apparently told someone else all about us, this David Todd. At the same time, my doubts were crystallizing into certainty.

Term ended, and I went home to my father at Falconbridge. It caused him some concern when I announced that I was going up to London alone to do some shopping, as I had never done anything of the kind before, but he agreed. I went out to a phone box and made an appointment with Mr Jaure.

Two days later, in a plush first-floor consulting room

overlooking Harley Street, Mr Jaure, a benevolent, elderly gynaecologist with white hair and a reassuring manner, confirmed that I was pregnant. Back at his desk, he consulted his diary.

'I could do it next Tuesday, if that suits you,' he said.

'Do what?' I said.

'Well, take away the baby, my dear. That's what you want, isn't it?'

I burst into tears.

'No it isn't!' I said. 'Leave my baby alone! I want him even if his father doesn't!'

The doctor tried to soothe me.

'If that's what you want, I'm sure Monsieur de la Tour will meet all the expenses of your confinement,' he said. 'He's an old friend, and I can say that with confidence. But I don't think that he could be expected to maintain the child after it was born. After all, he has his own family. And how would you manage for money? Much better to do as arranged and go through with the abortion. Plenty of time to have other babies later on when you're married to a nice young man.'

'I don't want his filthy money,' I said, picking up my handbag. I walked weeping into the street, where I narrowly avoided being run over by a taxi, which would have solved the whole problem immediately.

Chapter Nine

THIS, THEN, WAS what I had to tell Dominic, or rather a version of it which would portray his father in a reasonably good light. I felt instinctively that I must somehow preserve his father's image for him. I did not want him to think ill of Pierre.

The two young men in the garden of the Turl had abandoned me to my reverie and were talking to each other. I decided that I'd better make a move, or I wouldn't get back to London that night.

'Come on, Dom,' I said to my son. 'Back to the flat. Bye bye, Chris. See you again sometime, perhaps.'

Chris took my hand to shake it, and then put it to his lips. My son looked at him in surprise.

'Ay ay!' Dom said. 'What's going on, then?'

Chris flushed, and dropped my hand.

'Really, Dominic,' I said severely, 'Come along now, and stop fooling around. Bye bye, Chris. I'll give your regards to your father, shall I?'

'Er – yes, do,' Chris said. 'Thank you for the lunch, Mrs Shipton. I hope we'll meet again soon.'

'Mrs Shipton?' said Dominic. 'Nobody ever calls her Mrs Shipton. It was Hilary a short while ago, anyway.'

'By bye then, Hilary,' Chris said, escaping from my son's too-curious gaze. He departed briskly up the lane, and we followed at a more leisurely pace.

We stopped on the way back to the flat to buy wine and doner kebabs. Back in Dominic's sitting-room we pulled the curtains and lit the gas-fire and created a cocoon of intimacy. When he had uncorked the wine, he said 'What is it, Ma?'

'I don't know where to start,' I said. 'I have always let you believe, along with everyone else, that your father was dead, that he died in a road accident when you were a baby, and that I met and married Martin a short while later. Well, it wasn't true.'

And I told him a version of the real story, leaving out the arrangements that his father had made for him to be aborted, and my desperation and loneliness in my illegitimate pregnancy, which eighteen years ago was much more difficult than it might be today. Then, unmarried mothers were treated as though they were in disgrace, and subjected to disapproval and humiliation by hospital sisters and others. Today, single parenthood is often regarded as a kind of heroism.

My son drank his wine and watched me steadily, and at the end of the story, he said:

'Well, it isn't a great shock to me. I think I always really knew, inside me, somehow. Maybe when I was very young I heard something being discussed, I don't know. But I'd really like to meet my father. Is that possible?'

'Oh, no!' I said. 'He's married, you see, and has other children. His family doesn't know.'

'But I'm old enough to be discreet,' Dom persisted. 'Couldn't I arrange to meet him at his office, or at a restaurant? His family needn't know.'

My heart sank. And yet a part of me wanted it. I had always wanted to show Pierre our son.

'He might not want to see you or know you,' I pointed out.

'Well if he doesn't, he doesn't. But I'd like to go to France on my way back from Greece, and at least try.'

78

'And another thing,' I said. 'It was eighteen years ago. It may not be possible to find him. He may have changed his job, moved his office. He may even be dead.' The thought hadn't struck me before.

'Well, I'd like to try, anyway,' Dom said stubbornly. 'Don't you understand, Mother?'

I sighed.

'Yes, I do understand. I'll dig out his address – or what was his address, eighteen years ago – and send it to you. But promise me that if he refuses, that's that.'

Why did I want to protect Pierre, after all these years? Or was I protecting the frail bond between us, Pierre and me? Did it still exist?

'I'll just ring him at his office, and say that I think he knew my mother eighteen years ago, and I'm in Paris and should like to meet him,' Dom said. 'If he says no, then that's that.'

'All right,' I agreed. I trusted Dominic.

'But Ma – why have you suddenly come charging up to Oxford to tell me, after all this time?'

'Oh,' I'd forgotten. 'Yes. That's important. I had a letter, Dom, a sort of anonymous letter. Someone – I don't know who – knows about it all, and I was afraid that they might tell you, and I thought I'd rather tell you myself. Apart from telling you, they might do something else – a snide story in *Private Eye*, for example.'

'How contemptible!' Dominic was indignant. 'You must go to the police, Mother. Are you being blackmailed?'

'I don't know. Not yet. I don't know what the letter-writer wants,' I said. 'She – I've always thought of her as a woman, though I suppose that it might equally well be a man – has written to me twice before.'

I hadn't intended telling Dominic that, and I regretted it instantly.

'What about?' he naturally asked.

79

'Not about you,' I said. 'About totally other subjects. I'd rather not discuss them, if you don't mind. There are other people involved, and it's not really fair to them.'

'Is it going to make problems for you, Ma? In your job, I mean?'

Behind Dominic's genuine concern for me was a concern for his future at University, I sensed.

'I don't know, at the moment, Dom. About what the writer is hoping to achieve, I mean. But don't worry, about me or about your education. There's more than enough money to see you through. And as for me – I'm a survivor.'

It was true. I was, and I am.

Dominic kissed me.

'I'm sorry, Ma. That you should have had this worry, I mean. You've had a tough life, haven't you?'

Had I?

'What do you mean?'

'It must have been difficult for you, having me when you weren't married. Grandfather can't have been exactly delighted. I expect he thought that you were taking after Grandmother.'

'No, Grandfather wasn't delighted when I told him I was pregnant,' I said. 'But he adored you when you were born. Never forget that. And of course you'll inherit Falconbridge.'

'And you and Martin don't exactly get on,' Dom said.

'That's true, but we've achieved a way of life that works perfectly well,' I said.

We sat silently for a while.

'Tell me more about my father,' Dom said. 'What he looked like, what sort of personality he had. Do I take after him?'

I considered my son.

'Not very much,' I said. 'I think you're more like me. You've got his mouth maybe.'

I searched my memory to remember what had attracted me to Pierre, and described his charm, his style, his elegance, his authority, his tenderness, and my son – his son – listened with fascination. It grew dark outside, and a distant clock struck midnight, and I was reminded that I would not be back in London until two a.m., and I had to be at work the next day.

'I've got to go,' I said, and I kissed Dominic, and he patted my back tenderly, as his father had once done, and said:

'I'm glad you told me, Mother.'

He saw me into the car, and I began the drive home down the M40.

As I drove, I went over in my mind the extraordinary events of the day. It seemed a timeless age ago when I had driven along the same road in the opposite direction. So many things had happened during the intervening eighteen hours.

I had made love with a boy young enough to be my son, a boy who had discovered for the first time what making love was about. I felt stirrings of passion as I thought about Chris, and yes, love too. Oh, no! I mustn't let myself fall in love with him. It wouldn't do at all. He was young enough to be my son. Oedipus schmoedipus, I thought, so long as the boy loves his mother.

Did Freud have it all wrong? Was it really not sons who wanted to make love to their mothers, but mothers who lusted after their sons? Was that what the older woman's younger man relationship in France were all about? Women reach the peak of sexuality in their thirties, and young men at . . . Chris's age. He was bursting with it. It was exciting and revitalizing to have that tumescent urgency, imperative desire instead of the blasé sophistication of an older man. Oh, Chris, I loved you in spite of myself, and your leanness,

81

your hardness, your intensity, your gratitude . . .

There was a sickening bang, and I knew that I had hit the car in front, which had braked suddenly on coming upon a line of traffic. I shook silently for a few moments, then pulled onto the hard shoulder, and got out.

A belligerent young man with frizzy permed hair confronted me.

'Why don't you fucking look where you're going?' he demanded.

'I'm sorry. I was lost in thought about something, I'm afraid. Is there much damage?'

He ferretted in his car, and produced a torch.

'I'm okay,' he announced grudgingly. 'My car has a solid bumper. You've battered yourself a bit. D'you want to exchange names and addresses?'

'Do my lights and everything work?' I asked, feeling wobbly at the knees.

'Yes. It's just your bumper and a bit of bodywork,' he said.

'I won't make an insurance claim then, I'll just pay for it,' I said.

'Look where you're going, in future,' he said roughly. Then he smiled. 'Don't think and drive.'

I smiled back weakly, climbed in again and watched him drive safely into the distance before I started up. Don't think and drive. Mustn't think about making love with Chris. His bodywork wasn't good for my bodywork. In spite of myself, Chris's body came into my mind. He looked so young and vulnerable. Poor Chris. When did you last see your father? Who is your father? My father's house has many mansions . . . Chris . . . Christ . . . A visitation from the Holy Ghost, in the shape of a doctor with a syringe full of semen.

I remembered a poem by Rex Warner which I had read in my early teens. Something about *'the seed slipped in the membrane, quietly, without fuss . . .'* Chris had been conceived without intercourse. I wondered if other babies born by artificial insemination knew that they had been thus conceived. And I thought about something a doctor who wrote for the magazine had once told me. One of his patients was impotent but could have an ejaculation by masturbation. So his wife, who desperately wanted a child, was given a syringe and a test-tube, and instructed to scoop up the semen in the bed and inseminate herself. Incredibly, it had worked. But what if the child found out later in life how he had been conceived? Oh, I was scraped up off a blanket . . .

But Gerry O'Dwyer not only couldn't get it up, he couldn't even produce the semen to inseminate his wife, because Chris had been the child of an unknown donor. Unknown donor . . . unknown warrior. Selling his seed perhaps to pay for his medical studies. What must it be like, never to know your father? Dom was going to know his father, at long last.

I pictured the meeting between them. If Pierre realized from the brief phone call that Dom was his son, he was bound to be curious too, and would want to see him, wouldn't he? But perhaps he'd be apprehensive, wonder if demands were going to be made on him . . . I thought that he would probably take the risk. Perhaps he would take Dom to a good restaurant. What would they talk about ? Me?

'How is your mother? What does she do, now? Is she married? Are there other children?'

Pierre had other children. Perhaps Dom would learn about his half-brothers and sisters. Would father and son just part, forever, after one lunch? Or would Pierre be enchanted by Dominic (as Dom's mother, I was positive that he must be) and want to go on seeing his son, maybe want to settle something on him? Would Dom's meeting with Pierre lead to a meeting with Pierre for me? I more than half hoped that it might. I had a strong curiosity to see Pierre again, to see if I felt for him what once I had felt.

The darkness of the motorway gave way to the street lights of the outskirts of London. It was nearly two a.m., and there was hardly any traffic. I felt very tired. Tomorrow I had to go with God to visit an old people's home which had expressed an interest – well, actually that was too strong a term for it; they said they didn't mind, anyway – being adopted for God's 'Adopt a Granny for *Herself*' scheme. God would be bounding around with endless enthusiasm, as ever. Endless impotent enthusiasm, I realized. God had no children, so the magazine was his child. How did he feel towards Chris? A cuckoo in his nest. Another man's child who called him father, whom he pretended was his son. A false boast of non-existent virility and fertility. A fertility symbol . . .

No wonder Chris didn't want to go home. What a strange household. What an angry household.

Life, I decided, was really much stranger than fiction. Reaching the flats, I parked my car in its allotted space, toiled up the stairs – I didn't trust the lifts at night; if they stuck no-one would release you until morning – and put my key in the lock. As I walked towards the bedroom, I saw a light under the door, and stopped. Was it an intruder?

'Hello there!' It was Toby's voice. 'Is that you, darling?'

I recovered, and opened the bedroom door. Toby was sitting up in my bed in his pyjamas, with the bedside light on and photocopies of official-looking documents strewn all over the counterpane. For the first time ever, I felt resentful of him. I just wanted to slide between my own sheets and zonk out. I resented his uninvited intrusion into my bed, and probably into my body.

But 'Hello, darling, nice surprise,' I said, obeying the rules, and went over to kiss him.

84

Toby put his arms round me.

'You're late back,' he said. 'Are you okay?'

I turned my face away from him. Could he see the guilt in my eyes?

'Yes, of course,' I said. 'Why shouldn't I be?'

'You're very tense,' he said.

'I had a slight prang on the way back,' I said. 'Ran into the back of the car in front.'

'Were you hurt?' Toby turned me to face him, and looked into my eyes.

'No, not at all, just slightly shaken,' I said, hoping that he would attribute all my tension to the accident.

'What about the cars?'

'No damage to the other one, nothing much to mine,' I said.

'Get into bed, and I'll make you a cup of tea,' Toby said, getting out and gathering up his papers.

'Why are you so late? Was there a problem with Dominic?'

I started taking off my clothes.

'No, he took it very well. He said he'd sort of suspected, anyway. But he was out for the day when I arrived. I had to wait till he returned.'

'What a bore for you,' Toby said, putting his papers into his brief case. 'You're going to be exhausted tomorrow. Whatever did you do all day?'

'Oh, prowled around Oxford,' I hedged. 'I do feel a bit shaken after the accident, I'd appreciate that tea.'

'First or afterwards?' Toby asked, coming to take me into his arms.

My heart sank.

'First, please,' I said, kissing him politely but without enthusiasm, and sliding into bed.

Physically fatigued as I was, my mind felt feverish and active. I felt too keyed up for sleep, and was sitting up wishing that I had some sleeping pills when Toby returned with mugs of tea, and handed me one. He sat on the edge of the bed in his pyjamas, and I looked at him and thought again what an attractive man he was. And then I thought of Chris, and what an attractive boy he was.

Toby was saying something.

'What?' I said

'What did Dom say, exactly?' he said.

'Well, he was worried for me, and also for himself, I think, because if it became public and I lost my job, he didn't know if I could help him financially and see him through University. Of course I can. And he wants to meet his father.'

'Not a good idea.' Toby said instantly and firmly.

'Why not?' I asked aggressively.

'Well, you told me that his father was married, didn't you, and had a family? It could break up his marriage if it all came to light after all this time.'

I felt a hard ball of secret anger inside me. Toby was obviously identifying with Dom's father, imagining what it would be like to have the security of precious family life disrupted.

'What about Dom?' I asked. 'It's perfectly natural that he should want to meet his father. Anyway, he's a nice boy, and promises to be tactful and not do anything to upset the apple cart. Not that some apple carts wouldn't be better upset.'

'What do you mean by that?' Toby asked, sensing a hidden threat behind the words.

'Nothing,' I said, sliding away from it. 'I'm terribly tired, Toby. I need to sleep.'

He let it pass, took the mug away from me, slipped into bed beside me and started caressing my breasts. I felt rebellious and unwelcoming and lay stiffly, giving him no encouragement at all.

'What's the matter?' Toby asked.

'Nothing. I don't know, I'm out of sorts, I suppose.'

'What did the letter say, exactly?' he asked, thinking he knew the reason.

'It was very much like the others. Could have been mistaken for a genuine one, if it hadn't been signed 'Helen Turner.' It said something like 'Dear Hilary Toogood, I have a son of eighteen who is a student. My son believes that his father is dead, and that I was a widow when I married my present husband fifteen years ago. In fact my son was illegitimate, and his father is still alive. So far I have managed to keep this from him, but I don't know if I can do so indefinitely. Do you advise me to tell him in case he finds out from someone else?''

Perhaps it was a genuine letter,' Toby said.

'Oh, no, Toby. Not when it's signed 'Helen Turner', who gives a false address, and has already written to me saying that she has a lover who is a Member of Parliament, and a husband who likes little boys.'

'I say,' Toby said, laughing, 'For someone who sets up to sort out other peoples lives, you do have quite a cupboard full of skeletons.'

'It's not funny,' I said crossly. 'Anyway, most Problem Page editors had led fairly chequered lives, you know. If you've never known desperation, you can't really help people who are desperate, in my opinion.'

Toby yawned.

'Well, it's no good worrying, my love. I don't somehow think she's a blackmailer. I think that the extortion would have started before now.'

'But what does she want?' I asked. 'It feels like a nasty cat-and-mouse game.'

'I don't know,' Toby said. 'But I know what I want.'

So I lay back submissively, and pretended he was Chris.

Chapter Ten

THE NEXT MORNING I awoke to find the sun streaming over the black and white sprigged duvet.

'Oh, my God!' I said, sitting up abruptly. 'Toby, we've overslept. What time is it?'

Toby looked at his watch twice, then shot out of bed, and made for the bathroom.

'It's nine o'clock,' he said. 'I've got a client meeting at half past.'

'And I've got to go with God to visit an old folks' home in Streatham,' I said.

I made two mugs of instant coffee. Toby drank his while he used his electric razor, and I dipped myself in and out of a quick bath, threw on a navy print dress which I thought was appropriate for the old folk, and made it into the office by ten.

Ruth said, 'A gentleman has rung twice for you. He wouldn't give his name.'

My heart gave a lurch. Could Helen Turner be a man, after all?

'Oh, well, I daresay he'll call again,' I mangaed to say casually. 'I could do with some coffee. I overslept and had no breakfast.'

'Did you have a good day yesterday?' Ruth asked.

'Yes, but I was late getting home.'

As I walked towards my office, the phone started

ringing. Ruth picked it up, mouthed, 'It's him again –' and I said:

'Okay, I'll take it in my own office.' I went in, put down my bag and briefcase and picked up the receiver.

'Hello, Hilary Toogood.'

It was Chris.

'Chris! Was it you who rang before?'

'Yes, you're late,' he grumbled.

'What is it?' I asked, still slightly edgy.

'What do you mean, what is it? It's nothing and everything. It's thank you for yesterday, and its's I love you, and it's when can I see you again?'

'Oh!' I said.

'Hilary? Are you there?'

'Yes, I'm here.'

'I've thought of nothing except you and getting you into bed again since you walked out of the Turl with Dom yesterday evening. Have you given me a second thought?'

'I've thought about you a great deal. In fact,' I said, in a burst of honesty, 'I was thinking about you so hard driving home that I hit the car in front.'

'Hilary!' he said, with what sounded to me like unalloyed joy. 'Are you all right? Were you hurt?'

'No, I wasn't hurt,' I said.

'When can I see you again? Can I come up to London today and stay with you tonight?' Chris demanded.

'No!' I said. 'Chris, where are you? You're not within earshot of Dom, or anyone else, are you?'

'No, I've borrowed a friend's phone, and he's out,' he reassured me, 'When can I see you then?'

'I don't know.' I thought of Toby. It hadn't occurred to me that Chris would propose coming to London.

'Why can't I come up today?'

'It's Friday, and I usually go to Sussex on Fridays, for the weekend.'

'Don't go . Please don't go,' he implored me.

Could I stay? Toby would be out of town.

'I don't know, Chris,' I said weakly. 'I'm not sure.'

'Please. You don't have to go, do you?'

'It's not that. It's . . .' I couldn't tell him what it was. It felt like being unfaithful to Toby. But I wasn't married to Toby, that was ridiculous. I needed time to think about it.

'I do have to go to Sussex,' I said firmly. 'But possibly – just possibly, no promises – next weekend something might be arranged. But not London. You're not to come to my flat in London, d'you understand? But I might be able to come to Oxford. Dom's flat will be empty, won't it? He'll be in Greece by then.'

'Oh, yes,' Chris said. 'But promise. Please promise. Do come. Darling Hilary. I'm obsessed with thoughts of you.'

'Well, go and take a cold shower,' I said unkindly. 'Look, I've got to go now.'

'I'll write to you,' he said. 'May I? Please?'

'Yes, all right,' I said, rather ungraciously. 'Bye bye then, see you soon.' And I hung up.

By half past ten I had cleared the papers on my desk, and hurried down to join God in the chauffeur-driven car which was to take us to Eventide House. He had taken off his jacket, and sat in his shirt sleeves and red braces in the back of the car, waiting for me.

'Morning, sweetie,' he shouted, pecking my cheek.

'Good morning, Gerry.' I slid demurely into the car beside him, looking at him curiously. He looked just the same as he always did; loud, overbearing, sweating – and a eunuch. Yesterday I had been in bed with his son – no I hadn't, Chris, wasn't his son.

We crawled through the crowded, dirty streets of South London towards Streatham. After three quarters of an hour, the car pulled up outside a large detached

Victorian house with stubbly, stunted trees outside, and dingy net curtains obscuring all the windows. The paint was peeling, and there was a pile of sand and a rusty tank in the front garden. The building looked uninhabited and derelict. Gerry looked at it doubtfully.

'Are your sure this is the right place, sweetie?' he asked.

He rang the bell, and after a second ring a couple of minutes later, there was the sound of footsteps on lino, and the door was opened by a middle-aged woman in a very tight, very short, pale blue crimplene two-piece. Her sparse hair was bleached and permed and frizzy.

'Good morning,' she said. 'You must be *Herself*.'

'That's right,' God said, holding out a hand. 'This is Hilary Toogood, and I'm Gerry O'Dwyer.'

We stepped into the dark hall, which smelled strongly of cats and another pervasive odour I couldn't quite place. The only ornament was a vase of dusty plastic flowers on a tallboy at the foot of the stairs. There was no sign of life at all.

'I'm Matron', the lady, who had a strong Cockney accent, announced. 'The gerries are so looking forward to meeting you.'

'The gerries?' Gerry queried, confused.

'Geriatrics, dear, my old folk. I call them gerries for short. But not for long, unfortunately. Some of them don't have long with us.'

'Where do they go?' I asked stupidly.

Matron cast her eyes upwards.

'The Lord giveth and the Lord taketh away,' she said.

'You mean they pass away?' Gerry asked.

'You could say that,' Matron said.

We were still standing uncertainly in the hallway when a door to the left flew open, and we beheld a startling sight. A very old, totally bald lady rushed out and headed for the stairs. We knew it was a woman because she was completely nude. Her skin hung on her in folds and bags and pouches. Buttocks and breasts shook wildly as she rushed upwards. A middle-aged women in a navy overall pursued her with a dress in one hand, shouting:

'Mrs Baldwin! Mrs Baldwin! You're a very naughty girl indeed!'

At the top of the stairs, Mrs Baldwin halted and turned to face us, cackling. Her stomach hung on her like an apron, but not low enough to conceal the fact that she was bald in her pubic region as well. The nurse caught up with her, pulled the dress round her, and hustled her off somewhere upstairs.

Gerry and I stood open-mouthed. Matron didn't turn a hair.

'Some of the gerries are a little confused, dear,' she said. 'Now old Mrs Baldwin, she will keep taking her clothes off. Just hang on here a tick, will you, and I'll see if they're ready for you in the Residents' Lounge.'

She went through the door from which Mrs Baldwin had emerged, and I turned to God, giggling.

'Are the readers going to adopt a granny for *Herself*, or adopt a stripper for *Herself*?' I asked.

God shuddered. 'Unbelievable, isn't it,' he said. 'You don't suppose they're all like that?'

'Oh, worse, I should think,' I reassured him, cheerfully.

'Coooeee! You can come in now,' Matron called, and we moved towards the door through which she had disappeared.

It was a dark, high-ceilinged room with a large amount of empty floor space in the middle. Ranged round the outside edge of the room was a row of easy chairs with wooden arms, each of which was occupied by an old person. Some seemed to be asleep – at least, I hoped they were only asleep. One or two were regarding us with curiosity. We stood in the centre, the three of us, a small embarrassed group.

'This lady and gentleman are from *Herself* magazine,' Matron announced brightly. 'Remember I told you, their readers would like to take you out? Won't that be lovely?'

There was a long silence. I felt uncomfortable. Seeing an empty chair next to an old gentleman who appeared to be awake, I decided to take it.

'Hello, I'm Hilary Toogood,' I said.

'You'll have to speak up, I'm deaf,' he said loudly. He looked rather like a tortoise. Matron bore down on him, saying:

'Lost our teeth again have we, Mr Westcott? Dear me, we are absent-minded. You'll have to shout, dear,' she told me, 'he's posters deaf, I'm afraid, as well as – well, you know – a bit past it.'

'Can't stand that woman!' Mr Westcott shouted suddenly.

'Now, now, Mr Westcott. Naughty!' Matron reproved him.

An old lady across the room appeared to be trying to say something.

'Want potty, dear?' Matron asked her brightly. 'Right you are, just hold on a tick.' She went to the door.

'Nurse!' she shouted. 'Lady Havering wants potty.'

God stood in the middle of the room looking appalled. I addressed myself with determination to Mr Westcott.

'Do you have any family who visit you, Mr Westcott?' I shouted.

'My family doesn't visit,' he grumbled. 'Haven't seen them for fifteen years. That's all you get for working for them all your life. Never see them at all. Don't want to bother, they don't.'

'Would you like to have an adopted family, a *Herself* reader who would be like a daughter to you?' I bellowed.

93

'Certainly not,' Mr Westcott said, looking at me balefully. 'Don't want no more daughters. Can't stand the one I've got. Nothing but worry. Never did like her. Glad to see the back of her when she went off with that good-for-nothing boy. Course, I knew what she saw in him. Not his brains, I can tell you. Oh, no. Brazen little minx, she was! Haven't seen her from the day they went off together.'

'That's right, they don't want to know you when you're old, do they?' an old lady a couple of chairs away broke in. 'Thrown on the scrap heap, that's what we are.'

She glared at me, as though I were responsible, and a wave of antagonism seemed to flow round the other residents.

The door flew open and Mrs Baldwin, the lady of whom we had first seen all too much, came in. She was now wearing a shapeless cotton dress. The nurse behind her crossed the room and pulled Lady Havering to her feet to help her from the room. Age, I thought, was a great leveller.

Mrs Baldwin was standing right in front of me, jabbering incoherently but with evident animosity. I looked at her nervously and uncomprehendingly.

Matron came to my rescue.

'You're sitting in her chair, dear,' she explained. 'They all have their special chairs, and they can't stand anyone else sitting in them.'

'I'm so sorry.' I sprang to my feet, and Mrs Baldwin sat down in the vacated chair with a look of triumph.

'Of course,' Matron said 'they haven't got much in their lives, poor dears. A little thing like a telly would mean a lot. I expect that your readers could manage something like that for us. And we're always short-handed here. Never enough pairs of hands . . .'

'Sure, sure,' Gerry said hastily. 'A telly would be no problem, no problem at all.'

'Come and have a cup of tea in my office,' Matron invited.

In the hall someone was mopping up a large puddle in the middle of the lino. Lady Havering obviously hadn't made it to her destination.

'How are we going to manage about pictures?' I murmured to Gerry.

'We'll probably have to use models, sweetie,' he said.

Matron's office was positively luxurious compared with what we had seen up until then. There was a chintz sofa, and a television in one corner. As we sat down, a woman in an overall brought in a tray of coffee.

'We were going to call the scheme 'Adopt a Granny for *Herself*'', Gerry said, addressing himself to Matron, 'but some of the old folk don't seem too keen on being adopted.'

'Oh, don't you worry about that, dear,' Matron said brightly, pouring out an unspeakable coffee-and-milk mixture from the pot. 'They'll be all right later. Just a bit funny this morning, one or two of them. We all have our little ways, don't we? Now, about this television set . . .'

An hour later, we made our escape. It was a relief to get out of the dark and smelly house into the sunlight. Gerry directed the driver to a Dulwich pub he knew, where we drank double whiskies.

'My God!' Gerry said. 'I wish you'd never come up with this scheme, Hilary darling.'

He seemed to be serious. I looked at him open-mouthed.

'Would you prefer to drop it?' I asked hopefully.

'Certainly not,' Gerry said firmly. 'Nothing wrong with the idea, I suppose, just that you picked such an awful old folks' home. Surely you could have found a better one, sweetie?'

'Do you know how many homes Ruth rang round before she could find one which would cooperate at all?' I asked crossly. 'It took her days. Most of them said they'd have to ask the committee, or the local authority, or something, and the entanglement with bureaucracy was enormously frustrating and time-consuming. It took her the best part of a week's full-time work to find one which was willing to play ball without strings.'

'Well, there are strings – a new telly for Matron, probably a new roof by the time she's finished,' Gerry complained.

'So let's drop it,' I said.

'No, no, if it's all you can come up with, it'll have to do. I daresay if we can get one or two of the more presentable old folks out of there and sitting on a park bench watching *Herself* readers' children at play, it might be possible to get some pictures . . . using a soft-focus lens, of course,' Gerry said.

I had a fleeting mental vision of Mrs Baldwin sitting starkers on a park bench, and shuddered.

'I say,' I said. 'Mrs Baldwin was aptly named, wasn't she?'

And we both laughed, and Gerry ordered two more scotches.

When I got home that night, there was a smell of frying onions which made me remember that I'd had no lunch. Toby, a tea towel tucked around his waist as an apron, was making supper.

I stood in the kitchen doorway looking at him in surprise.

'It's been a funny, disjointed week. I keep thinking today's Friday,' I said.

'It is Friday,' he confirmed, tasting the dressing he was making for the salad.

'You usually go home on Fridays,' I said.

'Well, I decided to stay with you this weekend. You

96

seemed so strange last night, not yourself at all. I decided that you needed me.'

He kissed me briefly, and returned to crushing garlic.

'Oh!' I said, my first feeling of relief that I'd forbidden Chris to hurtle up to London as he had proposed. 'But I was going to Sussex.'

'You went last weekend,' Toby said. 'You can easily stay, can't you?

'I suppose so,' I said.

'You don't sound very enthusiastic.'

Toby put down the garlic grater and looked at me searchingly. I felt ashamed of myself. I wasn't playing my role of willing mistress at all well.

'Darling, I'm very enthusiastic, and of course I want to stay,' I said, putting my arms round his neck, and rubbing myself against him. He kissed me again, then put me gently aside and returned to his preparations for the meal. I went to telephone Martin to tell him that I shouldn't be returning to Falconbridge.

'Maybe not next weekend, either,' I said. 'we've got a lot of work on at the moment, and I'm very tied up. I don't think I'll make it.'

He didn't seem to mind.

'Did you see the psychiatrist?' I asked.

'Yes. Did you do it deliberately?' Martin demanded, 'Do what?'

'Choose a woman psychiatrist.'

'I didn't know it was a woman,' I said. 'I was only given the surname and initials. Dr E Raine, wasn't it?'

'The E stands for Elizabeth.'

'Oh,' I said. 'Does it matter?'

'Not really, I suppose,' he said grudgingly.

'Did you like her?'

'I suppose she's all right. I'm going to see her twice a week.'

'Can you manage that?'

97

'Well, of course it's difficult, but I should be able to, I think. For a while, anyway.'

'Good,' I said. 'See you in a fortnight, maybe.'

'Goodnight,' Martin said, and rang off.

Chapter Eleven

I WOKE EARLY the next morning, and lay watching Toby sleeping beside me. It reminded me of watching Chris sleeping a couple of days previously, and stirrings of sexual longing disturbed me. I felt under the bedclothes, and found Toby was hard. He stirred as I touched him, and I continued to play with him and nuzzle him, my own sexual feelings growing at the same time.

He lay, flushed with sleep and smiling indulgently as I climbed over him and started gently moving.

I climaxed in a couple of minutes, and he turned me onto my back and continued to make love until he too was satisfied.

'That's the way to wake up . . . with the sun streaming in, and a randy woman in bed beside you,' Toby said, caressing me idly and dozily as we lay side by side.

I slipped out of bed, and went to make breakfast. The smell of coffee percolating filled the flat. I fried bacon and eggs and laid a tray for two. When everything was ready, I carried the tray through to the bedroom.

'What shall we do today?' I asked Toby.

'If I were at home, I'd be mending the washing machine and putting up shelves in the boys' room,' he said.

'That reminds me –'

'No, no little jobs,' he interrupted me firmly. 'Jean finds me little jobs each and every time I'm home. She turns each weekend into a penance for having enjoyed myself with you all week, though she doesn't know that, of course.'

It gladdened my heart to hear it.

'Let's be thoroughly self-indulgent this weekend, and not do anything useful at all,' Toby suggested, 'I'll try and get some tickets for the Tom Stoppard play tonight, shall I? And would you like to go out to dinner?'

I lay beside him, playing with the hairs on his chest.

'You're a very sexy woman, you know,' Toby said, putting aside the tray carefully and unbuttoning my dressing-gown.

'Why don't we just spend the weekend in bed?' I suggested.

It was a heatwave weekend. When I picked the Sunday papers up off the mat the following morning, there were 'BRITAIN SWELTERS! UP, UP, UP GOES THE THERMOMETER' type headlines, and the flat was stifling.

We decided to take the car to Richmond Park, and sit in the sunshine. Unfortunately, half of West London seemed to have had the same idea. There were long queues of cars, and the car parks were crowded. Having arrived at the park, most people just sat in their cars, however. When we walked into the glade known as Isabella's Plantation, it was cool by the stream, and there weren't many trippers around.

We sat on the grass, and watched a family of four walking past. The mother was berating the children for something. They looked hot, exhausted, and out of sorts with each other.

'I think she's telling them to damn well enjoy themselves, or else,' Toby said, and laughed. His fingers caressed the nape of my neck. 'It's good to be here with you,' he said. 'I hate Sundays at home.'

'Why?'

100

'I don't know . . . she seems to make me do the things I find most boring. I don't suppose it's deliberate. I don't know, maybe it is.'

'What kind of things?'

'Well, when the boys were younger, we always took a Sunday afternoon walk, with me pushing the pram. She sort of had me on parade, all dressed up, showing off to the neighbours. 'This is my well-trained husband, my clean and well-dressed children.' I nearly went out of my mind with boredom.'

'It sounds sort of stultifying,' I said. Hearing Toby running down Jean was, I had to acknowledge, music to my ears.

'Did you want the children?' I asked.

'No. But I suppose I wanted the image of fatherhood.'

'Why did you marry her?'

'For all the wrong reasons. I decided very early in life that I was going to make a career in politics. I made the decision about the time I was President of the Oxford Union, I suppose. And it was quite obvious to me fairly early on that a wife who looked right was an enormous asset to a candidate. It was purely an intellectual decision, a career decision. She wanted children, and I suppose the image of a family man was even more useful. That was a career decision too, but I suppose all men want sons, don't they, to prove themselves and also to pass on their genes?'

'Couldn't you have waited to marry someone you loved?' I asked.

'Oh, I did love someone. Before I met Jean. But she didn't fit the image of a candidate's wife. So I gave her up. I still feel guilty about it.'

'Do I fit the image of a candidate's mistress?' I asked teasingly, but Toby took the question seriously, and looked at me ponderingly.

101

'No, you don't, he said. 'I chose you with my heart, not my head.'

I felt at the same time pleased, and perversely angry, that in some way I fell short of what Toby thought a mistress should be.

'In what way don't I fit?' I asked.

'I don't know.' He wasn't attentive enough to sense my anger. 'I suppose that a copybook mistress would be younger. And you don't look as sexy as you are.'

'I'm sorry I don't fit the bill absolutely,' I said, thoroughly nettled. 'Other people find me attractive and sexy, anyway.'

'I didn't say you weren't,' Toby said. 'Of course you are. You just don't flaunt it. But what exactly do you mean about other people?'

'Nothing,' I said.

'No, go on. What do you mean?'

'A handsome boy young enough to be your son found me overwhelmingly attractive in Oxford last week.'

'What do you mean, overwhelmingly?' Toby demanded.

'Nothing.'

'Hilary, I want to know. What do you mean?'

'Are you jealous?' I asked, pleased.

'Yes, I am jealous,' he said. 'Please tell me what you mean.'

'I don't mean anything,' I said, feeling fearful, and regretting having mentioned Chris.

'Hilary, I want to know the truth,' Toby said.

'There was a young man . . . I spent the afternoon in bed with him. But it didn't mean anything,' I said.

'How could it not mean anything?' Toby demanded loudly. He got up and started walking up and down.

'Sssh, Toby . . . someone will hear,' I said.

'I don't bloody well care if they do. You've been

screwing around with some young buck, and you expect me not to care?'

'I'm not married to you, you don't own me,' I flashed back, angrily.

'I don't own you, and I don't want to own you,' Toby said, drawing away from me, and I bitterly regretted having told him, and felt frightened and hurt.

'And you screw Jean, anyway, don't you?' I said.

'As a matter of fact I don't. She's frigid, and doesn't like it.'

'You mean that you would screw her if she wasn't?'

'No, I don't mean that. I'm not turned on by her at all, she's a cold and shallow woman. And she's not turned on to me, either.'

We were squabbling like children, but I couldn't stop.

'Maybe she's turned on to someone else. How d'you know she's faithful to you?' I taunted.

'Maybe she isn't. I couldn't care less, so long as she's discreet. I don't care a fig for her. But I do care for you, and I mind that you are. Why did you do it?'

'I don't know, Toby,' I said, moving towards him and putting my arms round him. 'I'm sorry.'

He didn't respond to my caress.

'Are you going to do it again?' he demanded.

I felt angry at the physical rejection, that my attempt at conciliation had been brushed aside.

'I don't know,' I said. 'If you really loved me, and we were married, I wouldn't. But you can't expect me to commit myself wholly to you when you won't commit yourself to me.'

'I simply don't understand the logic of what you're saying,' Toby said. 'And in any case, marriage is out of the question. I made that clear from the start.'

'You don't expect Jean to be faithful to you, and you're married to her, so why the hell should I be faithful to you, when we're not married?' I said.

103

'I didn't say I don't expect her to. I do expect her to. I said I didn't care if she wasn't. But she is.'

'How d'you know?' I asked.

'Well first, she doesn't like screwing, not at all, and then I shouldn't think that anyone would fancy her, anyway. And secondly, dependent wives have a lot more to lose than financially independent women like you,' Toby said.

'What a disgusting thing to say,' I said.

'What a disgusting thing to do,' he retaliated.

I burst into tears.

He sat on the grass seething and letting me cry for several minutes. Passers-by looked at me curiously. Eventually, he moved towards me, and took my hand.

'For God's sake stop snivelling,' Toby said, not unkindly. 'I didn't spend the weekend in London to have you crying all over me.'

'It's all too much,' I said.

'What's all too much?'

'Everything,' I said. 'Martin. Helen Turner. My life.'

'So change it,' Toby said.

'How can I change it?'

'I don't know,' he admitted.

'Oh, Toby, who is Helen Turner? And what is she going to do next? What does she want?'

'I don't know,' he said. 'But if you hear from her again, I think you ought to go to the police. Have you kept all the previous letters?'

'Yes,' I said. 'But what can the police do? She hasn't committed any crime. It's not as though she's asking for money.'

'Well, maybe a solicitor. It's harassment,' Toby said.

'I don't see what a solicitor can do either, not when we don't know who she is,' I argued.

'He could employ a private detective to find out,' Toby said.

104

We sat in silence for a while.

'Who could it be? What does she want?' I said

'Or he,' Toby said.

'I think of him as she because Helen Turner is a woman's name,' I said, in a confused sort of way.

'I need a drink,' Toby said, standing up.

'Toby, it doesn't make any difference, does it?' I asked, standing up too, and clinging to him.

'What?'

'Last Thursday, in Oxford.'

'Who was it?' he asked, his face darkening.

'A friend of Dom's.'

'Why did you do it, Hilary?'

'I don't know,' I said. I didn't. 'But it doesn't affect us, does it?'

'Come and have a drink,' he said abruptly.

I knew that it did.

Every batch of post which Ruth brought in from that time onwards made my heart thump with apprehension, and I would start flipping through it quickly to make sure that there was no letter from Helen Turner before I could breathe easily again, and read the ordinary letters with normal attention.

On the Wednesday, on top of the pile of opened letters stapled to their envelopes was an unopened letter in an unfamiliar hand, which had been forwarded from Falconbridge. It was marked PERSONAL AND CONFIDENTIAL and was addressed to Mrs Martin Shipton. It couldn't be Helen Turner, but I slit it open in some trepidation and glanced to the end to see who the writer was. It was Chris.

Chris had written me six pages of passionate and sexually explicit prose, pouring out his dammed-up longing and excitement onto paper. I looked at the date and postmark. He'd written it the previous Friday, expecting me to receive it when I went back to Falconbridge for the weekend. I felt annoyed with him for sending it there. For all he knew, my husband and I got on a lot better than in fact we did, and might well have shared our correspondence. If I had been happily married and had for a brief afternoon lost my head, I could have been landed in an an impossibly difficult situation by his letter. It was selfish and inconsiderate of him to have sent it there, I thought, or indeed to have written it at all.

I flipped through his ardent declarations of undying love and passion. One page was filled with nothing but 'I love you, I love you, I love you. . . .' written hundreds of times over. Other pages described the ways in which he would like to make love to me, if and when he were next allowed to do so. Towards the end, he burst into pleas that I should go to Oxford the following weekend, or that he should be allowed to come to London immediately. He ended by saying that he would telephone me on Sunday evening to know what I had decided.

Damn and blast, I thought. That meant last Sunday, and that he had telephoned Falconbridge. I hoped that he had had enough tact not to say anything out of the way. But how odd that he had not rung again. I buzzed Ruth.

'Ruth, has anybody rung while I've been out this week? There'a a young man, a friend of my son . . . he called last week. I don't know if you remember, he rang a couple of times early one morning and then just as I was arriving . . .'

'Oh yes, Hilary, I'm terribly sorry,' Ruth said. He's rung several times, I forgot to tell you. He said that you couldn't call him back, but he said he'll ring again at five o'clock this evening. It went clean out of my mind.'

'Oh, Ruth! You don't usually forget things.'

'No, I don't. But he wouldn't leave a name, or a message, so I didn't write anything down. I'm ever so sorry. Was it important?'

'No, it doesn't matter really,' I said. 'But if someone says they'll ring at a specific time, that is a message really, and I'd like to know.'

'Okay,' she said equably. 'The Matron of that Home's been on a couple of times, by the way. She says that the old folks don't mind being adopted, but are they going to be paid?'

'Paid?' I said. 'What for?'

'Don't know, really,' Ruth said. 'For having their pictures taken and everything, I suppose. One of them went on telly to talk about the last days of the Raj or something, and the Beeb gave him a fee for it.'

'Oh, my God!' I said. 'The whole thing gets more complicated and worse all the time. And God is now pretending that it was all my idea. Well, please tell her that if any of them appears in a photograph we will pay a small modelling fee. But we aren't paying them to go on outings with *Herself* readers. It's ridiculous. It's meant to be a treat for them.'

'That's what I did tell her, more or less,' Ruth said. 'I knew you'd say that. Oh, and God said to tell you that we've had a lawyer's letter about the health page.'

'What about?' I asked.

'I dunno, he said he'll send it for you to see. He said not to reply to it, just to draft something for Harry Ballsup and let him reply. He said he just wanted to alert you to it.'

'A fat lot of use that is, when he doesn't say what it is he's alerting me to,' I grumbled. 'Okay, Ruth, thank you. Put that young man through when he calls.'

Chris's call came at exactly five o'clock.

'Hilary?' he sounded young and uncertain.

'Chris? I've just had your letter. You really shouldn't have written it. It could have caused an awful lot of trouble for me,' I upbraided him.

'You should have had it at the weekend, but you weren't there, were you?' he said.

'No, I wasn't.'

'Where were you? Were you in London? I could have come up to see you. Didn't you want to see me? Was it just an excuse?'

'No, it wasn't an excuse, I had intended going to Falconbridge for the weekend, but something cropped up,' I said.

'Oh, work,' he said, sounding relieved. I let it pass.

'You shouldn't have written to me at Falconbridge,' I said, 'My husband might have opened it.'

'I only knew Dom's address there. I didn't know the address of your London flat,' he said. 'And I didn't like to ask Dom before he left.'

'Did he get off all right?'

'Yes, he did,' Chris said. 'Hilary, darling Hilary, please come to Oxford this weekend.'

'I don't think I can,' I said.

'Why not? Please, Hilary. You can if you want to.'

'I ought to go to Sussex. I didn't get there last weekend.'

'Please leave it. One more week won't hurt, will it? Please come to Oxford. Or let me come to London.'

'No!' I said sharply. 'There are other reasons, anyway, Chris. This whole thing isn't a very good idea, actually.'

'You just don't like me,' he said miserably.

'I do like you, but . . .'

'But what?'

'There are other factors involved,' I said stubbornly.

'You mean the difference in our ages? I wouldn't have thought that you were the kind of woman to whom that mattered.'

Oh, clever Chris.

'It's not that . . . It's difficult to discuss it over the phone.'

'That's why I want to see you,' he said plaintively.

'Well, let me think about it. Can I ring you?'

'No, but I can ring you. When?' he said, instantly.

'Ring me on Friday, at five.'

'Okay. Hilary –'

'Chris, I've got to go now, I'm sorry. If you have to write to me again, and I'd rather you didn't, please mark it 'Strictly Personal' and send it to my office.'

'Right you are,' he said blithely. 'Till Friday, Hilary darling.'

'Bye bye,' I said.

I hung up. What was I doing? I was mad. I should have told him that it was all finished. But perhaps I owed him some kind of explanation. Or was it just that I wanted to see him again?

I sighed and turned to the correspondence on my desk.

Chapter Twelve

On the Thursday evening, the heatwave evaporated into torrential rain. Toby had spent the night with me, and his car was being serviced. He had only a light suit with him, so we got up early on the Friday, and I drove him to the Battersea flat which he nominally occupied, to pick up his raincoat and his luggage to go back to his constituency for the weekend. It was still pouring, and he kissed me goodbye through the car window.

'See you Monday,' he said.

I drove on into the office. Gerry was ahead of me, perched matily on the corner of Ruth's desk, drinking coffee with her.

'Sorry I'm late,' I said. 'You don't often come slumming, Gerry. To what do I owe the honour of this visit?'

He waved a letter at me.

'The long arm of the law, sweetie. They're after our money. Bring in some coffee for Hilary and me, Ruthie, will you?'

He followed me into my office. I took off my raincoat, and hung it up.

'You remember the feature on fertility?' he said. 'We ran a piece on the couple who had a baby after seven years fruitless marriage, when she had had the new fertility treatment. Our doctor commented on the types of case the treatment might be suitable for.'

'Mr and Mrs Borer,' I said. 'I remember. There were some smashing pictures of them with the baby.'

'Yes,' said Gerry. 'Only unfortunately, sweetie, Mrs Borer isn't the legal Mrs Borer.'

Ruth brought in the coffee, and I tried to understand what he meant.

'You're telling me that they're not married?' I said.

'That's right, they're not.'

'Well, they've been together for seven years, so what does it matter? The doctors obviously thought that it was a stable relationship, or they wouldn't have prescribed fertility drugs.'

'Did you know they weren't married?' Gerry demanded.

'No, I didn't. I don't suppose the feature writer did, either. The lady calls herself Mrs Borer, and we don't ask to see the marriage certificate of everyone we feature in the magazine.'

'Well, unfortunately in this case, the legal Mrs Borer is suing us for libel. She says that Mr Borer deserted her and her two children five years ago, and she says that this article holds her up to ridicule and contempt.'

'I don't see that it's libellous,' I argued. 'The other lady is undoubtedly calling herself Mrs Borer, and she must be Mr Borer's common law wife. I don't see there's a case at all.'

'Well, Harry Ballsup thinks there may be. There was a case in the nineteen thirties, apparently, where an aggrieved wife won damages against a newspaper which had published a story about her husband and a young lady calling herself his wife, when she wasn't.'

'We aren't living in the nineteen thirties,' I said. 'What does the legal Mrs Borer want, anyway?'

'A retraction.'

'In other words, she wants to embarrass the who is living with her husband,' I said heatedly. 'I'll be damned if I'll have anything to do with it.'

'Harry thinks we ought to publish a paragraph,' Gerry said doubtfully.

'Well I don't, ' I said.

Gerry tapped his teeth with his pen.

'Okay,' he said, at length. 'We'll try sending a strong letter back, and see what happens. If she thinks she'll have to take us to court, she may back down. But if she carries on, we're not going to shell out, sweetie. You'll have to put a para in.'

'Over my dead body,' I said, and Gerry wandered off.

By the Friday afternoon, when the second post had been dealt with, it was obvious that Helen Turner had left me in peace for the week. Perhaps with the three letters she had shot her bolt? It seemed too much to hope for. It had a feeling of incompleteness, too. I somehow felt certain that I was going to hear from her again. In a way, I almost wanted to. I felt like a mongoose confronting a snake, waiting for the next strike. But the mongoose is quick and quick-witted and can often win, I reminded myself. I felt threatened by her, but if only I could see her, I could deal with her.

At half past four, Ruth buzzed me.

'There's a young man to see you Hilary,' she said.

'Let him in,' I said absently. And Chris stood squarely in front of my desk, looking at me quizzically, rainwater dripping from his anorak onto the carpet.

'Chris! What are you doing here? For goodness sake take that wet jacket off,' I said.

He struggled out of it, and I took it from him.

'May I kiss you?' he said.

'I'm afraid not, anyone might come in. Do you want a cup of tea?'

'Yes, please.' He looked around curiously. 'So this is the lair of Hilary Toogood.'

I ignored the remark.

'What are you doing here?' I asked.

'I said I was going to phone you at five, remember? I decided to come, instead.'

I buzzed for tea, and Ruth brought in two cups. Chris sat in one of the low chairs by the coffee table, and I took the one opposite him.

'You don't look very pleased to see me,' he said.

'I don't think I am pleased to see you.'

'Why not?'

'I didn't invite you.'

'You do like to control everything, don't you?' he burst out.

'Do I?' I was surprised.

'Hilary, I want to talk to you. Not here . . .' he waved his hand round. 'It's all too . . . Please, can we talk about it somewhere privately?'

I thought about it. Toby had gone to Wales for the weekend, I knew. I sighed. I knew how it would end.

'Okay, Chris. I'm going to knock off in a few minutes; you can come back to my flat and have a drink. But that's all, mind.'

He gave me a dazzling smile. I went over to clear up my desk, and he followed me.

'Dear Hilary Toogood,' he said, looking at the large sheaf of letters so addressed. Then, putting on a funny voice:

'My problem is that I'm in love with a married lady . . .'

The telephone buzzed. Ruth said: 'Gerry's here, Hilary.'

I said, 'Tell him . . .' but it was too late. The door opened, and Gerry came in.

He stopped short in his tracks on seeing Chris.

113

'Chris! Whatever are you doing here?' he said. He looked from Chris to me, and back again. I felt that my cheeks were burning, and hoped that they weren't.

Chris said easily, 'Hello, Dad. I came to deliver a couple of things to Hilary from her son. He left them with me when he went off to Greece.'

Gerry said, 'I didn't know you two knew each other.'

I said, 'Oh, we met when I went to see Dominic in Oxford last week, before he went off to Greece.'

'I didn't know you were coming home this weekend,' Gerry said to his son. I kept forgetting. Chris wasn't his son.

I'm not coming home, actually, Dad,' Chris said. 'I'm staying with a mate.'

We all three stood irresolutely for a minute or so. Then I said, 'I'm so sorry, Gerry, can I do something for you? What was it you wanted?'

'Nothing important, really,' Gerry said. 'I forgot to mention this morning that Harry suggested you should make a statement that you accepted the article in all good faith, believing that the lady was in fact the legal Mrs Borer.'

'I'll see him about it on Monday,' I said.

'Good girl.'

Gerry paused, then looked at his watch, and said, 'Well, I'd better be off. I've been summoned to have a drink with the Snow Queen.' He turned to Chris. 'If you're staying in London, try and come and have Sunday lunch with us. Your mother would like that.

'Okay, Dad, I'll try. I'll give her a ring, anyway.'

'Goodnight, all,' Gerry said, and withdrew.

There was a short silence after his departure. Then I said, 'Do you think he suspected anything?'

Chris shook his head. 'I'm sure he didn't.' He shrugged. 'Doesn't matter, anyway, does it?'

'He is my boss, Chris.'

'So what?'

I sighed. 'Oh, it doesn't matter, I suppose. Maybe I *am* hung up about my age.'

Ruth stuck her head round the door.

'Goodnight, Hilary. Good weekend.'

'And to you, Ruth. Goodbye.'

I stuffed work for the weekend into my briefcase, and Chris humped on his anorak and picked up his plastic bag.

'I hope you don't think I'm the mate with whom you told your father you were spending the weekend,' I said.

'I'll wait till I'm invited,' he said, looking at me sideways from under his eyelashes. He followed me demurely to the car park and got into the passenger seat beside me.

We drove home more or less in silence. I was partly thinking about Gerry, and wondering if he had suspected anything, and partly picturing a scenario where I found Toby in the flat, as I had the previous weekend, and he and Chris confronting each other. The previous weekend was the first time that Toby had ever stayed in London with me like that, however, and I didn't really believe that it would happen again.

Nevertheless it was with a feeling of relief that I opened my front door to find the flat reassuringly empty.

'Jesus Christ!' Chris said, looking round the flat. Why is it all in black and white? Don't you lead a highly colourful life?'

'Maybe my life is too colourful, and this is a restful background,' I said glibly. Maybe the silly statement was even true. But I didn't really believe it. 'No, that's silly,' I said. 'The black and white decor grew accidentally at first, but then consciously. I like it.'

'I like it too,' Chris said. 'It's got great style. Really great. But then you've got style too, Hilary. May I kiss you now?'

115

I didn't reply, and he took silence for assent. He took me into his arms, and kissed me passionately. Pressed against him, I could feel his erection

'Let's go to bed, Hilary,' he said urgently. 'Please.'

'I've got to talk to you first,' I said, disengaging myself firmly. 'Come and sit down and have a drink, Chris.' I led the way into the sitting-room.

I think it was the word first that made him follow me docilely, with the air of someone willing to endure whatever I wanted to lecture him about. First. So long as there was an afterwards.

I gave him a beer, and poured myself a whisky, and sat some way from him, in an armchair, wanting distance between us. He lay back on the sofa, watching me through half-closed eyes, relaxed, one jeaned leg thrown over the other, playing with the laces on his sneakers.

I took a deep breath.

'Chris, I like you very much, you're a sexy young man, and I enjoyed making love with you,' I said. 'But I'm not going to have an affair with you. The reason is that I already have what my magazine calls a live-in lover. More or less live-in, anyway.'

Chris looked alarmed.

'Where is he?' he said, taking a large gulp of beer.

'He's away for the weekend at the moment, at least I think he is,' I said. 'He stayed in London last weekend. But I can't run two affairs, and I don't want to.'

'Do you love him?' Chris asked, getting straight to the point.

'I think so.'

'Were you just being kind to me?'

'No – well, I don't think so. Only partly, anyway. I wanted you.'

'You were being kind,' he said miserably.

I put down my drink, and went over to sit by him.

'Chris, you are an eminently attractive young man.

Don't be silly. I'm not a charitable institution. I didn't go to bed with you out of kindness. You know how much I enjoyed it.'

He took my hand.

'Well, come to bed with me now,' he suggested.

I sighed.

'I've just been telling you that I'm not going to have an affair with you.'

'Okay, I accept that. But come and say goodbye.'

'Chris, you're incorrigible.'

He rubbed his erection, which I could see straining through his jeans.

Hilary, you don't know how much I want you,' he groaned.

I hesitated.

'This is positively goodbye. You do understand, don't you?'

'Yes, anything.'

I unzipped his jeans, and bent my lips towards him.

An hour or so later, I remembered Martin. By that time, we were in the bedroom. I got up, and groped for my clothes.

'I've got to ring Sussex,' I told Chris. He lay smiling contentedly as I pulled a dressing-gown around me, and went to the sitting-room to telephone.

Mother Shipton answered.

'I've called to say I'm stuck in London again,' I told her.

'I see, Hilary. I think Martin wanted a word. Can you hang on a minute?' she asked.

I heard her calling Martin, and there was muffled conversation. Then Martin came on the line:

'Hilary? Mother says you're not coming down to-night.'

'That's right,' I confirmed. 'I'll see you next weekend.'

'I hope so, it's breaking-up and prize-giving,' he reminded me.

'Oh, yes. I'd forgotten. Well, I'll certainly be there,' I promised.

'I've cancelled the August trip,' Martin said.

'What August trip?'

'The boat I was going to take with the boys, on the Broads.'

'What boat?'

'I told you all about it, Hilary. I arranged to take a cruiser on the Broads with half a dozen of the senior boys. But I've decided that I've got too much work on. After talking about it to Liz.'

'Liz?' I said. 'Liz who?'

'Liz Raine, the psychiatrist. What's the matter with you, Hilary?' Martin asked me. 'Are you feeling all right?'

'Yes, I'm fine,' I said. 'Sorry, Martin. I'd forgotten about the psychiatrist. And if you had told me that you were taking a boat on the Broads with the boys, I'd forgotten that too. But I'm sure you're right not to. Have you told the parents?'

'Yes. It wasn't confirmed, anyway, so no-one's been inconvenienced,' Martin said. 'We'll see you next Friday, then, shall we? You'll be in good time, won't you?'

'I'll be in good time,' I promised.

So it was Liz, was it, I thought. Well, she seemed to be effective. Of course he shouldn't take the boys on a boat, when temptation would dog him daily. How had I failed to remember that that was what he had planned? Obviously Liz listened to him, and I didn't. Well, she was paid to.

Chris, wearing Toby's bath-robe, padded into the sitting-room on his bare feet.

'Come back to bed,' he invited.

Chapter Thirteen

WE STAYED IN bed for the next thirty-six hours. Occasionally I made forays to the kitchen to fetch food or mugs of coffee. There was a period of about eight hours, I think, when Chris slept. The rest of the time he explored my body with incredulous delight, and made love to me so many times that I was sore and aching, my skin was blotched and there were dark circles under my eyes.

On the Sunday morning, I soaked myself in a hot bath while he shaved.

'Anything can happen after a bath with Badedas,' he quoted from the advertisement, eyeing me as I lay exhaustedly in the foam.

'No, it can't,' I said firmly, 'I'm tired, and you're being sexually greedy, and I'm going to send you back to your mama for lunch.'

'Can I come back to you tonight?' he asked hopefully.

'No, you can't, Chris. I'm sorry, but we aren't having an affair. It's got to end.'

He crouched by the bath and blew the foam aside so that he could see my breasts.

'The worst of it is, I'm afraid you mean it,' he said.

'I do, Chris.' I took his face in my hands. 'I like you very much, and it's been great, but we're worlds apart.

A generation apart to be exact, I'm afraid. And that's it.'

'I don't think you could have made love with me like you did if you'd really loved that guy,' Chris said.

'You mean Toby?'

'Yes.'

'Well, I do love him. But I have this stupid feeling that it's mean and ungenerous not to give myself when someone wants me as badly as you did –'

'It is, it is, you're right!' he interrupted.

'No, shut up, Chris. Oh, I'm all confused. But this can't go on. It has to be goodbye. So leave me be, will you, there's a dear.'

To my surprise, a tear trickled down my face. Chris looked at me tenderly, and wiped my face with the flannel.

'Can I write to you? You might change your mind,' he said.

'I'd rather you didn't.'

I got out and started drying myself, and he held me with gentleness but without passion, and I buried my face in his shoulder.

'Thanks, anyway, Hilary,' he said. 'I'll never forget you.'

'Good,' I said. 'I'll cook you breakfast before you go.'

By eleven, he had departed, leaving me with a pile of greasy plates and the Sunday papers scattered all over the floor. I collected them up, and decided to lie on the bed and read them before tackling the washing up. I must have been more exhausted than I realized, because I fell into a deep sleep. When I awoke, it was evening.

I got up and went to clear up the kitchen. I moved around as if in a dream. I stacked the dishes, tidied the sitting-room, got into my nightdress and went back to bed.

If I had been wide awake, I might have noticed that Chris had left his anorak in the hall cupboard.

The next day, I awoke early and refreshed. The rain had stopped, but the plants in the hanging baskets on the balcony still dripped wetly. I was ravenously hungry, and remembered that I had not eaten since breakfast the day before, I made toast and boiled eggs, laid a tray and pampered myself like a convalescent after illness.

I was early setting out for work, and the offices were empty when I arrived. I put the coffee on to percolate, and started catching up on reading unsolicited manuscripts.

Ruth arrived late, looking frowsty, as if she had been dragged through a bed backwards. She probably had. Her hair was all over the place, her blouse buttoned wrongly and there were shadows under her eyes. I looked at her with some disfavour. I didn't think she'd had a bath.

'You look as if someone's been giving you a rough time,' I said, very unfairly considering the way in which I had been spending the weekend.

Ruth smiled wryly.

'An orgy, actually,' she said.

'You mean a gang bang?'

'Something of the kind. Lovely,' she said, and drifted out dreamily to fetch the post.

No letters from Helen Turner. Hooray. A sense of relief, and a good start to the week.

And then, at eleven o'clock, the call came.

'There's a lady calling, long distance, won't give her name, says it's personal,' Ruth said.

Thump, thump, thump went my heart.

'I'll take it, Ruth.'

'Hello?' The voice on the other end of the phone sounded young, a bit tremulous. 'Is that Hilary Toogood?'

'Yes, speaking.' I waited.

121

'You don't know me. At least, we've never met. My name is Jean Abbott.'

Funny, that was a familiar name. Who was she? Jean Abbott! Oh my God, of course. Toby's wife!

'Yes, Mrs Abbott?' I said cautiously.

'You know my husband I think,' she said.

'Mr Abbott . . .' I said. 'Do you mean Toby Abbott?'

'I do,' she said crisply.

'We've met,' I said.

'Well, I think we've got things to talk about, Miss Toogood,' Jean Abbott said. 'I'd like to meet you.'

'Oh.' I said. 'What is it about?'

'I think you must have a very good idea. I'm coming up to London on Wednesday, and wondered if you were free in the afternoon?'

I flipped through my diary.

'Well, I could be free, Mrs Abbott. But where do you suggest? I don't think my office is a very suitable place. How did you get my number, by the way?'

She ignored the last question.

'I don't intend to come to your office,' she said. 'I suggest that we meet at Harrods Dress Circle coffee bar, at three thirty.'

I was taken aback.

'Could you make it four?' I asked. 'I've someone coming to see me at . . .'

'No, three thirty. I shan't be staying overnight, and I have to get a train home.'

'Okay. How shall we know each other?'

'I'll be wearing a red dress, and will wait for you at the entrance to the coffee shop,' she said.

'See you on Wednesday, then,' I said.

'Goodbye, Miss Toogood.'

She hung up, and I sat looking at the telephone. Was she Helen Turner? Why hadn't she said so? All Helen Turner's letters had borne London postmarks. Had she been in London, posting them? What else had she been doing in London? Watching Toby and me? I felt panic-stricken at the thought. How could she have known about Dominic? Toby must have told her. That meant he'd told her about me, discussed me. But how could she have known about Martin? Had she had me investigated by a private detective agency? She must have. That must be it. I felt angry, exposed, shaken and frightened, all at the same time.

I rang Toby.

'Are you in a meeting?' I asked him.

'No, what is it? What's happened? You sound odd. Are you ill?'

'No. Toby, Jean's just rung me. Did you know she was going to?'

'Oh, my Lord. No, no I didn't. What did she say?'

'She asked me if I knew you. I said cautiously we'd met. She wants me to meet her in Harrods on Wednesday.'

'In Harrods? Whatever for?'

'Tea.'

'Why?'

'She said she wanted to talk. She wouldn't say more. But Toby, she knows. About us, I mean. And I think she's Helen Turner.'

'Oh,' he said, sounding shocked. 'But how could she? How could she know?'

'I don't know, but Toby, I'm frightened.'

'Don't worry, it'll be all right,' he reassured me. 'I don't know what it's all about, but I'm sure it'll be all right.'

'Toby, did you tell her about us?'

'No, I've never mentioned you.'

I was sure he was telling the truth.

'Look, darling,' Toby said. 'We'll talk about it to-night, shall we? It's not a good idea on the phone. I'm on an extension, and so are you, and anyone could overhear.

I'm sure it'll be all right. She can't know anything, not really. Don't worry. What time will you be back tonight?'

'Late, I'm afriad,' I said. 'I've got to interview a new cookery sub-editor at five thirty.'

'Well, I haven't got much on today. I'll be back early,' Toby said, 'so I'll get some food and have dinner waiting for you. We can talk properly then.'

'Okay, see you,' I said.

I tried to put it out of my mind and concentrate on my work, but I didn't succeed.

I sensed that Toby was seething when I walked into the flat. I attributed it to anxiety about Jean. There was the smell of cooking, but he was sitting drinking whisky.

'Do you want one?' he offered, waving his glass as I entered the room. I nodded, and he poured me a large measure. I sat on the sofa opposite him drinking it.

'Tell me about it,' he suggested, so I went through the story again, and he listened in silence.

'Well, I've never mentioned you to Jean at all,' he said finally, 'so I just don't know how she knows. She was a bit different at the weekend, maybe, a bit more distant perhaps, but then she usually is distant, and I didn't think anything in particular.'

'She knows somehow,' I said. 'But how?'

Toby shook his head. 'I don't know. But I wonder . . . I wonder if Helen Turner could have written to her, too?'

'Oh,' I said. It hadn't occurred to me. 'I suppose it's possible. I don't like it, Toby. It's frightening, and it makes me feel trapped, sitting waiting and wondering what she's going to do next. Helen Turner, I mean. And Jean, I suppose.'

'Perhaps I ought to ring her,' Toby said.

'No, don't,' I said. 'If you do, she'll know that the first

124

thing I did was to tell you. It may only be a suspicion, after all. She may not actually know anything.'

'What are you going to say, if she asks you outright?' Toby said.

'What do you want me to say?'

'I don't want a divorce, Hilary. I know that attitudes are different, now, but it would inevitably be a setback to my career. I don't think Jean wants a divorce, either, or she'd have tackled me about it instead of you, I reckon. I'm a bit puzzled about what it is she does want. But I don't think she wants a break-up. She'd be worse off, there isn't anyone else in her life, and it wouldn't be good for the children. What has she got to gain by it?'

'What has she got to gain by summoning me to Harrods?' I asked.

'That's what's so strange. Maybe it's just feminine curiosity.'

'Or maybe she's Helen Turner, and this is the crunch,' I said.

Toby lit his pipe, and sat smoking in silence. I noticed that he was making little gestures of impatience and anger.

'Is there something the matter, Toby? You look angry.' I secretly hoped he was angry with Jean.

'There's an anorak in the hall cupboard,' he said.

'Oh,' I said feebly. *Bugger* Chris. Had he left it deliberately? If I hadn't been so tired yesterday, I would have noticed it.

'It's that boy's, isn't it?' Toby asked.

'What boy?'

'Oh, come on Hilary,' he said wearily. 'Don't lie to *me*, please.'

'Yes, it is,' I said.

'He was here at the weekend,' Toby said.

'Yes, he was. And I ended it, Toby. It was goodbye.'

'So why did he leave his anorak?'

125

'I don't know. The young do strew their possessions about, you know. Are you very angry?'

I went over and sat by him and slipped my hand under his arm and rested my head on his shoulder. He was cold and resisting.

'Toby?' I said.

'I'm furious,' he said.

I sighed, and sat up. His anger kindled anger in me.

'Well, we're not married, Toby. I don't belong to you, and you don't want me, not really,' I said.

'I don't want you if you go whoring around with boys young enough to be your son,' he blazed at me.

I burst into tears and left the room. How dare he! But I knew that I had broken the rules. All those years ago, Pierre had told me yes, of course, infidelity is accepted in a wife, if the passions have blown cold. But in a mistress, never.

I sat at my dressing-table, repairing my make-up, and fuming. It was all too much, and not fair at all. Was there anyone in the world who truly loved me? Not Toby. He put his precious career first. Not Martin, for certain. Dominic? Maybe, but I wasn't even sure about that. And sooner or later he would lose his heart to some girl, and I should be forgotten. On top if it all, I was being persecuted not only by Toby's wife, but by the invisible Helen Turner. I felt that my life was escaping from my control.

Toby stuck his head round the bedroom door.

'The meal's on the table,' he announced.

I went and put my arms round him.

'Toby, please forgive me,' I said.

But he couldn't.

I stood at the entrance to Harrods Dress Circle coffee bar at twenty-five past three, watching the women arriving and mentally rehearsing our conversation. I was determined not to be on the defensive. She had taken me by surprise on the telephone, and had had control of the call from start to finish, but I was determined that at this meeting she was not going to make me feel like a guilty child, caught with its hand in the cookie jar.

Okay, so I saw her husband. But if he were attracted to me, it was because there was something lacking in his relationship with her. And I hadn't seduced him, anyway. Quite the other way round. He was an adult human being, responsible for himself, and I wasn't going to be held responsible if his behaviour made her unhappy.

Half past three came and went. I began to think that she had thought better of it. Then at twenty-five to four she arrived, a little breathless.

'Hilary Toogood? I'm sorry I'm late. I had to wait in a queue for a taxi. Shall we go in?'

We collected some tea, and sat down at a table. We studied each other silently for a minute or two. The first thing that struck me about her was how thin she was. Bony, almost skeletal. Her red cotton dress hung loosely on her. She had no tits at all, flat as a boy. No wonder Toby enjoyed mine.

'You're older than your picture in the magazine,' she announced.

'It's an old picture, and retouched,' I said cheerfully.

'How long has your affair with my husband been going on?' she said.

A girl hovered nearby, clearing tables. When she was out of earshot I said, 'What makes you think I'm having an affair with your husband?'

'Oh come, Miss Toogood. Please don't pretend. It's not necessary.'

'Won't you call me Hilary?' I asked. Why did I say that? I wondered.

'Then you must call me Jean,' she responded automatically. 'All right, then, Hilary. How long has your affair with my husband been going on?'

'Why are you asking *me*?' I countered. 'If you think that your husband is having an affair, why not ask him about it?'

'We aren't going to achieve anything if you fence like this,' she said.

'What do you want to achieve?' I asked.

She considered the question.

'I asked myself that before I came,' she said. 'I wanted to meet you – partly curiosity, partly wanting to size up the enemy, I suppose. You seem less of a threat now I've met you. You aren't so attractive as I'd imagined.'

'Nor are you,' I said, stung into aggression.

'I'm not going to divorce him, you know,' she said.

'Toby doesn't want a divorce,' I said.

'Oh,' she said. 'You've discussed it, then. What about you? D'you want to marry him?'

'I'm married already', I said.

'Are you?' she said. 'Now that I didn't know.'

I looked at her in some surprise.

'Mrs Abbott – Jean – may I ask you, does the name Helen Turner mean anything to you?'

'Helen Turner?' She thought about it, and shook her head. 'No, I don't think so. Is she another?'

'Another what?'

'Another of Toby's women. You don't think you're the only one, do you?'

'No, of course not,' I lied. Don't show surprise, don't give her that satisfaction.

'He's always been a womanizer, you know. Runs strings of them,' she said, with some bitterness.

I shrugged.

'But Helen Turner . . .' she returned to the question. 'No, it doesn't mean anything to me. Who is she?'

I was sure she was speaking the truth.

'I don't know,' I said. 'I've had a couple of letters from her. I wondered if you – have you ever had a letter from her?'

'No, I haven't,' she said definitely.

'Oh. Well how did you know . . . what made you think that Toby and I were having an affair?'

'I knew that he was having a fairly serious affair with someone. He was never at the Battersea flat when I rang it. Then one night, when I rang, there must have been a new chap staying in the flat, and he left the receiver on the hall table, and I heard him saying to one of the other men, "It's Toby's wife. What do I do?" And I heard the reply. "He's with Hilary Toogood as usual. The number's stuck up by the phone. Tell his wife he isn't in yet, ring him there, and he'll call her back and say he's just got in." Or something like that. The name Hilary Toogood rang a bell, and I remembered I'd seen it in the magazine at the hairdresser's.'

It rang true.

'It's been going on a long time, hasn't it?' she said.

'Maybe a year, I don't remember exactly,' I said. It seemed pointless to go on denying it.

'That's a long time, for Toby. I knew,' she said. 'I've lost two stones, worrying about it.'

Her arms, indeed, looked like those of a Belsen camp inmate. Her cheeks were hollow. But strangely, I did not feel guilty at all.

'I noticed you were thin,' I said.

'I've always been skinny. I couldn't afford to lose the weight I've lost. No wonder Toby doesn't fancy me.'

'Doesn't he? I thought the boot was on the other foot.'

'Okay, so I don't enjoy sex. But when I got worried, I tried to seduce him. I couldn't'.

My heart gladdened to hear it. But she wasn't Helen Turner.

129

'What do you want, Jean?' I asked.

'I didn't know you were married,' she said. 'Are you happily married?'

'Not that it's any of your business, but no, I'm not.'

'Are you going to take my husband away from me?'

'I'm not going to do anything,' I said. 'Toby isn't a possession, a rag doll to be snatched one from another between us. He is possessed of free will.'

She sighed. 'You want him, don't you?'

'Toby doesn't want a divorce.' It was the only crumb of comfort I could offer her.

'I hope not,' she said. 'He isn't going to get one, anyway. I shan't divorce him. So if you're hoping that I will, you're wasting your time.'

'Is that what you came to tell me?'

'Oh, I was going to tell you all sorts of things,' she said. 'Appeal to your better nature. Tell you about the boys, how they need their father. I won't do it. I don't think it would have any effect, anyway.'

'Do you want to say anything else?' I asked. She shook her head. We got up, and at the door to the restaurant she offered me her hand. I hesitated, then took it.

'Goodbye, Hilary,' she said. 'I don't suppose that we'll meet again.'

'Goodbye,' I said. 'Put some weight on. For your own sake.'

'I'll try,' she said. And smiled briefly. And went.

After she had gone, I went to the negligé department and bought an extraordinarily expensive, very sexy nightdress with which to tempt her husband.

Chapter Fourteen

I DROVE DOWN to Falconbridge on the Friday morning. It was a lovely afternoon for prize-giving, which went without a hitch. When the last small boy, dwarfed by his oversized trunk, had been scooped up by doting parents and disappeared in the car down the drive, the house was quiet and echoing, as I loved it. Mother Shipton was spending a large part of the holidays with her sister in Southgate, and Martin told me that he had decided to take the boat on the Broads after all.

'I thought the psychiatrist had advised you not to,' I said.

'Liz doesn't hand out advice,' he said. 'Unlike you, she believes that people are responsible for their own decisions, and must find their own solutions. *I* decided not to take the boys on a boat. But I'm going to take a boat on my own for a few weeks, to think things out.'

I was nettled by the comparison.

'I think that people are responsible for their own decisions too,' I said. 'And I don't think I do hand out advice, unless you're talking about the magazine. I suppose some people might regard the replies to the letters as advice. What are you going to think out, anyway?'

'Us, among other things,' Martin said. 'Liz says . . .'

'Liz says, Liz says,' I said. 'I seem to have heard about Liz all weekend.'

He flushed, and the conversation ended. I spent a lot of the rest of the weekend in solitary walks along the seashore, and did not see him again before I returned to London on the Monday.

The fourth letter from Helen Turner arrived towards the end of the week. I was flipping through the post, almost lulled into thinking that there were to be no more, when I came upon it.

'Dear Hilary Toogood, (it read)
'I am very worried about my younger sister. She has never known a secure home, and perhaps this has made her rather unstable. She is really my half-sister. My parents' marriage broke up when I was young, and she is the daughter of my mother's second marriage. She is about ten years younger than I am, and now I think she has become a lesbian. She is living with a woman in Hertfordshire, and has been the cause of this woman's marriage break-up. How can I help my sister? Do you think that I should offer her a home with me? My own marriage is not happy, and my husband and I live separate lives. I feel guilty because I have not helped my sister in the past. She had made more than one suicide attempt, which is some indication of how disturbed she is.
'Yours sincerely, Helen Turner.'

My hand shook as I read the letter through for the second time. It was Jan, all right. Jan to a T. How on *earth* did she know? I felt a great upsurge of anger. Who the hell was Helen Turner, and what the hell was she trying to do to me? Frighten me, worry me, make me feel guilty? Make me go rushing round the country to get in ahead of

132

her and tell Toby, and Martin, and Dominic and now Jan that somebody, somewhere knew all, and might tell? What did bloody Helen Turner *want*? To drive me out of my mind?

I resisted an impulse to crumple the letter and throw it in the waste paper basket. Instead I unlocked the drawer where the first three Helen Turner letters nestled like a cache of baby vipers, added the latest one, and rang Toby.

'Toby, it's another letter. I feel at the end of my tether. Are you free for lunch? I need a shoulder,' I said miserably.

'Of course,' he said immediately. 'How about Tuttons in Covent Garden at one o'clock?'

Toby was waiting for me in the downstairs area of the restaurant with a bottle of wine opened when I arrived. Since my meeting with Jean the week before, things between Toby and me seemed to have settled down a bit. He had been relieved that we had not had an acrimonious slanging match, I think. (In *Harrods*? He really had no idea.) He even seemed to have forgotten about Chris. Things were almost back to normal. Well, that was the way it felt, anyway.

He squeezed my hand, and poured me a glass of wine.

'What did she say this time?' he asked.

'It's Jan, my sister. You know, I told you about her. She lives with this lady bee-keeper in Hertfordshire. The woman's husband marched off with great shouts of "Lesbians!" It would make a good newspaper story if something like the *News of the World* got hold of it, which they haven't up to now, and of course the fact that she's my sister would be bound to be dragged in.'

'Well, there's nothing that you can do about it, is there?' Toby said. 'Presumably Jan isn't going to leave her – mate, or whatever you call her.'

133

'No, she's not,' I said. 'I must confess, I thought it was all a hoot at the time. Jan lives in a Renault 5, you know. She always says that the world is divided into cave dwellers and tent dwellers, cave dwellers being people like me, who have to put down roots, and settle for as long as possible, and the tent dwellers being people like her, who can't bear to stay put, and are always on the move. She packs all her possessions – every single thing she owns – into the back of this rickety little car which has been involved in God knows how many accidents, and she mooches round the world as the spirit moves her.'

'She seems to have settled down now. In a cave, or perhaps in a bee-hive,' Toby pointed out.

'Oh, I don't suppose she'll stay there forever,' I said. 'She stopped there last summer, when she was motoring up the A10 and her car broke down just outside the bee-keeper's gate. She went in to ask if she could use the phone, and bingo! She and the lady of the house fell for one another.'

'It's ridiculous,' Toby said, laughing. 'If Jan were a man instead of a woman, it would be just like a short story out of *Herself*.'

'Truth really is much stranger than fiction,' I said.

'Are you going to tell her that somebody else knows all?' Toby said.

I sighed. 'I don't know. We don't communicate much, and I don't see that she would do anything about it. Perhaps I should try. I did go to see her once, last autumn. It was something to do with our mother's will which needed sorting out. Jan's girlfriend was wearing her bee-keeping veil, and looked spooky. She behaved like a witch too: I expected to be swept out of the house with her broomstick. She was so unfriendly. Perhaps a nasty queen bee is a better simile. I don't really want to get stung again.'

'Perhaps she thought that Hilary Toogood would disapprove of a lesbian alliance,' Toby suggested. 'Perhaps the bee-keeping veil was a sort of protection, like dark glasses.'

'No, I just think she looks better wearing her bee-keeping veil than she does without it,' I said unkindly. 'I think her husband was probably glad of an excuse to leave her, anyway. Both she and Jan are mad as hatters. They talk to the bees, tell them when there's a death in the family, and generally carry on in a thoroughly superstitious way. With any luck, Jan will have got itchy feet and moved on again before anybody cottons on to the story.'

'I think you ought to see a solicitor, anyway,' Toby said. 'You've been making light of it but it's obviously harassment, it upsets you, and it ought to be stopped.'

'Yes . . . But I'm sure a solicitor would recommend hiring a private detective, and I'm not sure I want to.'

'You've got to do something,' Toby said.

'You're right, of course. I'll talk to a solicitor about it, anyway,' I said.

It was only a day or so later that Harry Ballsup came to see me about the wretched Mrs Borer, who was demanding that we publish a lengthy statement designed to cause maximum embarrassment to the lady who was calling herself Mrs Borer.

'I won't do it,' I said to Harry. 'It's sheer malice. There are hundreds – probably thousands – of ladies up and down the country who are using the surnames of the men with whom they're living, and whom they're not able to marry because some dog-in-the-manger or rather bitch-in-the-manger of a first wife won't give her husband a divorce.'

Harry looked at me thoughtfully.

'You wouldn't have a personal axe to grind in all this, would you?' he asked.

I flushed.

'I have a lot of sympathy for Mrs Borer number two,' I said. 'What has she done to be embarrassed in public by this spiteful first wife? She hasn't committed any offence, has she?'

'It used to be called jactitation,' Harry said. 'The false assertion that one is married to someone one isn't married to.'

'Mrs Borer number two hasn't made that assertion,' I protested. 'She's simply calling herself Mrs Borer. It's different.'

Harry sighed. 'It may cost us money,' he said.

'Let's try holding out a bit longer anyway, Harry. If we have to, in the end, we'll publish the most inconspicuous paragraph possible. It will be so long after the original article has appeared that no-one will be able to remember to whom it refers anyway.'

'Okay, done. How about a drink, Hilary? I'm parched.'

'This company is divided into those gentlemen who are paralytic and incapable of working in the afternoon, and those gentlemen who are paralytic and incapable of working all day. Okay Harry, but while you're drinking it, maybe I can pick your brains and ask you for some advice on a personal matter,' I said, handing him a tumbler containing a triple gin and tonic.

'With pleasure, Hilary. Don't tell me you're going to get yourself divorced? And all the marriages Hilary Toogood has pontificated on, to have your own come apart would be a turn up for the book.'

'I don't pontificate on marriages,' I said, annoyed that for the second time within a week I was being accused of it. 'No, it's some letters I've been receiving.'

'Oh. Pity,' Harry said. 'I thought I might be in with a chance, there.'

'My attentions are otherwise engaged, I'm afraid,' I said.

'What about the letters, anyway?' he said.

'Well, I've had three – no, four. They're all from the same woman. Or man, I suppose. Whoever it is, the letters are all signed "Helen Turner". She writes from a fictitious address. I know it's fictitious, because I tried to reply to the first one, and my letter was returned. The letters all refer to things in my private life which I thought that nobody, but nobody, knew about. I can't imagine how anyone could know about them, either, without doing an immense amount of poking round, maybe even employing a private detective agency . . .'

'Can I see them?' Harry asked. 'You did keep them, I suppose?'

'I'd rather not show them to you,' I said.

'But you have got them?'

'Yes,' I said reluctantly.

'Well, why not go to the police?'

'What would the police do? I'm not being blackmailed. And anyway, I can't. One of the letters refers to somebody else who did something which could be the subject of a criminal investigation.'

'Oh,' Harry said. I watched him, sprawled on my sofa in his rumpled suit. He was obviously slightly shocked.

'Well, if you don't want me to read them, I'm not sure how I can help,' he said. 'I suppose it's harassment, but then she's sending them to you, and not to anyone else. Has your secretary seen them? Are they libellous, or are they true?'

'My secretary hasn't seen them. They're true enough, I'm afraid,' I said.

'Ouch,' Harry said.

I made up my mind.

'Harry, you're an awful old gossip, but I'll trust you not to gossip about this,' I said. 'Will you look at them?'

'Of course,' he said.

I unlocked the drawer, fished them out, and handed them to him. I busied myself refilling his glass and giving myself a whisky. Then I pretended to read some papers on my desk. I didn't want to watch him while he read them.

It seemed an eternity until he'd finished. He set them down, and thought for a long time.

I could bear the silence no longer.

'What d'you think?' I asked.

He shook his head.

'I don't know. It's extraordinary. Is it really – does it really bear a resemblance to your own family, your own life?'

I nodded.

'But Hilary, who else knows?'

'What do you mean?'

'Who else knows you as well as that? Who knows *all* about you?'

'Nobody,' I said. 'Obviously some people know some of it, but nobody knows all of it. At least, I didn't think they did. Unless, as I said, someone employed a private detective agency.'

Harry shook his head. 'It's not possible, Hilary. A private detective agency simply couldn't find out all that. Not things out of the past. Not even a good detective agency, and they're simply not that good. No, you must have told someone yourself, without realizing it.'

'I haven't. Nobody. Not everything.'

'Have you ever been psychoanalysed, for example?' he asked.

'No, I haven't. My husband is having psychiatric treatment at the moment, but the letters started coming

138

before that. In fact, the letters led to the treatment, in a way.'

'Perhaps you talk in your sleep,' Harry suggested, picking up one of the letters and looking at it again.

I shook my head.

'It has to be someone close to you, Hilary, unless . . .'

'Unless what?'

'No, it's not possible.'

'What's not possible?'

'Hilary, I don't quite know how to say it.'

'Come on, Harry, spit it out. What is it?'

'Don't take offence, will you? But have you noticed . . . the writer's initial are HT. HT – Helen Turner. But also HT – Hilary Toogood. Hilary, is it possible – you couldn't have written them yourself?'

I looked at him in silence. Suddenly tears were streaming down my face, and I was weeping uncontrollably. Harry looked at me in an alarmed way, set down his glass, came over to sit by me, and put his arm round me.

'Don't cry, Hilary,' he said. 'Don't worry.'

'It's not true,' I said. 'I didn't write them, Harry. But when you said it, I knew that that was what had been worrying me secretly for some time. Am I going mad? Is part of me doing something that the other part of me doesn't know about? Am I suffering from schizophrenia?'

Harry handed me a clean handkerchief, took my whisky glass and poured into it a large measure. He sat down opposite me and studied me carefully.

'If you're really worried, you're quite sensible enough to consult a psychiatrist,' he said eventually. 'But I've known you for quite a long time, Hilary, and it's my guess that you aren't suffering from any mental disturbance at all. I wanted to float the idea to see what your reaction would be. It seemed to me to be the reaction of a perfectly sane and normal person. I don't think that the insane have doubts about their own sanity. That's a wholly sane reaction, though of course I'm not an expert.'

I gulped my whisky.

'I think you may have to employ a private detective to track down Helen Turner,' Harry said. 'Have you kept the envelopes that the letters came in?'

'I have the last two, but not the earlier ones,' I said.

'Okay, well if there are any more, be sure to keep the envelopes, and handle them as little as possible,' Harry said 'Where were they posted?'

'London postal districts,' I said. 'One came from N21, and the other from SW1.'

'That's a pity,' Harry said. 'If she were using the same post box each time, it might make matters easier. Look, if you don't want to go to the police, what I suggest you do for a start is to make a list of all the people close to you who just might know some of these things. Put absolutely everyone on it that you can think of – don't leave anyone out. Don't omit someone because you think he or she likes you and wouldn't write the letters, or because you think he or she doesn't know all the things the the writer knows.'

'Okay,' I said.

'After you've compiled the list, we can go through it and see if there are any useful leads to follow,' Harry said. 'And try to keep calm and keep cheerful, Hilary. If you haven't had a blackmail demand by now, you may not get one. Have you ever thought that the writer's objective may be to frighten you, or to make you doubt your own sanity, as in fact you have?'

I shivered.

'It's horrible to think of being hated so much that someone wants to do that to you,' I said.

'Yes. What about the MP's wife?' Harry asked. 'The wife of the man she says you're having an affair with?'

I looked at him in surprise.

'You're cleverer than I gave you credit for, Harry Ballsup,' I said, and indeed he was. Most lawyers, in my opinion, fall into one of two categories – clever and crooked, or honest and thick. I had put Harry in the second category.

'As a matter of fact I've met the MP's wife. And yes, she springs naturally to mind. But I don't really believe that it is her.'

'Why not? She has reason to hate you, doesn't she?'

'Yes, she does. But she rang last week, and we met for tea in Harrods. I sprang the name Helen Turner on her, and she didn't react at all. Either she's innocent, or she's an exceptionally good actress, quite wasted as a house-wife.'

'Tea in Harrods,' Harry said, laughing. 'Why on earth?'

I shrugged. 'She suggested it.'

'Oh, well – pity; she seemed the most obvious candidate. Never mind. Compile that list for a start, then we'll talk about it again, if you like.'

'Okay, and thank you,' I said.

'I deserve another gin,' Harry said.

'You won't tell anyone anything, will you?' I asked anxiously, refilling his glass.

'Of course I won't,' Harry said. He kissed my cheek. 'And don't worry, Hilary, it'll all come out in the wash.'

141

Chapter Fifteen

EARLY THE FOLLOWING Saturday morning, I drove through the grey streets of Islington en route for Hertfordshire and Jan's house. When I had rung her she said briefly yes, she would be there at the weekend, what was it about? I said I'd be along on Saturday to discuss it, and she said okay, and hung up briskly. She hadn't invited me to lunch, but I supposed that I could get something in a pub somewhere.

The house was up a small country road off the A10. I couldn't think where on earth Jan had been heading for to take her along this unlikely by-way. Her Renault 5, with one punctured wheel, was parked outside, and there were several old wooden boxes, two rusty tricycles and a string of grey washing outside the house. A dirty-faced child wearing only a tee-shirt and wellington boots stood sucking the corner of a small blanket and eyeing me with hostility as I parked and approached the house.

'Hello,' I said. 'Is Mummy in? I'm Jan's sister.'

The child surveyed me blankly. The front door lacked both bell and knocker, so I banged with my knuckles on the wood. A head appeared at an upstairs window. It was the cross-eyed bee-keeper.

Oh, it's you,' she said. 'Jan! She's here already.'

I waited several minutes and then my sister, wearing a

man's towelling bath-robe over her nightdress and with her hair uncombed, opened the door.

The front door gave directly onto the living-room, which was littered with broken toys, buckets of dirty nappies, newspapers, empty bottles and dirty mugs. In the corner of the room a baby in plastic pants sat in a playpen playing with two cats and grizzling intermittently.

'You're early,' my sister said, in an unwelcoming way. 'D'you want some coffee?'

She disappeared through the door at the back of the room to make it, while I drew back the curtains to let some sunlight in, cleared the toys off a couple of chairs so there was somewhere to sit down, and made a space on the table for the coffee mugs. The child with the blanket had followed me in, and stood looking at me silently. I found it disconcerting. The bare wooden floor was dusty. He sat down on it and continued to regard me.

All the furniture and wood surfaces in the room were stripped wood, unpolished and unpainted. There were no carpets and what upholstered furniture there was showed springs at odd and uncomfortable angles. I sat on a stripped wooden chair with arms, which was the most inviting piece of furniture there was.

'What's your name?' I asked the child, to break the uncomfortable silence.

He considered, removed the blanket from his mouth, said 'Tarquin', and put the blanket back in again.

'Tarquin?' I said, unbelievingly. 'And how old are you, Tarquin?'

'Got no daddy,' Tarquin confided. 'My daddy went away. Got a Jan, though.'

'I see,' I said. 'Is that your baby sister?'

Jan emerged with two mugs of coffee, which she put down on the table. She removed a cat from a chair, and sat down. I noticed that there were cat turds in one corner of the room near the playpen, which doubtless accounted for the appalling smell. I was glad that I hadn't been invited to lunch.

'Is it Mother's will again?' Jan asked.

'No, it isn't,' I said. 'It's some letters I've been receiving.'

At this point the baby's grizzles turned to screams. I was reminded of a heading one of our less literate sub-editors had put on a mother craft article: 'HOW TO DEAL WITH A GRISLY BABY'. Jan ignored the noise. I could not hear myself speak, and my nerves were beginnning to shred. The baby looked so extremely unappealing that I could not bring myself to pick it up. I certainly couldn't have done so without making some effort to clean it up and make it more comfortable.

When the roars threatened to deafen us, Monica, the lady bee-keeper, swept into the room and across to the playpen. She too had obviously just got out of bed. She was wearing a raincoat over her nightdress, and her feet were bare. She cast a baleful look at Jan, and swept up the baby with an impatient gesture.

'For God's sake, Jan, couldn't you have done something about her?' she demanded. And then – 'Oh, shit!' She had stepped in it.

Jan started to laugh, and Tarquin joined in. Monica looked furious. With the baby under her arm, and her shitty foot held off the ground, she hopped towards the kitchen door, and slammed it resonantly behind her.

'Peace at last,' Jan said, lighting a cigarette.

I said, 'D'you mind if I open the window?' and did so, without waiting for an answer.

Jan said, 'I'm just about fed up with her!' in a low and vicious mutter. A cat, tail waving, wound its way among the litter on the table. I hastily removed my coffee cup.

'Jan, I've been having these letters,' I said. 'They're signed by someone calling herself Helen Turner, but

144

actually that's a fictitious name. I don't know whether they're leading up to blackmail or what, but she knows an enormous amount about my private life. The last one concerned you.'

'What does she know?' Jan asked.

'She knows things which I've never told anyone, and which I believed that no-one knew,' I said. 'Things going way back into the past, which a private detective couldn't possibly have found out. I don't know how she knows them. I simply don't understand it.'

'And she knows about me, too?' Jan said.

I nodded. 'Jan, I don't normally smoke, but could I possibly have a cigarette now? This room smells, not to put too fine a point on it.'

'It's the cat shit,' Jan agreed absently, pushing across to me a packet with two cigarettes in it.

'Is that all you've got?' I asked.

'Monica's got some more, it's all right,' Jan said. 'But how could she know about all those years back?'

'Who?'

'Helen Turner, did you say her name was ?'

'About all what years back?' I said, thoroughly confused.

'Well, you said she knew about me too, didn't you?' Jan asked.

'Yes.'

'Well, it was years ago that it happened. How could she possibly know?'

'Jan, I don't know what you're talking about,' I said.

'Oh, my God. I thought when you said she knew, that you knew too, since she'd written to you,' Jan said.

'Jan, could you just tell me plainly what it is you're talking about?' I asked

'I'm talking about the accident, but never mind.'

'What accident?'

145

Jan looked at me impatiently. She peered under the table.

'Tarquin, go and help Mummy with the baby,' she ordered.

'No.' Tarquin had masturbated himself to a delightful erection, and was clearly enjoying himself.

'Tarquin, go and help Mummy at once!' Jan commanded

He got up reluctantly, and went out of the room. Jan got up, shut the door behind him, and said

'I may as well tell you, I suppose. Do you remember when we were younger – I was about ten, and you had recently had Dominic, and you brought him to see Mother for an occasional weekend, and we used to cycle round the country lanes together?'

'I vaguely remember it,' I said. 'But I don't really see what this has got to do with Helen Turner. I don't think you've understood me, Jan.'

'Yes, I have,' she said. 'This Helen Turner has somehow found out that I'm a murderess.'

'You're what?'

'That hole in the wall – a man drove into it. The wall, I mean. And it was my fault.'

'But how?'

'I was playing around on my bicycle, fooling around riding without hands in the middle of the road. A van appeared suddenly, coming rather fast. He had to swerve to avoid me, and he went through the wall. He was dead on arrival at the hospital, so they never knew it was me.'

I struggled to take it in.

'Who else knows?' I asked.

'No-one, no-one at all. Except Helen Turner.'

'She doesn't know,' I said.

'But you said that she wrote to you. Can I see the letter?' Jan asked, a bit impatiently.

'I haven't brought it,' I said truthfully.

'But she did write to you about me?'

'Yes, but not about any accident. About your living with Monica.'

'About my living with Monica?' Jan repeated. 'But what about my living with Monica?'

'Monica's husband did go off accusing you both of being lesbians, and it would make quite a good Sunday newspaper story.'

'That's outrageous!' Jan said indignantly. 'What business is it of anyone else's if we happen to be gay?'

I surveyed the squalid scene and thought that 'gay' was the last word I should apply to it.

'That's what her letter was about, anyway,' I said.

'And you came all the way over to tell me that?'

I sighed. 'I don't know what she's going to do, Jan. It might be blackmail, though she hasn't asked for any money yet. I don't really know what she wants. But if she gives the story to the *News of the World* or to *Private Eye*, you'll be besieged by reporters and it won't be very comfortable for you.'

Jan shrugged. She was plainly relieved.

'So what?' she said.

'Are you happy here?' I asked.

'She gets on my tits sometimes.'

'Monica?'

'Yes. I think I'll be moving on, soon.'

'Oh well,' I said, 'If you do that, there won't be a story, of course.'

She thought for a few moments.

'I'm not sorry I told you, anyway,' she said. 'It's always been a burden, and it feels a bit better to have got it off my chest, even if it's only to you.'

'Thanks very much,' I said.

The door flew open and Monica, now wearing jeans, marched in and put two bowls of lumpy greyish liquid down on the table. She stuffed the baby into a highchair

147

in front of one bowl, and Tarquin pushed the cat off a chair and sat himself down in front of the other.

'Would you like some breakfast?' Jan offered. Monica pointedly ignored me.

'No, I'd better be going,' I said. 'Keep in touch, won't you, Jan? Let me know where – how you are, and everything?'

'I will.'

Jan accompanied me to the door and, somewhat to my surprise kissed me. It was a relief to step out into the sunshine again.

On the way back to London, I went over Jan's revelation in my mind. Did she really think that she was responsible for a man's death? What a burden to carry round all these years. Had she been responsible? Was it possible for her to be prosecuted after all this time?

Clearly Jan couldn't be Helen Turner, anyway. Her confusion had been genuine, she hadn't intended to tell me. Unless it had been an extraordinarily clever dissemblance. Unless, unless, unless.

I started making a list in my head of the people I knew who knew anything about me, and might be Helen Turner. Okay, Jan. And Monica, I supposed. She certainly disliked me enough, though I wasn't quite sure why. I supposed that she and Jan must talk in bed the way that husbands and wives talk, so she had proably heard a fair amount about me. But Jan didn't know as much as Helen Turner knew. She didn't know about Toby, for instance.

Then there was Toby. Could he be Helen Turner? The idea was ridiculous. What on earth would be his motive? It was out of the question. But Harry had told me to make a list of *all* my acquaintances, so I supposed that I should have to include Toby's name. Jean, Toby's wife . . . well, logically she had the most reason to hate me, so she should certainly be suspect number one. But I had watched her closely when I mentioned the name Helen Turner in Harrods, and she hadn't looked guilty to me.

Dominic? Absolutely not. I refused to include the name of my son on the list. He probably knew a great deal about me, and probably had some inkling about Martin, but I simply didn't believe that Dominic would write me anonymous letters. Chris? Impossible, I'd only met him when I went to talk to Dominic. Unless he had written me the letter about Dominic in order to get me to go to Oxford, and then had been waiting, intending to seduce me. Could he possibly have engineered the whole thing? No, it was too fantastic for words.

Chris's father, God? As my boss, God knew me fairly well, but not that well. What possible purpose could there be in his sending me the Helen Turner mail? Unless he had a sick mind, warped by impotence, and got some kind of kick out of frightening me.

Who else at the office? Ruth knew me better than anyone, of course. She certainly could have guessed at a lot of Helen Turner's revelations. Did she resent me, hate me secretly? Surely she was too preoccupied with her own bizarre life to involve herself in mine?

Who else was there? Martin, I supposed. But one of the letters had been about him. Surely he wouldn't have written that himself? Or would he, to put me off the scent? Martin's mother, Mother Shipton? She was too attached to her son to drag up such distasteful memories.

Who on earth else was there? The Snow Queen, in her remote and palatial office? I hardly ever saw her. Did she regard me as some sort of threat; was she trying to drive me out of the company, out of my mind? Mrs Carstairs, the astrologer? She was mad as a hatter, anyway. And she had seemed to know something about the letters when she had been in my office a few weeks ago.

The whole thing was ridiculous. By now I'd forgotten

149

whom I had thought of at the beginning, but trying to count them up on my fingers, I thought that there were eleven people on the list. And I didn't believe that it was any one of them.

Of course, if this were an Agatha Christie novel, it would be all of them, eleven people who hated me, all meeting and piecing together their separate bits of information to form a composite Helen Turner. But this wasn't an Agatha Christie story, it was real life, and the idea was just absurd. I really was going round the twist.

There must be someone else whom I'd forgotten. Or maybe Harry was wrong, and Helen Turner wasn't someone who knew me well, but an anonymous, malevolent woman, watching me from somewhere separate, maybe surveying my flat through binoculars, bugging my phone, determined to possess me and my life and let me know how much she knew . . .

Oh, that was really paranoid. Don't let her do this to me. There must be a rational, commonsense explanation for the whole thing. Hang on to commonsense and reason. Hang on to sanity.

But commonsense and reason weren't leading anywhere in dealing with bloody Helen Turner. What else was there? No, no, not the police. Not a private detective. Extra sensory perception? Clairvoyance? Astrology?

Astrology? I thought about Mrs Carstairs again.

'Drop by my flat any time, dear, I'd love to see you.'

I looked at my watch. It was still only two o'clock, on a Saturday afternoon, and I was by the King's Cross roundabout. I swung my car south towards Battersea.

Chapter Sixteen

MRS CARSTAIRS LIVED in Queen's Mansions, one of those cavernous red-brick blocks of flats facing onto Battersea Park. When I rang her doorbell, there was a long silence. At first I thought that she was out. Then there were scuffling sounds, and Mrs Carstairs inspected me through her peephole.

'Hilary, darling! What a nice surprise!' she said, opening the door to admit me to her hall. 'Lovely to see you, come on in. Would you like a cup of tea?'

I followed Mrs Carstairs into her sitting-room, which was dark and cluttered. Mrs C collected books about the occult, and also pictures of animals. Her walls were covered with terrible paintings of livestock – kittens, tigers, dogs, horses, birds, elephants and other wildlife – in every conceivable mood, style and frame, ranging from Woolworths to an original John Skeaping. I sat down in an overstuffed armchair and she stood in front of me, looking very ordinary and not at all exotic in her baggy skirt and Marks and Spencer blouse and fluffy slippers.

'I'd love a cup of tea,' I said gratefully, and she went to put the kettle on. I read a book of Sun Signs, and checked to see if it said that I was compatible with Toby until she reappeared with a tea-tray set with bone china, and a plate of sandwiches.

'I thought you looked hungry, dear, so I made a couple of sandwiches,' Mrs C said, and I found that I was very hungry indeed. She watched me indulgently as I carved a swathe through the food, and then she said:

'It's lovely to see you, Hilary darling. Is it just a teeny chat, or is there something special on your mind? My copy's not late this time, is it? I let you have it all before I went to America.'

'Your copy isn't late, and I'm afraid I'd forgotten – how was America?' I asked.

'It was fine, just a flying visit, dear. One of my regular clients, the head of a big corporation, was thinking of making a new acquisition, and he wanted to talk to me before he did so, I had to tell him that the time wasn't right at all, the stars were very inauspicious for him. Besides, between you and me and the gatepost, dear, I'd heard one or two things about the company he was thinking of taking over and well, I wouldn't touch it with a barge pole, myself.'

'So did he take your advice?' I asked, fascinated by this glimpse of Mrs C as a business consultant.

'Oh yes, dear, and he won't regret it, I can tell you. You can't lose anyway, by taking no action, not in most cases, not in my experience, anyway. And the fact that he sent for me indicated that he had doubts about it himself, didn't it? If in doubt, leave out, that's my motto.'

'I'm sure you're right,' I said.

Mrs Carstairs said, 'But what about you, dear? Are you thinking of making a takeover bid for something? Or changing your life in some way?'

'No, not really,' I said. 'But I do have something – a problem – on my mind.'

'Would you like to see what the cards have to say about it, dear?' Mrs C invited. She had the tact and discretion not to make an effort to draw me out on the nature of the problem.

152

'I'd love to,' I said.

'Righty-ho, then. I'll just take this tray out to the kitchen, then I'll get the cards out,' she said, and she removed the cups and plates, and reappeared a few moments later with a packet in her hand.

Mrs C pulled a rather dusty coffee table between us, and unwrapped a large pack of Tarot cards from the piece of black velvet in which they were wrapped.

'Let's just find the Queen of Wands. That's you, dear,' she said. 'Here she is. Now, will you shuffle the cards, and cut them into three piles to the left, using your left hand. That's right. Think hard of the problem to which you want to know the answer, won't you, dear? And listen hard. Among the interpretations the answer should lie, but it may not be obvious. You may have to listen for it, do you know what I mean? It's sometimes cunningly concealed, as the bishop said to the actress.'

Listening to her I thought, not for the first time, that Mrs C reminded me of the nurse in *Romeo and Juliet*. Good-natured, garrulous, earthy. She couldn't be Helen Turner. I simply didn't believe it.

'All right, dear, now we must concentrate,' Mrs C said. She drew the curtains and lit two candles which she placed on the coffee table between us.

'Now think very hard of the problem that is bothering you. That's you, there in the centre. You're a dreamer, with the gift of vision. You may not be as you appear to the world. You live a great deal in your imagination, perhaps too much, dear.'

Mrs C took the next card from the top of the pack.

'This covers you. It's the Nine of Wands. That's unusual. Are you waiting for something, dear, something you're a bit apprehensive about? Clearly there's some anxiety here.

'I think you have experienced some kind of worry recently, and you are bracing yourself for something else. I

153

don't quite understand this. Does it mean anything to you?'

'Yes, it does,' I said.

'Don't worry, dear,' Mrs C said. 'You're perfectly capable of looking after yourself. It'll be all right, I'm sure it will. Let's look at another card.'

She picked another card off the pile I had assembled, and said, 'This crosses you.'

The card was labelled 'The Lovers', and showed a man and a woman who looked like Adam and Eve, with a Godlike figure above them.

'Oh dear,' Mrs C said. 'You've got the Lovers reversed. There's some kind of marriage break-up here, dear. The course of true love isn't running entirely smooth. Take care you don't make the wrong decision, won't you?'

Was it Toby's marriage breaking up? I hoped so.

'How's hubby?' Mrs Carstairs asked.

'He's okay,' I said noncommitally.

'Perhaps it's not *your* marriage breaking up then, dear?' Mrs Carstairs suggested.

I did my best to keep a deadpan expression. I did not want her interpretation to be coloured by my reactions. Did I really believe in it all?

'Well now, what have we here?' Mrs C asked. 'It's the Knight of Wands He's a fair young man, and I think you know who he is, dear. He came galloping into your life fairly recently, didn't he? But he's brought some kind of rivalry or conflict with him. We'd better mind that hubby doesn't find out about him, hadn't we, dear?'

She gave me a dreadful wink, and I felt a chill sweep through me. It was Chris, of course. But how did Mrs Carstairs know about him? Was she Helen Turner after all? In the flickering candle-light her face looked different, frightening.

'Mrs Carstairs,' I said, 'Does the name Helen Turner mean anything to you?'

She gave me a long, questioning look.

'Helen Turner?' she repeated. 'No, I don't think that it means anything to me, dear. Should it? But I think it means something to you. Would you like to tell me more about it?'

'No, no,' I said. 'I just wondered. Please go on with the reading.'

'Well now, here's the King of Swords,' Mrs Carstairs said. 'He's a dark-haired man. The situation is not perfectly straightforward. There could be something to do with a lawsuit here. Do you know who this card represents, Hilary? If you do, a certain amount of caution is necessary. Don't be too trustful. He may not have your interests at heart.'

Was it Martin? Martin had dark brown hair and brown eyes. Was Martin going to be involved in a prosecution after all? Or was it someone else? Toby answered the same description, of course.

'Now here's the crowning card, dear,' Mrs Carstairs said. 'It's the High Priestess. Ah, there are some hidden influences at work here. You haven't got to the bottom of things yet, have you? There is some mystery here. In fact it's all rather puzzling.

'And now this is the Tower. Well, well. There are going to be big changes in your life, Hilary. Be prepared for them. They will be all for the best, as you'll realise later. Don't worry about it. It's a long time since I've seen that card, though.

'Do you want me to go on, or have you heard enough?' she asked. 'There are four more cards which you can have if you want them.'

I still didn't know about Helen Turner.

'Please go on,' I said.

By now, Mrs Carstairs had arranged the cards in a cross

155

around the central card with which she had started. She went on to make a line of cards alongside this.

'Here's the Five of Cups,' Mrs Carstairs said. 'You're a bit worried about something in the past. Or is it someone – a person who has just come into your life again after a long, long interval? There may be some regrets here. And now there's the Two of Pentacles. Something to do with letters and messages. You'll have to be careful how you handle this situation. There's some opposition, some difficulties. Take care what you put in writing.'

'What did you say?' I said. 'Something about letters?'

'Did I?' Mrs Carstairs said.

'Yes, you did,' I said. Was she in a trance, or something?

'Take care in the way you deal with them, that's all, dear,' Mrs Carstairs said.

Was she warning me? Or threatening me?

'What do you mean?' I asked.

'You go dancing through life, don't you, dear?' Mrs C said. 'But you don't always feel like dancing and smiling. You put a brave face on things sometimes. This card has to do with messages, letters. All those letters you get . . . it must be a great strain.'

'Who are they from?' I asked.

'That isn't revealed,' Mrs C said. 'Let's see if the cards are going to tell us more. What's next?'

She turned over a new card.

'Do the letters come from a man?' she asked. 'There's a young man here, the Knight of Pentacles. He loves you. Does he love you enough? I think you want his love. But take a little care, dear. Things may not be entirely what they seem.'

'I don't understand,' I said.

'Well, let's look at the last card,' Mrs Carstairs said. 'Oh. It's the Queen of Swords. A dark woman, perhaps an older person. Is she connected with the question in some way?'

'Is it you, Mrs Carstairs?' I asked. 'Please tell me if it is. Don't play with me.'

Mrs Carstairs said, 'I don't know the answer to your question, dear. Do you think that I am the Queen of Swords? If you think so, then maybe I am.'

'Please don't tease me,' I said. 'I really need to know.'

'I never tease, I don't know what you mean,' Mrs C said. 'I hope it's been helpful, dear. I can't do more. That's the last card.'

We sat in the gloom for a couple of moments. I sighed. Mrs Carstairs blew the candles out, and the room was almost entirely dark. She moved across it, like a cat through the clutter, and pulled aside the curtains. Late afternoon sunshine streamed in, and the mood was broken.

'Let's have a noggin, dear,' Mrs Carstairs said, becoming her everyday self again. 'We've been altogether too serious, haven't we? Can I give you a tiny sherry?'

I drank the glass of sickly sweet sherry, and went over in my mind what she had said, while Mrs Carstairs chattered inconsequentially about America, lunar influences, rival astrologers and the paucity of her fee, which she still thought God should increase. I am afraid that at last she noticed my inattention, because she ground to a halt and said, not without sympathy:

'You look tired, dear. Have you still got something on your mind?'

I sighed. 'I suppose I have, Mrs C. I'm sorry, I was listening, really.'

'If you want to talk about it, do feel free,' Mrs Carstairs invited. 'Mum's the word, of course, dear. You can rely on me absolutely to keep anything you say confidential. You'd be surprised the things I hear, really, but it's all locked away, I never breathe a dicky-bird, not to a living soul.'

For a fleeting moment I was tempted to confide in Mrs Carstairs about the letters, but I resisted the temptation. It wasn't that I didn't trust her. It was that I didn't want to reveal that much of myself. I didn't want her to get that close to me. At least, that's what I told myself.

'Thank you, Mrs C dear,' I said, 'but it's being dealt with. There's a lawyer advising me, I mean, and I'm not really supposed to discuss it at the moment. I know you'll understand. Thank you for the sherry, and thank you for reading the cards for me. It was really helpful, I appreciated it.'

'Did you find the answer that you were looking for?' Mrs C asked, giving me a penetrating look.

'I don't know,' I said. 'I need to think about all the things you said. I think you were probably right, the answer is there somewhere, but I need to think it over, to digest it inwardly, before I recognize it.'

'Any time you want another reading, do come again,' Mrs Carstairs said. 'I'm always pleased to see you, Hilary. You've always been one of my favourite customers. It's a lovely magazine, *Herself*. And such nice people working for it.'

We made conventionally polite noises at each other, and I took my leave.

It was by now early evening, and it had been raining while I had been indoors in that dark and candle-lit room. The earth smelled fresh.

Traffic was beginning to build up as people were coming into London for a Saturday night out. I drove west along the Embankment, up the road by Earl's Court, and parked at the back of the block of flats.

As I walked up the corridor towards my flat, I saw a huddled shape by my front door. I froze. It looked like a

158

corpse. The body stirred, however, and scrambled to its feet.

'Hello, Hilary,' said Chris. 'You don't look pleased to see me.'

He had been sitting on the floor of the corridor outside my front door, his back against the wall. He now stood in front of me, looking rather vulnerable and uncertain of himself.

'You gave me a fright,' I said. 'What were you doing, sitting there?'

'Waiting for you,' he said.

I found my front door key.

'What do you want?' I asked.

'Ah, what do I want, what do I want,' he repeated. 'Do you really want me to tell you?'

'No, I don't think so, and I'm afraid it's not on offer, anyway,' I said.

'Oh,' He stood uncertainly in the doorway as I let myself into the hall of the flat.

'Since you're here, you'd better collect the anorak you left behind,' I said.

'Oh, is this where I left it?' he said. 'Good. I wondered what had happened to it.'

'You mean you didn't know that you'd left it here?'

'No, I didn't know where it was.'

'It caused a lot of trouble, anyway,' I said.

'I'm sorry,' he said. He sounded as though he meant it.

'Chris, if you were hoping to stay the weekend, you can't,' I said. 'So let's get that straight from the start.'

He shrugged.

'S'matter of fact, I just came to say goodbye, sort of,' he said.

'Oh.' I felt a bit deflated. 'Well, so long as that's clear, would you like a drink? I'm going to have one. I've done a lot of driving today, and I need one.'

'Yes, please.'

'What do you want?'

'Have you got a whisky and coke?'

I gave him one. I poured myself a neat whisky, to take away the taste of Mrs C's sweet sherry.

Chris said, 'I've got a girlfriend, Hilary, a really smashing girl, and my love life is absolutely fantastic, suddenly. I wanted to say thank you, because it's all your doing. S'matter of fact, I'm meeting her later this evening, but she has been away for a couple of days and isn't getting back to London till eight, so I thought I'd come round and see you before I met her at the station.'

I felt an unexpected surge of jealousy.

'It didn't take you very long to recover from your grand passion for me,' I said, in a rather prickly way.

'Yes, but don't you see, it was loving and being loved by you that made me realize – oh, all sorts of things. That I was lovable, and that I could do it, and that – oh, anyway, I feel really grateful, and wanted to say so,' he said.

'"Gratitude is a lively sense of future favours", Walpole said. But in this case, there aren't going to be any future favours,' I said, still smarting from the hurt of being so easily replaced. I felt rejected and sore. I was almost tempted to seduce him, to prove that the young woman, whoever she was, really knew nothing about the subject of seduction whatsoever. I had to admit that I found it galling that Chris, whom I had cast in the role of unrequited lover, refused to accept it and had simply trotted off and replaced me, seemingly with the greatest of ease.

'You aren't hurt, Hilary, are you?' he asked anxiously.

'No, of course I'm not hurt,' I lied. 'Who is she, anyway?'

'Her name's Henrietta, and she lives a couple of doors away. I've never noticed her much, before, but last weekend I was home, and she came round and my parents

160

were out, and before I knew where we were – wham! We were in bed together. It was incredible.'

'What if your parents had come home unexpectedly?' I asked.

'That's what she kept saying, actually. But they didn't. And it was really great. She's got the most enormous tits,' Chris confided, making me feel absolutely furious. I thought he was comparing her with me. How dared he?

'The French don't think much of big tits,' I said childishly. 'They think small, firm ones are really beautiful.'

But Chris disregarded me. He was obviously reliving in his mind the pleasures of his most recent sexual encounter.

My anger turned to chill displeasure.

'When you've finished your drink, Chris, you'd better go off and meet this over-endowed nymphette,' I said. 'I've had a heavy day, and really need some peace.'

'Are you angry?' he asked. 'I thought you'd be really pleased. It's all thanks to you, anyway.'

'It's all a bit like *Der Rosenkavalier*,' I said.

'What's that?'

'It's a Strauss opera about a young knight who was chosen by a married lady to carry a rose to a young girl, with whom he falls in love. Was Henrietta a virgin, by the way?'

Chris flushed slightly.

'No, she wasn't,' he said, a bit defensively. 'Why, is it important?'

I shrugged. 'I just wondered.'

'Would you like to say goodbye properly?' Chris asked me.

'What do you mean?'

'Well, in bed?'

'Certainly not!' I said. 'Chris, you really are the end.'

161

He smiled disarmingly. 'I just thought it would be a memorable farewell,' he said.

'It's not like shaking hands, you know,' I said.

'May I kiss you goodbye, anyway?' he asked.

'You may give me a filial sort of kiss, on my cheek,' I said. He got up, set down his glass, and did so. He stood in front of me, looking at me quizzically and tenderly. I was sitting in front of him, on a low chair, and at eye-level was the bulge in his faded jeans. I was tempted there and then to unzip his jeans, and use my mouth, my tongue, all my considerable skills and artifices to detain him so that he would be late for Henrietta, not go to her at all . . . But I didn't do so.

'I there's ever anything I can do for you, Hilary – I don't mean sex, I really mean anything I can do to help you at any time, I want to do it. I really like you, you know,' Chris said.

I set down my glass, stood up, and kissed him properly and satisfyingly on the mouth.

'I like you, too, and I've been behaving rather badly, I'm sorry,' I said. 'There you are, that's farewell, then. And don't forget your anorak, this time.'

'I'd better go, before my jeans split,' he said, patted my bottom, and went to the hall cupboard to get his anorak. He went out through the front door, holding his anorak in front of him. I heard the front door crash shut, and thought that this time, he had really gone out of my life.

Chapter Seventeen

IT WAS IRONIC, therefore, that Helen Turner's fifth letter arrived on the following Monday morning.

'Dear Hilary Toogood, (it read),
'I have been married for some years to a man I do not love. My husband and I live apart from Mondays to Fridays, only spending occasional weekends under the same roof, and for some time I have been having an affair with another man.

'Now a third man has come into my life, a much younger boy, young enough to be my son, in fact. We have made love together, and he is ardent and passionate, and of course wants to continue the affair. What do you advise? Which of these men do you think I should really be happy with?

'Helen Turner.'

I felt, when I read it, a kind of angry resignation. I sighed deeply, and looked out of my office window, and wondered how on earth anybody knew about Chris, and felt infuriated and resigned and frightened at the same time. Had Helen Turner been watching my flat on Saturday? Had she seen me take Chris in with me? Had she been watching through the sitting-room window? It wasn't possible, my sitting-room was five floors up, and wasn't overlooked. Had she got the room bugged, perhaps, or were there hidden cameras? It was preposterous, but I could think of no other explanation.

I studied the envelope. It had been posted on Saturday morning, in fact, in Kilburn. So it had been sent before Chris ever came to my flat. Well, on Saturday morning I had been out in Hertfordshire seeing Jan and Monica, so I could not have posted the letter myself. At least *I* could be ruled out as a suspect. I smiled wryly at the ridiculous logic of eliminating myself.

Should I tell Harry that another letter had arrived? I was loath to let Harry know this further detail of my most private private life. I didn't feel I could discuss this latest letter with Toby, either. I felt alone, at bay, and sick to the bottom of my heart.

I decided to have some strong, sweet coffee as an antidote to shock, and was just going through the door into Ruth's room to put the percolator on when I collided with God, coming in the other direction, in a hurry. His shirt was hanging out of his trousers, leaving a patch of bare tummy visible, and he seemed to be in a fair state of perturbation.

'There you are!' he cried. 'It's a pretty kettle of fish you've landed us in now, sweetie!'

It felt as though my heart had stopped, but I managed to sound calm, I hoped.

'What's the matter, Gerry?' I asked. 'I'm just going to put some coffee on. You sound as though you could do with a cup, too.'

'It's your beastly "Adopt a Granny" scheme,' Gerry accused. 'It's completely backfired. The most awful thing has happened.'

I forebore from arguing about whose scheme it really was, and said:

'Let's keep calm and have a cup of coffee, Gerry dear. Let me just put the percolator on, and then you can sit

164

down in my office, get your breath back and tell me all about it.'

Gerry grunted, threw himself down on the sofa in my room, and lit a cigarette. I dealt with the coffee, and went back to join him.

'Now, what's it all about?' I asked.

'I had a call first thing this morning from the photographer who was taking the pictures for the "Adopt a Granny" feature,' Gerry said. 'He spent a whole day taking various old folk to different places, together with *Herself* readers and their children, and taking happy snaps.'

'So?' I said.

'Well, he took one old boy to the park on top of Streatham Hill – you know, where the model dinosaurs and things are. There was Mr Millerson – that's the old boy – and two little girls of eleven and twelve, sisters, Lorraine and Sharon Smith. He took pictures of Grandpa benignly watching while they rode donkeys, played hide-and-seek round the dinosaurs, and so on.'

'Where was the girls' mother?' I asked, a nasty suspicion beginning to form in my mind.

'She was at home, looking after the girls' baby brother. She was only too glad to get the kids off her hands for the morning. The photographer had originally intended to get her in the shots too, but when he saw her, he said she was cross-eyed and sharp-featured, and on the whole he thought he'd get better pictures without her. Her took one of her with a soft-focus lens from a long way away, waving off the girls and old Mr Millerson as they departed up the road.'

'So what happened?'

'At the park, everything was fine. The girls appeared to enjoy it all immensely, and the old boy was most cooperative. But when the photographer returned the girls to their mother, the two little horrors reported that they didn't like their adopted grandpa at all, they thought he was rude. And when their mother asked what they meant, they alleged that while our photographer had been walking back to the car for more film, their charming old adopted grandpa had exposed himself to them behind the bushes, and had tried to persuade them to hold his cock.'

'Oh, dear,' I said feebly. 'I'll go and get us some coffee.'

I was back in a minute with two strong cups, and Gerry produced a hip flask and laced them both liberally with whisky.

'I'd like to castrate the old bugger,' he said.

'Shutting the stable door,' I told him. 'What did the girls' mother do?'

'She had hysterics, screamed at the photographer, is going to ring up the Managing Director this morning, threatens to sue, bring charges, and so on and so forth.'

'What about the old boy, Mr Millerson?' I asked. 'Did he admit it?'

'The photographer had dropped him off first at the Home,' Gerry said. 'So he doesn't know anything about it. Yet.'

'They might have made it up, of course,' I said. 'The girls, I mean.'

'I asked the photographer about that,' Gerry said. 'He said it was possible, but although he didn't much care for Lorraine and Sharon, and gave it as his opinion that it wouldn't have been the first cock they'd seen by a long chalk, he thought that they were probably telling the truth. He said he had vaguely noticed that when he got back from the car after changing the film, the old boy looked a bit pink and excited.'

'Pink?' I said

'In the face, of course,' Gerry said.

'What a start to the week,' I said. 'Well, don't worry,

Gerry. I'll go and see Mrs – what did you say her name was?'

'Smith.'

'I'll go and see Mrs Smith, and tell her how bad it would be for the girls to go to court to give evidence. It would be bad for them, actually. I'll try to persuade her to accept a sum of money to "give them a treat to take their minds off it", and I'm sure we'll hear no more about it.'

'How much money?' Gerry demanded.

'A hundred?'

'Too much. If she thinks there's any real money in it, she'll get greedy.'

'Perhaps you're right. Okay, I'll try twenty, go to fifty if I have to. And for God's sake – I mean, for heaven's sake – could you please kick that photographer in the balls, and tell him never to take kids anywhere without their mother or a chaperone ever again? It could be an accusation against him, next time.'

'There isn't going to be a next time,' Gerry said. 'I've decided to drop the "Adopt a Granny" idea. I'm sorry, Hilary, I know it meant a lot to you, but I don't think it's such a good idea as it sounded when you first put it up to me.'

'Gerry, it was your idea,' I said.

'Oh, no, sweetie, I distinctly remember the morning you put it up,' Gerry said. I could see that he really believed it. I sighed.

'Let me have a note of Mrs Smith's address, will you?' I asked. 'I'll try and get to see her this afternoon.'

'That's a good girl,' Gerry said, relieved. 'You can take my car and chauffeur, if you like. How about some more coffee?'

I buzzed for Ruth, who came and replenished our cups. When we were alone again, sitting quietly drinking the hot coffee, I said,

167

'Gerry, does the name Helen Turner mean anything to you?'

Gerry gave it his consideration.

'It's not that new receptionist, is it?' he asked. 'The one with the amazing breasts?'

'No, it isn't the new receptionist,' I said.

'Give up, then', he said. 'Who is it?'

'I don't know,' I said. 'I just wondered if you'd ever heard of her. I've had a couple of letters signed "Helen Turner", and I think they're cod letters.'

'What about?' Gerry asked.

'Oh, just the usual kind of problem letters, but when I tried to send a personal reply, the address didn't exist,' I said.

'Well, that's quite common, isn't it, sweetie?' Gerry asked. 'I mean, for someone to use a false address, and expect to see the answer on your page the next week?'

'Yes, but there has been more than one, and I was curious,' I said. I watched him closely, and the name seemed to have had no effect on him at all. I didn't believe that he could be Helen Turner.

'Have you talked to Harry about Mrs Borer?' I asked, to change the subject.

'Yes, I've agreed with him to play it your way for the moment,' Gerry said. 'Thanks for the coffee, sweetie. I'll send you Mrs Smith's address. Let me know how you get on, won't you?'

'Right you are,' I said, and began on the day's letters.

Travelling out to Streatham in solitary state in the back of the chauffeur-driven Rover, waves of anger and depression about Helen Turner assailed me. What did she want? I was reminded of Freud's 'What do women want?' and wondered if he felt as desperate as I did at not being able to fathom the answer.

I soon found that I held the key to what Mrs Smith

168

wanted. She settled happily and gratefully for twenty pounds, which I produced in cash from my handbag and placed on her sideboard. I left amid protestations that *Herself* was the 'book' which Mrs Smith preferred to all others, and that she would read it with even greater interest from now on. Her daughters were wicked girls to say the things they had, she said. She would give them a good talking to, and they wouldn't repeat them further.

It was the rush hour by the time we were wending our way back. We met a great stream of traffic crawling out of London. It was too late to go back to the office, so the chauffeur turned westwards to drop me off at my flat. As I stepped out onto the pavement, a taxi drew up behind us, and Toby jumped out of it.

'Hallo,' he said, when he saw me. 'You're travelling in style. Have you been promoted?'

'No, just doing a bit of bacon-saving,' I said. 'I need a drink, badly. I'll tell you then.'

The lift had broken down, so we plodded up the stairs, and it reminded me of the first night that Toby and I had been to bed together. Then the lift had also been out of order, and we had had to walk, one behind the other, feeling shy because we both knew how the evening was going to end.

I said, 'D'you remember the first time, Toby, when we had to walk?'

And he said 'Yes, I do. It was quite astonishing.'

I said 'Astonishing? How?'

And he said 'When we got in, rather out of breath after hiking up all those stairs, you said "Would you like some coffee?" and I said "Yes, please", and then you said "You don't really want coffee, do you? Wouldn't you rather go to bed?" And before I knew what had happened you had all your clothes off, and there we were. I'd never met anyone so direct and lacking in coyness before. I liked it, anyway.'

I laughed. 'Did it shock you?'

'I suppose it did, a bit,' Toby said.

He put his key into the lock, and we went into the flat.

'Do you want to go to bed now?' I asked. He hesitated, and I saw that he didn't.

'It doesn't matter,' I said. 'I'm not dying from frustration. Just in need of a little comfort, maybe. I can manage just as well if you give me a drink and hold my hand.'

'Not another letter?' Toby said.

'I'm afraid so.'

'Bloody hell, this is beyond a joke. You'll have to go to the police. What is it this time?'

'Oh, Toby . . . Let's have a drink first, shall we?'

He poured us two whiskies, and handed me one in silence. He sat beside me on the sofa, and waited.

'I didn't mean to tell you about it,' I said. 'But I really need to talk to you, or to talk about it to someone, and I'd rather it was you than anyone.'

'What was the letter about?' Toby asked.

'About Chris. The boy in Oxford,' I said.

'How in hell does she know about that?'

'God knows. I wish I did,' I said miserably.

'You don't suppose he does, do you?' Toby asked.

'What?'

'When you said "God knows". You don't suppose that it could be Gerry O'Dwyer, the all-knowing God?'

'Chris is his son,' I said slowly. 'But no, I don't think so, not really. I tried the name Helen Turner on him this morning, and it evoked no reaction at all.'

'What did the letter say about the boy wonder?' Toby demanded.

'Not much. She just knew about him,' I said.

'Knew what about him, though?'

I sighed. 'Knew that we'd – that I'd made love with him.'

'When?' Toby demanded.

170

'Well, you know . . . when I told you about it.'

'And since then?'

'Not since then.'

Toby looked at me searchingly.

'He's been here again, hasn't he, Hilary?'

'You're behaving like a bloody prosecuting counsel!' I burst out. 'Okay, yes, he's been here again. But just to collect his anorak. Nothing else. We didn't screw.'

'Was it this last weekend?'

'Yes, it was. I went out for the day on Saturday, and when I came back, he was waiting. He had one drink, collected his anorak, and went.'

'I don't believe you,' Toby said.

'Well, it's true.' I felt angry and frustrated and resentful. I started to cry, but they were tears of rage and self-pity, and Toby moved away from me.

'Oh, shut up,' he said.

'What's sauce for the gander is sauce for the goose,' I attacked.

'What do you mean?'

'How did you spend your weekend, anyway? With another woman.'

'I don't call Jean a woman. She's sexless.'

'What about the others?'

'What others?'

'She said there were others, other women.'

'Oh.' Toby got up and poured himself another whisky. He waved the bottle at me. 'Want one?'

I held out my glass to him in silence, and he poured a large quantity of neat whisky into it.

'Are there?' I asked.

'At the moment, you mean?

'There are, aren't there?'

'Not at the moment, no.'

'But there have been?'

171

'Oh, come on, Hilary, you must have known that there were women before you, mustn't you?'

'You told me there weren't. Is that all I am, just one of a series?' I said.

Toby sat down beside me again.

'What's the matter with you, Hilary? You're not usually like this. You're behaving like – you're behaving like bloody Jean, actually.'

'You started it, about the boy wonder,' I muttered.

His face darkened, and I knew that it was a mistake.

'Are you going to see him again?' he demanded.

'No, I'm not. I didn't invite him or intend to see him on Saturday. He left his anorak behind, and he came to fetch it. I'm sorry about it, but that was all that happened. He is out of my life forever. He understands that, and as a matter of fact, he's got a girlfriend his own age, anyway.'

'Oh,' said Toby. 'That's why it's all over, is it?'

'That's nasty,' I said.

'I know. I'm sorry.'

We sat in silence for a few moments.

'Shall I take you out to dinner?' I offered.

'What a liberated lady!' he said. 'Delightful. Makes me feel like a kept man. I'm certainly not going to refuse. Where shall we go?'

'Don Luigi, in the King's road?' I suggested.

'Do you want to shower? I'll ring and book a table.'

'Yes, please.'

I got to my feet, but the whiskies had made me unsteady. Toby held me as I stumbled, and I buried my face in his shoulder.

'I'm sorry,' I said, but I wasn't sure quite what I was apologizing for.

'It's Helen Turner,' Toby said. 'She's unnerved you, and I'm not surprised. You've got to do something about her.'

'Toby . . . you haven't any idea who it might be, have you?' I asked.

He shook his head.

'Harry – the lawyer – suggested that I might be writing the letters myself,' I said.

Toby held me away from him, and looked at me. Tears, unbidden tears this time, rolled down my cheeks. He took out his silk handkerchief and wiped them away.

'That's silly, isn't it?' he said gently. 'And do stop crying. You're always in tears these days.'

'I'm not writing the letters myself, you know,' I said.

'I know that.'

'I'm not mad, Toby, I'm not.'

'I know that, too.'

Toby kissed me, gently and consolingly at first, and then with more passion and urgency. He unbuttoned my dress and fondled my breasts, and I took off the rest of my clothes, and he threw aside his trousers. I sat down on the Casa Pupo rug by the window, and he sat beside me and caressed me, and then pushed me back and was into me. His breathing had just quickened, when the doorbell rang.

'Bloody hell!' Toby froze.

He took himself out of me and off me, and I lay, naked and shivering, feeling the roughness of the rug buckled under my back.

'Who is it?' he asked.

'I don't know. I'm not expecting anyone.'

The bell went again, a long peal.

'I'll have to answer it.'

I pulled my dress over my head, slipped my feet into my sandals and stood up. I scooped up Toby's trousers and my underclothes, and handed them to him.

'I suppose Jean might have a private detective,' I said. 'Why don't you go and lock yourself in the bathroom? I'll give you a knock when I know who it is.'

173

He nodded, picked up his tie from the sofa, and padded out. I kicked his shoes under the chair, ran my fingers through my hair, and went to the front door.

When I opened it, I didn't at first recognize the figure who almost fell into the hall. She leaned against the wall, her face in shadow, saying nothing. I turned the light on and looked at her.

It was Ruth, but it wasn't surprising that I hadn't realized it at first. My normally cool, well-groomed secretary was dishevelled, with a face swollen with bruises and eyes heavy with weeping. Her hair fell in lank strands over her blotchy complexion, her tights were ripped and wrinkled, and her dress was stained. Her handbag strap was broken, and it dangled from one hand.

'Ruth! Whatever's happened to you?' I said.

'I – I –' She slipped down the wall.

'Come and sit down.'

I put my arm round her, and helped her into the sitting-room.

'Come on, sit on the sofa here. You look as though you need a drink. But rest a minute first. Have you been in an accident?'

'Something like that.' Her lips were cut and bruised, and she mumbled indistinctly.

'Do you think you need to go to hospital? I'd better not give you a drink if you might need an anaesthetic.'

She shook her head.

'Don't need hospital. Want a drink.'

'Are you sure there are no bones broken? Do you want whisky or brandy?'

'Whisky, please.'

I handed her the glass, and stroked her hair back from her forehead to look at the extent of her injuries.

'What happened, Ruth? No, don't tell me for a moment. Just rest. You can tell me in a minute or two.

174

I'm just going to get a bowl and some first aid things, I'll be back in a minute.'

I went through to the bedroom. Toby stood there. He was now fully dressed.

'Who is it?' he asked.

'It's Ruth. She looks as though she's been in an accident.'

'Does she need to go to hospital?'

'She says not. I don't think so.'

I got out the first aid box and filled a small bowl with water.

'Shall I wait in here?' Toby asked.

'I don't think it matters,' I said. 'Ruth won't mind you seeing her, I don't think.'

He followed me back into the sitting-room. Ruth was lying on the sofa with her feet up, sipping the whisky.

'Ruth, you know Toby, don't you?'

'Hi, Ruth,' he said.

'Hello, Toby,' she mumbled.

'Don't try to speak for a minute or two, let me wash the cuts,' I said. She shut her eyes, and I gently cleaned her face with moistened cotton wool.

When I'd finished, it didn't look nearly so horrifying as when she'd arrived. A little blood goes a long way, and when I'd removed it, it was clear that her injuries were fairly superficial, and there wouldn't be any long term scarring.

'Do you want to talk about what happened, or not?' I asked.

'It was a bloody Arab,' she said. 'Can I have another whisky?'

'Do you want us to call the police?' Toby asked.

'Good God, no!' Ruth was horrified. 'They'd probably book me.'

'Book you? What for?'

She shrugged.

'Book the agency, anyway,' she said. 'They sent me to this guy – he's renting a flat two floors up. He was okay at first – gave me a drink, paid me, was perfectly civil. Then he started wanting different things. I said that he should have told the agency if he'd wanted special services. He got angry. I got frightened. And when I wouldn't do what he wanted, he beat me up.'

'What did he want?' Toby asked.

Ruth shrugged again.

'Nothing so outrageous, really, I suppose. He wanted me to beat him, and I didn't want to, but I did. Then he wanted . . . oh, I think what he really wanted was to find something that I wouldn't do, so he had an excuse to beat me up.' She started to cry again.

'Ruth, don't you think you expose yourself to the risk of this kind of thing, or even worse, by taking the agency work?' I asked.

She nodded miserably.

'I'll probably get murdered someday,' she said.

'So why go on?'

'It's the excitement,' she said.

Toby said, 'Hilary's right. It's too risky, Ruth.'

'I'll think about it,' she said. 'I'll certainly think about it, after this.'

'Where did you say he lived?' Toby said.

'Two floors up. I got away from him, and staggered out, and I remembered that you lived here, Hilary, because of the time when you had flu and I brought those proofs round, so I managed to make it to your front door.'

'I'm glad you did,' I said. 'But Ruth – have you been to this block of flats before?'

'No, I don't think so. Why?'

Helen Turner was never far from the top of my mind, these days. The suspicion had come to me that if Ruth

176

had been visiting her clients in the block regularly, she might well have been watching me, too.

'Do you know who Helen Turner is, Ruth?'

'Helen Turner? No, does she live in this block? The name rings a bell somehow,' she said.

'How?' Toby asked.

'I don't know. Maybe she's one of our regular crank correspondents, or something,' Ruth said. 'Why?'

'Oh, nothing,' I said. 'How are you feeling?'

'Better,' she said. 'I say, I'm awfully sorry to burst in on you like that, and collapse dramatically on your doorstep. I hope that I didn't interrupt anything.'

Toby and I looked at each other.

'Obviously I did,' Ruth said. 'I'm terribly sorry. I'd better take myself off.'

'Nonsense,' I said. You'd better rest a bit longer. You clearly aren't fit.'

'I'm perfectly okay now, really,' Ruth said. 'It was the shock more than anything else, you know. I'd better be going.'

'Can I drive you somewhere?' Toby asked.

'It's okay, the agency pays for taxis. The porter will call me one. No problem. Really, I'm perfectly okay, and I feel embarrassed about making such a fuss,' she said.

When she had left, Toby and I sat in silence for a few minutes. The passion which had possessed us half an hour previously had evaporated.

'Poor Ruth,' I said. 'Poor, crazy, mixed-up Ruth. I do feel sorry for her. What's it all about?'

'I was watching you both as you were sitting together on the sofa,' Toby said.

'And?'

'Oh, nothing.'

'Yes, there was something.'

'Well,' he said. 'I thought that you were rather alike.'

'Alike!' I said. 'Ruth and me?' I felt as though he had

suddenly and without warning hit and winded me. 'What do you mean?'

'Nothing. I wish I hadn't said anything.'

'Oh, no.' I said. 'It didn't slip out accidentally. You clobbered me with it, Toby. Ruth is a prostitute. Are you saying that I'm one, too?'

'I didn't say that,' he said.

'But that's what you were meaning, wasn't it? That Ruth and I sell ourselves, or allow men to use us?' Anger rose in me. 'Well, is that what you meant?'

He shrugged and turned his back on me as he poured himself a drink.

'All right, Toby, I do allow you to use me. But not for money. For love. Because I love you. And you don't love me, do you? You just make use of me. And Jean. And probably a whole lot of other people too.'

Toby's knuckles were white as he gripped the glass. I felt frightened at having angered him so much, particularly as he was going away on a business trip in a couple of days' time.

Chapter Eighteen

GOD HAD ASKED me to a dinner party at his home the following Tuesday week. It had never happened before. I wasn't sure if it was a gesture of gratitude for having settled Mrs Smith of Streatham and her potential lawsuit, or a consolation prize for having abandoned the 'Adopt a Granny' scheme (which by now he had convinced himself had been entirely my ill-conceived idea), or simply that he was short of a single woman, or a woman he could ask on her own, anyway, to make up his numbers. Toby was away for three weeks on a so-called Fact Finding Mission to one of the warmer regions of an Iron Curtain country, so I was glad of the diversion.

God was in his heaven in fashionable Canonbury. On the appointed evening, I parked my car outside his large Georgian house, and knocked at the heavily-restored front door.

It was opened by a buxom lady in a flowing Indian dress, beneath which rippled rolls of fat. She was what my mother would have called a bottle blonde.

'Hilary Toogood!' she cried. 'I knew you instantly, from your picture in the magazine. I've heard so much about you. It's lovely to meet you in the flesh.'

'You must be Marjorie,' I said, avoiding "in the flesh". I realized that this must be Chris's mother, and tried to see the resemblance between him and this lady who so much called to mind an overstuffed horsehair sofa. He was very fair, so perhaps she wasn't a bottle blonde, after all.

She showed me into the drawing-room, where a small group of people were already assembled. Gerry had drawn his guests almost entirely from United Magazines. There was the Snow Queen, our Managing Director, and her husband, a distinguished-looking man in his forties. Harry Ballsup was standing by the drinks cupboard.

'Hallo, Shirley, I didn't know you were going to be here,' I said. Somehow Shirley was a particularly incongruous name for the Snow Queen, who was a singularly cool, elegant and sophisticated lady. She must have been born at about the time that Shirley Temple was at the zenith of her popularity, I guessed. If I was right, her Christian name betrayed her lower middle-class origins.

'Hilary, darling,' She greeted me with a kiss. 'You know Dennis, my husband, don't you?'

'We met at that competition – the flower arranging thing,' he reminded me, and I shook hands with him.

'You know Harry, of course,' God said. 'He's buying a house just down the road.'

I waved to Harry, and accepted a glass of white wine from Gerry. The wine was cold, but not really cold enough. As I drank it, I studied my surroundings. It was conventional Canonbury trendy, from the bare wood floors, scattered with rugs, to the stripped wood furniture and uncomfortable Victorian chairs. There were glass shelves on either side of the fireplace, with expensive and elaborate hi-fi equipment, and a video tape recorder. A television set was in its own cabinet. The hard and lumpy looking chairs, obviously recently re-upholstered, were supplemented by giant floor cushions, covered in Indian fabric, a relict of the previous decade when Habitatty furnishing had been the fashion.

I sighed. The middle-classes in that area certainly knew how to make themselves uncomfortable.

Marjorie's flowing Indian dress was in contrast to the Snow Queen's elegant white silk sheath, and my own delicate voile print. Gerry was wearing a suit, but the other men wore casual jackets and no ties.

Gerry was extolling the virtues of the wine he was serving, and inviting guesses as to its country of origin. I thought it was probably Australian, but didn't like to say so.

'It's English!' he announced triumphantly, when everyone had politely suggested German, Hungarian, Austrian and French. 'From the Isle of Wight! We're just starting to produce some very good wine in this country, you know. You'd never have guessed, would you? Of course, we've been producing wine in England since the Middle Ages. There used to be vineyards round Oxford.'

I noticed Harry regarding him quizzically. Harry caught my eye, and moved nearer to me.

'D'you know much about wine?' he asked.

'Not really. Do you?'

'I'm afraid not. Do you play bridge?'

'No, I'm afraid I don't.'

Having drifted up two conversational cul-de-sacs, I felt I had to make an effort.

'Are you moving here from another part of Canonbury, or from somewhere outside the area?' I asked.

It turned out to be the right question. Harry's wife had left him, I discovered to my surprise, and he had sold his suburban home and bought two flats: one for himself, and one for his son. The floodgates were opened for him. He longed to talk to someone about his wife and her desertion of him, and all I had to do was to make sympathetic noises occasionally. He let it all out, totally oblivious to the other guests, who were still discussing vintages, sources of cheap wine in bulk, quantity discounts and wine clubs. Harry and I settled ourselves uncomfortably on a lumpy Victorian sofa, and I listened to his tale of woe. Having only seen him in an office context previously, it surprised me to discover in him something so human as a broken marriage.

'Why Canonbury?' I asked, when I could get a word in edgeways, and this unleashed another flood of stories about his grandparents, who had lived in the area, and who had brought him up, it seemed. As I listened, sipping my drink and nodding encouragingly from time to time, it occurred to me that perhaps bores might be defined as people who were interested largely in themselves. Having started off by sympathizing with him over the loss of his wife – her rejection of him had obviously been a very painful and scarring experience – I began to find myself sympathizing with her, instead. How on earth had she stood him for as long as sixteen years?

After about half an hour, we were shepherded through into the dining-room to eat. To my surprise, I saw that the table was laid for ten people, although there were only eight of us. As we began to sort ourselves out, I heard voices in the hall. The door flew open and Chris burst in, followed by a young woman.

'Chris darling! You're late,' his mother greeted him.

'Sorry, Ma,' he said, kissing her cheek.

'And really, you might have changed out of your jeans,' she remonstrated. 'This is my feckless son Chris, everyone, and this is Henrietta. Now, darlings, whom don't you know?'

Chris stood beside his mother, and for the first time looked at the rest of us. Our eyes met, and I saw his slight look of shock. He recovered rapidly and said,

'Well, of course, I know Hilary. Dominic and I are at Oxford together. I didn't know you were going to be here tonight, Hilary. How are you? Have you heard from Dominic recently?'

He shook hands with everyone, introductions were made, and we seated ourselves. I was sitting between God and Dennis, Shirley's husband. Shirley sat on the other side of God, and Henrietta was sitting opposite me. She had untidy, tangled red hair, and a rather pre-Raphaelite appearance. When the puppy fat disappeared, she would probably be a very good-looking woman. She was wearing a low-cut white cotton blouse, and a printed skirt, and her breasts were clearly visible. Chris had manoeuvred himself to sit beside her, and he couldn't take his eyes off them.

Henrietta started talking, and my first impression of her potentially good looks was destroyed by her voice. It was harsh and ugly, with a strong Cockney inflection.

'This guy said to me "I hear you're the best stylist that this salon's got". And I said "That's right". And he was a – you know – TV type, and while I did his hair, he told me about his girlfriend committing suicide. He came back and found her, two weeks ago, and it was really heavy. It absolutely – you know – spooked me.'

I hoped that the distaste I felt for Henrietta wasn't showing on my face. How on earth could Chris have been attracted to someone like that? She was dreadful. I supposed it was the tits.

The first course was a mélange of horrid sea-foods, reeking with garlic. I pushed it around with a fork, and managed to swallow a mouthful or two, eating plenty of bread with it. It was followed by *coq au vin*. The talk turned, inevitably, to money and property prices, with everyone being self-congratulatory about their perspicacity in buying before the boom. Chris hardly looked at me. He was clearly dazzled by and besotted with his unspeakable little hairdresser. I felt piqued but decided to be particularly gracious and charming.

Marjorie brought in the last course, which was obviously her *pièce de résistance*. It was a pyramid of meringue and fruit and whipped cream, which she bore in triumphantly, amidst polite exclamations of admiration. She obviously had a sweet tooth. No wonder she was so fat. Gerry poured out a sickly sweet white wine to accompany it. I tried to refuse both the wine and the pudding, but Marjorie was not to be denied. She insisted on heaping a section of the pyramid onto my plate.

'Only about two thousand carlories,' the Snow Queen said, *sotto voce*, grimacing sympathetically as we both contemplated it glumly.

'You ought to take up jogging, soon lose it all again,' Gerry urged us heartily. 'I do two miles every morning, feels heaps better for it.'

'I'd be embarrassed to be seen by the neighbours,' the Snow Queen confessed.

Gerry said, 'Well, there are other ways of getting exercise, if you know what I mean, eh?' guffawed, and dug me in the ribs. I smiled faintly.

'It's as good as a six mile walk, I'm told,' Harry contributed.

'What is?' Marjorie had been in and out to the kitchen, fetching yet more cream with which to anoint the gooey confection.

'Gerry is recommending making love as a way of losing weight,' Dennis explained. There was a slight awkward silence, as we contemplated our hostess. I remembered that Gerry was impotent, and that that was a form of weight reduction denied to her, although none of the other guests knew it. Perhaps I imagined their embarrassment, but mine was real, and I felt constrained to break the silence.

'David Bailey makes love daily,' I said foolishly.

The Snow Queen said, 'What?' and Gerry said, 'What are you talking about, sweetie?'

I said, feeling silly, 'David Bailey, the photographer, you know. That's what they say about him.'

'Reminds me of "Toby Abbott's got queer habits"'
Dennis said.

I couldn't believe my ears.

I thought I really must be going mad.

Keep quiet, keep calm, you'll find out what he really said in a moment. Just don't say anything.

'Who's he?' God said.

'You know. That MP fellow, works in PR, always hanging around magazine offices,' Dennis said. 'Good-looking bloke, but smarmy, too much of a tailor's dummy for my liking.'

'Of course, I know him,' the Snow Queen said. 'He put up the money for that investment competition one of the magazines ran. Well, he didn't put it up personally, he got it out of the sponsor for us, if you know what I mean.'

'Well, you know the story that was going round about him a month or two ago, don't you?' Dennis said. 'I think the rhyme originated then.'

'What story?' Gerry asked.

'The one about the pictures of him and the other fellow in bed with the Right Honourable Lady Minister.'

'No, really? Not the Minister of Education?' Marjorie asked, enthralled.

'The very same lady. Apparently the pictures showed her in the middle, and Toby and the other fellow – another MP, can't remember his name at the moment for the life of me – one each side. All three were starkers, and the Right Honourable Lady had an erect prick in each hand. Someone was trying to sell the pictures to the *News of the World*.'

'But the *News of the World* couldn't publish them!' I burst out. 'I mean, if they exist, they must be obscene. What was the point?'

'Well, don't you see,' Dennis explained kindly, 'they weren't offered for sale for publication, but simply as evidence of goings-on in high places. The Right

Honourable Lady is a bit of a groupie, enjoys a small gang bang, and friend Abbott – well, he's AC-DC, as they say.'

'What's AC-DC?' Henrietta asked. Only she said 'Icey Dicey'.

'Icey Dicey means he likes it both ways, ma'am,' Dennis mimicked back to her; unconsciously, I'm sure – he was too much of a gentleman to intend rudeness. 'It means he enjoys it with both ladies and gentlemen. Toby Abbott's got queer habits.'

'I say – have you heard the old joke: "You can kiss a nun once, you can kiss a nun twice, but you mustn't get into the habit"' Gerry broke in. There was a general laugh, and Marjorie started collecting up the pudding plates and putting on coffee.

I still felt unable to take it in, or believe in it. There must be some mistake, of course there was. I looked at Chris. Had I ever mentioned Toby's name to him? Would he connect Toby with the dinner-table gossip? But he had displayed no flicker of interest in the scurrilous story, and was still concentrating wholly on Henrietta. The story had obviously meant nothing to him whatsoever.

I felt increasingly like Alice in Wonderland. These things weren't really happening. I wasn't really hearing right. Any minute I should wake up and find that I was in bed with Toby. I dug my fingernails into the palms of my hand surreptitiously, hurting myself, hoping to wake myself out of the nightmare. But nothing happened. I was awake. It was true, but incredible. These strangers were talking about Toby. It was one of those gossipy dinner party conversations, people showing off about knowing inside stories, having inside information. They didn't know that I knew him, it was pure chance.

We returned to the sitting-room, and Harry Ballsup pulled over an Indian cushion and sat at my feet. He kept looking up at me with the eyes of a spaniel. He had taken my idle sympathy at the beginning of the evening for encouragement. Unfortunately he was looking for further opportunities to rabbit on and on and on about his wretched wife.

'I'd love to show you my house,' he was saying. 'You obviously have such marvellous taste, I can tell that from your clothes, maybe you'd give me some ideas on decoration and so forth. I'm not much good at that side of things. Now my wife –' and he was off again.

I suddenly felt that I could stand it all no longer. I didn't like these people. I didn't want to sit and listen to their silly gossip. Why should I stay when I didn't want to? Chris and Henrietta had retreated to a far corner of the room, and were engaged in an intense whispered conversation. Apart from greeting me, he hadn't addressed a word to me all evening. I felt miserable and impatient, and hoped it didn't show.

Coffee had been served and cleared away, but it was still only eleven o'clock. I got up and said to Marjorie, 'Where's the loo, please?'

She said, 'I'll show you,' and accompanied me out of the room.

When we got outside, I said, untruthfully, 'Marjorie I hope you won't think me terribly rude, but I've got the curse frightfully badly, and dreadful stomach cramps, and I think bed with a hot-water-bottle is the only thing that's going to help at all. Would you mind frightfully if I crept away? You could explain to Gerry for me, couldn't you? I don't want to break up the party, so maybe I could just disappear?'

'Of course,' Majorie said. 'I'm so sorry, dear. Is there anything I can do to help? Would you like to lie down on my bed for a bit?'

'No, I'll just pop into the loo, and then I'll be off,' I said. 'Thank you so much for that delicious dinner, and such a magnificient pudding. You must give me the recipe.'

'I think you made a conquest with Harry,' Marjorie said, with all the satisfaction of a hostess who finds herself a matchmaker. 'He seems very smitten.'

I was appalled. 'He's a super person,' I said falsely, 'obviously terribly cut-up about his wife.'

'Yes, poor dear,' Marjorie said. 'Well, I'm sorry you're feeling off-colour, but I do understand, I often feel like that myself. I hope you'll come again when you're feeling better.'

I spent a few moments in the lavatory as part of my excuse, slipped out of the house, and breathed great gulps of the night air with a sense of relief. The whole evening had been a bad dream. I didn't believe that it was true at all.

Chapter Nineteen

THE SUMMER WAS ending. The tide of tourists eddied out of London. Taxis became easier to come by. As the state schools reassembled, elderly lollipop men sprouted at the crossings like a plague of garden gnomes. They all seemed to be in their eighties, and caused immense traffic jams as they ambled into the middle of the road, balefully waving their STOP CHILDREN CROSSING sticks.

'I'd support that movement any time,' I said tartly to Gerry's chauffeur who had picked me up one morning. Late for work, we waited interminably in one of these hold ups.

I had not seen Martin for weeks. I went down to Falconbridge most weekends, and spent lovely solitary days reading in my tower room, and walking along the coast. Each time I arrived, I expected to find him returned, but each time I found the house empty except for the staff. The cleaners came and spring cleaned during the long Summer holiday, and the secretary came in and dealt with the mail. Once I saw her, when I was arriving, and she said:

'Oh, Mrs Shipton – do you know when Mr Shipton will be back?'

'No, I don't,' I said. 'Do you need him?'

She hesitated.

'Well no, not really. I mean, there's nothing I can't

cope with. But – well, do you know where he is? I mean, he usually leaves me an address and phone number, just in case, but he hasn't, this time.'

'I know he took a boat on the Broads. We could probably find out, if you need him,' I said.

'I know about the boat, but I thought he'd be back after that. It's where is is now,' she said.

'No, I don't know,' I said, feeling irritated with Martin for his irresponsibility, and for putting me in the embarrassing position of having to admit to his secretary that I didn't know where my husband was. 'But his mother is staying with her sister in Southgate in North London. I could give you that phone number, if you like, and you could ask her.'

'Oh no, it's not urgent,' the woman said. 'I'm sorry to have bothered you. I expect he thought it didn't matter; after all I have your office number, and I can always get into touch with you in an emergency, can't I?'

She turned away, rather pink, and I wondered if she were a little in love with Martin. If so, she was doomed to disappointment.

'He's bound to be back a week before term starts,' I said consolingly. 'It's not long now, is it?'

'It's a late start this year, the twenty-fifth,' she said. 'I'm sure he'll be back soon.'

Toby was also due back soon, from his fact finding tour. I had resolved not to ask him about the photographs the minute he crossed the threshold, but to wait, and hold back till an appropriate time.

Helen Turner seemed to be taking a break, too. I had heard nothing from her since the letter about Chris. Was it significant? Did it link up with the fact that Martin and Toby were both away? Could it be either of them? Then I heard that Mrs Carstairs was away, and my suspicions were diverted to her. In fact all the world seemed to be on holiday, except me.

190

Harry Ballsup had drifted into my office and asked sympathetically how things were. Had I had any more correspondence? He wanted to know. 'Only about a hundred letters a day,' I said rather irritably, indicating the pile in front of me.

'I mean – you know – anonymous ones,' he said, picking up a reader's letter from the top of the pile, and reading it.

I was irritated by this, by the way his breath smelled of alcohol, and, irrationally, by his reference to Helen Turner. It wasn't fair, since I had asked for his help about her in the first place.

'No, I haven't, and I'm sorry, Harry, but I'm very busy at the moment,' I said. 'Like Greta Garbo, I want to be alone.'

'Okay, okay, sorry,' he said, putting down the letter and backing away. 'Only trying to help.'

'I know, Harry. I'm sorry. It's just that it's a bit frantic at the moment. Please don't be offended.'

But he was.

When Toby returned he was due to go back to Jean in Wales, but he was going to tell her that the duration of the trip was longer than it had actually been and spend a couple of nights with me en route.

He arrived laden with duty free liquor, which he said apologetically he'd have to take on to Wales unopened as part of the alibi. He had bought me a giant bottle of Courrèges Empreinte as a consolation prize.

I made him dinner at home that evening, because I knew that after a couple of weeks of hotel and restaurant eating, he'd prefer it. He looked sun-tanned and fit, and watching him as he ate appreciatively the lamb I'd cooked, and the late raspberries (why do all men prefer raspberries to strawberries?) I felt envious and irritated. Why couldn't he have taken me with him? I hardly ever took holidays, mainly because I had no-one to go on holiday with, since Dominic had grown up. Fact finding tour or whatever fancy name he gave to it, Toby had obviously just had a super holiday, and had never given me a second thought. The anger built up in me, and by the time we went to bed, I was seething.

Toby drifted round the bedroom unhurriedly, reading *The Economist* to catch up on what had been happening while he was away, blithely unaware that I was lying there like a dormant volcano, about to erupt at any minute.

He sat on the edge of the bed in his pyjamas, still placidly reading. It added to my fury. After three weeks separation, I would have expected him to be passionate. The fact that he showed no signs of unappeased appetite probably meant that it hadn't been unappeased.

'Who has been holding your cock in the last three weeks, then?' I asked nastily.

That actually did distract his attention from *The Economist*. He noticed the edge in my voice, and eyed me in some alarm.

'Why are you so angry? What's it all about?' Toby asked nervously. Perhaps he had known me in pre-eruption mood before.

'Don't you know?' I asked, feeling further aggravated. He eyed me warily.

'Are you about to have the curse?' he asked.

'I'm going to have a cigarette,' I said.

Since I never smoked, Toby took this to be a very bad omen indeed. As I padded off to the sitting-room to find a cigarette, he looked extremely apprehensive. I thought grimly that I was doing precisely what I had made up my mind I would not do, but I simply couldn't help it. I had intended to broach the subject coolly and reasonably, and listen to what he had to say. And I wasn't doing anything of the sort.

I came back into the bedroom with a cigarette and an

ashtray, and sat up in bed, puffing away furiously.

'Now, do you mind telling me what all this is about?'
Toby asked.

'With whom have you been having it off in Rumania,
or wherever it was that you went?' I asked. 'Was it a
woman, or a man, to start with?'

'I don't know what you're talking about,' Toby said.

I maintained a hostile silence. I told myself that it was
dignified, but actually it was hostile.

Toby took the cigarette away from me, stubbed it out,
and took me in his arms.

'Hilary, what's upsetting you?' he asked. 'Is it pre-
menstrual tension, or is it something more?'

'I was at a dinner party,' I said, 'and they started
talking about you.'

'Who did?'

'Everybody. The other guests.'

'Who were they?'

I didn't reply.

'What did they say?'

'It was about the photographs.'

'Oh.'

Toby released me, and sat quietly, his hands on his
knees, looking at the floor.

'It's true, then?' I said.

'I don't know what they said, do I?' he said.

'That these pictures of you in bed with a woman and another man were being hawked round Fleet Street. That
she was in the middle, holding each of you by the cock.'

'It's roughly true,' Toby said.

'How can it be roughly true? Either it's true or it isn't.'

'Okay, so it's true.'

'How on earth did they come to be taken?' I asked.

'Jack – the other guy – had one of those cameras you
can fix up and then whizz round to be in the picture
yourself, and he did it for a joke,' Toby said.

'But why? And how on earth did someone get hold of them to try to sell them to the *News of the World?*'

'They were taken some while ago, and the silly bugger didn't destroy them, although he told me that he'd destroyed both the pictures and the negatives. One of his ex-girlfriends, who had a key to his flat, went in to collect her things and found them. She was the vindictive type, so she took them, and passed them on to some crook who tried to sell them. One of the papers rang me up about them, but fortunately nothing much was published. There were one or two heavily-veiled allusions to it in the gossip columns which provided a snigger for people in the know, but it really remained an in-joke.'

'When did all this happen?' I asked.

'Oh, about six months ago, I suppose.'

'You mean that six months ago you were having group sex at the same time as having an affair with which you told me was exclusive?'

'No, no, the pictures were actually taken a couple of years ago. It was six months ago that they were being offered around, and the newspaper items appeared.'

'And you didn't trust me enough to tell me about it,' I said.

'It wasn't a question of not trusting you. I just knew you'd be furious, and you are,' Toby said.

'Of course I am. What about Rumania? Who have you been screwing there? And did you have the chap in the pictures as well as the woman, as they said?'

'Oh God,' Toby said. 'Does it matter?'

'Of course it bloody well matters. Are you queer? Do you know what they were saying, that evening? "Toby Abbot's got queer habits".'

'I don't like that word,' Toby said.

'What word? Queer? Perhaps you prefer gay?'

'Would you use either of them in your columns?' he flared. 'Aren't you always preaching acceptance of people for what they are?'

'I don't preach at all,' I shouted. 'I do say you shouldn't pretend to be what you aren't. You're nothing but pretence, it seems to me.'

'What about you?' he countered. 'You're hardly in a position to preach about pretending to be what you're not. Look at all the cover-ups in your own life. But Helen Turner's got the measure of you, hasn't she? Whoever she is.'

'I hate you!' I screamed, and I hit him in the face with the flat of my hand. I was about to hit out again when he caught my hands by the wrists, and held them down tightly, so that I couldn't move.

'Control yourself, please,' he said, in a hatefully calm voice. 'Do you want the neighbours to hear, and call the police? It would damage you as well as me, you know. I think you're really sick, if you want to know. Are you sure you aren't writing those letters yourself?'

My tears welled up and overflowed. When I stopped struggling, Toby let go of me, got up wearily off the bed, and went over to the chair where he had left his clothes. I lay back, shaken with paroxysms of weeping.

'What are you doing?' I asked.

'I'm going.' He was dressing rapidly.

'You can't. Jean isn't expecting you. You told her that you'd be away until the day after tomorrow.'

'I shall go to the Battersea flat for a couple of days,' he said.

'Please don't go,' I said.

He ignored me.

'Toby, please.'

He didn't speak another word. He picked up his suitcase, and I heard the front door slam behind him. I lay feeling sorry for myself. Was there something wrong with me, that my husband preferred little boys, and my lover other men? Was I really sick, or mad?

I cried myself to sleep.

Chapter Twenty

THE NEXT DAY I hoped all morning that Toby would telephone me, and thought of very little else. There were no phone calls at all. I felt too miserable to go out and eat lunch, so I drank a glass of white wine and ate cottage cheese in my office. At about four o'clock, I picked up the phone and dialled the Battersea flat. There was no reply.

When I arrived home, I half expected to find Toby waiting there for me. When I found the flat empty, a wave of loneliness and unhappiness spread through me. I went into the bedroom to change out of my office clothes, and something made me look in the wardrobe where Toby kept his things. It was empty. He had obviously returned to the flat during the day and collected his clothes.

I went through the rest of the flat, rushing from room to room, looking for traces of him. He had not left me a note, but he didn't seem to have taken anything except his clothes and the spare electric razor he kept in the flat. The records and cassettes that he had bought were still there, and odd things like his Anglepoise lamp and garlic squeezer he had bought. I poured myself a stiff whisky, and picked up the telephone.

I dialled the Battersea flat again. The phone rang for

quite a long time, then a man's voice answered. It was not Toby.

'Can I speak to Toby Abbott, please?' I said.

'Who is it?'

'Hilary.'

There was a pause.

'I'm awfully sorry, he doesn't seem to be around,' the young man said. He sounded rather nervous.

'Can you tell me when he'll be in?'

There was a longer pause, and muffled mutterings.

'I understand he's left for Wales,' the man said.

'Oh.' I didn't believe him at all. I thought Toby was standing right by him.

'Look, please let me speak to him,' I said desperately. 'I only want a quick word. Please.'

'He's not here,' the young man said stubbornly.

'Oh, God. Well, if you see him or hear from him, will you ask him to ring me? Please? It's really important. Will you do that?'

'Certainly I will.' A note of sympathy had crept into his voice.

'When – when do you expect to see him again ?' I was crying.

'I don't know, but I'll certainly pass on your message. I say, are you all right?' He sounded concerned.

I tried to pull myself together.

'Yes, yes, I'm all right, but I do need to speak to him. Please tell him.'

'I will, I promise.'

'Thank you. Thank you very much. Goodbye.'

I hung up, and went into the bedroom, and threw myself onto the bed, weeping noisily. It made me feel better, and when I'd got a lot of it out of my system, I lay feeling quietly sorry for myself.

When the phone rang, I ran joyfully to answer it. My

disappointment was intense on hearing a man's voice which was not Toby's.

'Hello, Hilary. Harry. I hope you don't mind me calling you at home. I got your number off the office list. I was sitting thinking about you, and thought I'd call.'

'Harry,' I said apathetically. 'No, I don't mind. What is it?'

'Do you remember you said at Gerry's dinner party that you might be good enough to look at my house, and give me some advice? I know it's a frightful imposition, but I'd really appreciate it if you had a few minutes to spare to cast an eye over it, and tell me what you think. And perhaps we could have a spot of dinner somewhere afterwards?'

'Oh, Harry.' I tried to pull myself together. 'Normally I'd love to be of help, but I'm afraid at the moment I'm really up to my eyes in it. Dinner's a bit difficult too, because – well, as you know, there's this bloke I live with. He was away on a business trip when Gerry asked me to dinner, otherwise I expect I should have brought him.'

'Oh, I see.' He sounded crestfallen. 'I thought that as you were on your own at Gerry's dinner, the affair must be all over. I hope you didn't mind me asking, anyway. Most frightful cheek on my part.'

'No, not at all,' I said. 'I'm sorry not to be able to help with the house.'

'Please don't worry about it,' Harry said. 'Never mind. Perhaps later on if you do have any time to spare, you'd let me know?'

A minute or so later, with further expressions of regret on both sides, I managed to hang up. Blast Harry, I thought. While he had been on my phone, Toby might have been trying to ring me. I looked at the instrument hopefully, willing it to ring again. It didn't.

I didn't feel hungry, and couldn't be bothered to read

or even to listen to music. I went to bed and pulled the covers over my head. Sleep didn't come, I lay thinking about Toby, and wishing unsaid all the things I had said the night before. Would I ever see him again?

The rest of the week passed like a bad dream. Every time the phone rang, I expected it to be Toby, and it wasn't. Every post I hoped would bring a message from him, and nothing came. I found his home telephone number in *Who's Who*, and rang him at home in Wales one afternoon, but Jean answered, so I hung up without speaking.

Then on the Friday morning, at about half past seven, there was a ring on the doorbell. The postman handed me a registered packet. I signed for it, and saw it was addressed in Toby's writing. Trembling with anticipation, I opened it. Was it a peace offering, a small piece of jewellery, perhaps? He had given me a watch, once, when mine had broken, and a pendant on another occasion.

Inside the envelope was Toby's key to my front door. And that was all. No message of any kind. I kept looking inside the envelope for a note, but there was absolutely nothing.

I sat looking at it for a time in a kind of numb despair. It was really the end, then. I wanted to cry, but I couldn't.

I went into the office and did my day's work like an automaton. In the afternoon, I decided to drive down to Sussex for the weekend. It could not be lonelier or more depressing than the flat, and Falconbridge held no associations with Toby for me, so it might be less painful. At least I felt secure there, and free from the waves of panic and isolation which threatened to engulf me.

A couple of hours later, I sat in the long queue of traffic leaving London. As evening came, I was parking in the gravel drive, and opening the front door apprehensively. If Martin had arrived back, I decided that I would only stay the night, and head back to London the following day. But in his study the piles of mail were still untouched. There was no evidence of his presence at all. I felt an overwhelming relief.

I went up to my tower room, and sat for a long while in the rocking-chair, looking out of the window. Autumn was coming, and a strong wind off the sea was blowing the leaves into little eddies. There was a slight mist, too, and it enhanced the feeling of alienation and isolation.

I felt desperately unhappy and alone. Nobody knew or cared where I was or what I was doing. I might be dead for all anybody cared. Toby wouldn't mind if I were dead. Or would he? Maybe he'd be sorry then for having treated me so cruelly.

That was the first time that I thought of dying. There seemed to be nothing to live for, no point in going on living. Dominic – well, Dominic would grieve for a bit, of course, but he was grown-up and independent really, he didn't need me. Nobody needed me.

And Toby would be sorry, maybe, if I were dead.

I poured myself a large whisky. I had had no lunch, and it went instantly to my head. I sat in the rocking-chair, watching the room come towards me and recede. Darkness was beginning to fall. Darkness and night, night and sleep, sleep and death. Death was just a long sleep, after all. A blissful sleep, from which I need never wake up. No more deadlines. Ha! Deadlines were appropriate. No more letters, no more hassle, no more Helen Turner. If I killed myself, would I kill Helen Turner?

I drank more whisky, and felt thoroughly fuddled. I couldn't work it out. I wasn't Helen Turner. I knew that I wasn't Helen Turner. So if I killed myself, Helen Turner would still be alive. I arrived at this point with a feeling of triumph. Would she be sorry that I was dead?

Toby would be sorry that I was dead. It was all his fault. I hated him.

It didn't hurt, if you cut your wrists. The blood just flowed out gently. Of course the actual cutting must hurt a bit, but not after that. It just flowed out gently, and then you gradually lost consciousness, and went to sleep. Into a coma. Death is an irreversible coma . . .

It wouldn't hurt if I cut firmly and quickly. There would be a quick pain, and then it wouldn't hurt.

I felt terribly tired. I heaved myself out of the chair, and went to the bathroom to look for a razor blade.

The razor was in the bathroom cupboard where I had left it. It was a G2.

I looked at the razor, and at my reflection in the mirror of the cabinet. My face looked pale and blotchy. I didn't recognize myself.

How bloody stupid, I thought. Bloody razor. Stupid safety razor, bloody useless for cutting wrists. Bloody bloodless razor.

In a fury, I seized a bottle of mouthwash from the cabinet, and hurled it onto the tiled floor. It broke, and there was a pleasant, mildly antiseptic smell as the liquid spilled over the tiles. I picked up a jagged piece of the glass.

That would do.

I fumbled with the buttons on the sleeve of my blouse, and couldn't undo them. Didn't want to get blood on my blouse, anyway, I pulled it off, and threw it onto the laundry basket.

Then I pushed the glass edge down onto my wrist.

It hurt a lot. Blood streamed down my left hand. I held it over the wash-basin, and watched it flow into the bowl. Instinctively I held the cut with my right hand to ease the hurt. Blood trickled between my fingers into the basin.

I knew that I ought to cut my right wrist too, but my left wrist and hand were hurting too much. I felt faint and dizzy. I sat on the cork-topped stool and watched the blood swirling down the plug-hole.

201

And then I heard the footsteps coming up the stairs.

'Hilary!' I heard Martin's voice calling me. It seemed a long way away.

'Hilary!'

I don't know whether it was seconds, or minutes. Martin was in the doorway. I saw his expression in the mirror, as he took in first the mess of spilled mouthwash and broken glass all over the floor, and then me sitting by the basin, then the blood.

I think he said 'What's happened?' I think he tied a towel tightly round my wrist. It was partly the alcohol and partly the shock and partly the loss of blood. The next couple of hours seemed all confusion and noise. Being jolted in the ambulance, and the bright lights and white tiles of the hospital casualty department.

And oh, my wrist hurt. The young doctor put a local anaesthetic into it, and then stitched it up. I saw him in the corner with Martin then: mutter, mutter, mutter. I was wheeled through seemingly endless corridors and put into a small room by myself. Another injection and then oblivion.

'Mrs Shipton! Mrs Shipton!' A very young, very plump nurse was standing by me.

I opened my eyes.

Then I remembered, and closed them again.

'Come along now, Mrs Shipton dear,' the nurse said.

There was a rustle, and another voice this time:

'Mrs Shipton! Wake up now, dear.' The voice had a not-to-be-denied authority, and I opened my eyes again.

Sunlight was streaming into the small room, and there were voices in the background. Sister, in dark blue, was standing by the side of my bed, the plump probationer beside her.

'That's better!' Sister said brightly. 'Now, how do we feel this morning? We let you sleep late, but we need to have you awake now, because doctor will be along to see you shortly.'

I felt terrible. My head ached. I felt extremely fuzzy, and my wrist hurt like hell. I said so.

'Well, it's only to be expected, isn't it?' Sister said, without too much sympathy, I thought. 'You did have rather a lot to drink before you had that nasty accident, it seems. Wasn't it lucky your husband found you when he did? You could have died, you know, dear. Now, how about a nice cup of tea?'

'I'd like that,' I said, and at this faint gesture of human kindness, tears started to pour down my cheeks.

'Cheer up now, Mrs Shipton dear,' Sister said. 'Nurse will get you a cup of tea, and you'll soon be right as rain. What are you worried about?'

'I don't know,' I said.

'Was it an accident, dear?' she asked, giving me a penetrating look.

I closed my eyes.

'Yes it was, of course,' I said eventually.

'Well, why are you crying?'

'I don't know, I don't feel well. My wrist hurts.'

'You'll soon feel better. Your wrist will hurt for a bit, but doctor's done a beautiful bit of embroidery, and you shouldn't have much of a scar,' Sister said. She fussed around the bed, tucking in the bedclothes.

'Now, after you've drunk your tea, nurse will give you a bit of a wash and tidy up, and then you'll see doctor.'

I lay back and drank my tea, and listened to the noise of voices outside, and occasional laughter. The events of the night seemed like a bad dream. Noise, confusion, bright lights and blood, my blood, my life seeping out of me. It seemed unreal, but the actuality of it was confirmed by my throbbing head and aching wrist.

The morning was peaceful. There were sunbeams, and the sound of birdsong in the garden outside. The sunshine began to warm me, and cold death receded.

Chapter Twenty-one

SOMETIME DURING THE morning, the young houseman who had stitched the cut came to see me. He looked at the wound cursorily. The black stitches looked like a giant spider attached to my wrist. He covered it over again, and with not very well simulated casualness asked me how the accident had happened.

I was vague, and he was suspicious. He looked deathly tired. He had obviously been summoned from his bed in the night to attend me, and I felt guilty about it, and about demanding his attention now, all through my own stupidity. In the end, I said

'Look, I'm terribly sorry. I feel dreadfully guilty. It wasn't an accident. I'm sorry to have kept you from your bed in the night, and I'm sorry now to be occupying this bed and your time and the nurses' time. I was really stupid.'

'Stop apologizing,' he said. 'It was stupid, but it was born of desperation. Would you like to tell me what it was about?'

I cried, and he held my hand. My good hand.

'It's usually a man,' he prompted me.

I nodded.

'Is it your husband?'

I was silent.

'If it was someone else, do you want me to let anyone know that you're in here?'

My heart leapt with joy at the prospect. If someone else were to ring Toby, not me, I couldn't be held responsible, could I? And he would be sure to come and see me. But I couldn't. Some stubborn pride held me back. Or perhaps it was fear that Toby wouldn't come and see me, even if he knew. I shook my head.

'Look,' the young doctor said, 'I'm awfully sorry, but I'm not terribly good at this kind of thing.' He was frightfully young, he looked not much older than Dominic. He was wearing a tie with MCP and a little pig symbol on it, I noticed. Perhaps his girlfriend had given it to him.

'I think we'll keep you in hospital over the weekend for a nice rest,' he said. 'And then after Dr Stone has seen you on Monday, you can probably go home.'

'Oh, no,' I said involuntarily. 'I'm perfectly all right, really. I've put you all to enough trouble. I'd like to go home now.'

'I'm afraid that's not possible,' he said. 'I can't take the responsibility for discharging you. You could discharge yourself, of course, if you insist, but why not just have a quiet time and a rest for a couple of days?'

'But why can't I go now?' I persisted childishly.

'Well, you've told me that it was attempted suicide, and so you have to be seen by a psychiatrist,' he said reluctantly. 'It's Saturday now, and I don't feel justified in disturbing his golf. He'll be in on Monday morning. I'd like to keep you in till then.'

I didn't relish the thought of being interviewed by the psychiatrist. It smacked a little of being reported to the headmaster, I thought. But the prospect of being looked after for a couple of days didn't seem so bad, after all. So I said

'Okay then. And thank you for all your kindness.'

'All part of the service,' he said, and was gone.

205

I dozed off, to be awakened to choose my meals for the day. I chose them, dozed off again, and was awakened to be served an execrable lunch, which bore no relation at all to the menu I had chosen. When I mentioned this apologetically to the ward maid who brought it, she laughed. She was a jolly, coloured lady with frizzy hair.

'You don't want to take no notice of them menus, darling,' she said. 'They bring those menus round, and the patients, they spend ages choosing, and then they send up the same meals for everybody, see?'

I attempted to eat the sausage roll and dried-up baked beans, but I couldn't have summoned up an appetite for caviar at that point. After lunch I fell asleep again, and awakened when the door crashed open, and Sister said:

'Here's your husband, dear, and another visitor.'

Martin came in, looking different from the way I remembered him. He looked sun-tanned and fit, and was wearing some casual clothes which I hadn't seen before. His plum-coloured Tricel polo-necked sweater was quite different to his usual style of dressing.

With him was a short, grey-haired woman with a round face, who was hanging back somewhat hesitantly. She was wearing a red cotton summer dress and had bare legs and flat-heeled sandals. For one moment, I thought that it was Mother Shipton, but this woman was younger. She was just a couple of years older than me, perhaps.

'Hello, Hilary, how are you?' Martin said.

'Not too bad, thanks, but they want me to stay in over the weekend,' I said.

'I know,' Martin said. 'We've just spoken to Sister. Hilary, I don't think you've met Liz, Liz Raine, have you?'

Liz Raine. The name sounded familiar, but I couldn't remember in what connection. Then it came to me.

'Liz Raine! Now I remember. You're Martin's . . . you're Martin's psychiatrist.' I held out my hand.

She shook it, and smiled at me.

'I was Martin's psychiatrist, but I've handed the case over to a colleague.'

'Oh. I see.' I didn't really. There was a short, awkward silence. Had Martin brought her to see me instead of the hospital psychiatrist I was supposed to see on Monday?

'They said – the houseman said that I should have to see a psychiatrist before I was discharged,' I said. 'Is that what this is about?'

'You told him that you cut your wrist deliberately,' Martin said accusingly. He had obviously heard it from Sister.

'Yes.'

'Wasn't that a little unwise, Hilary?' He was as stuffy, patronizing, parental and infuriating as ever. Irritation welled up in me.

'It probably was,' I said in an exasperated sort of way. 'But I'm fed up with all the lies.'

'All what lies?' Martin said.

'I don't know. Anyway –' I turned back to Liz Raine. 'Is this a professional visit, please? If so, perhaps we could talk alone?'

'It isn't a professional visit,' she said. 'I just came along to see you as a friend of Martin's.'

'A friend of Martin's!' I don't know why I was so taken aback.

'Why did you do it?' Martin asked.

'Why do you ask?' I challenged him.

'Are you going to try it again?' he asked aggressively.

'Martin –' Liz said.

'I'm not going to try it again,' I said, 'but I don't suppose you'd care if I did, anyway. In fact, I'm not sure why you bothered to bring me here last night. Why didn't you just leave me alone?'

The antagonism between us was almost tangible. Liz Raine said, probably to ease her own embarrassment:

207

'Is there anything you want that we can do for you, Hilary?'

'That's kind of you, but I don't think so, thank you,' I said. Then I felt suddenly aware of the shapeless short cotton hospital gown I was wearing. 'Well actually, I would like a few personal things from home, my sponge bag and a couple of night dresses, maybe. If I give you a brief list, perhaps Martin's secretary could find them and drop them in for me.'

'Of course.' She rummaged in her bag, and found a pencil and a piece of paper.

'Why did you stop treating Martin?' I asked her. The communciation was now between the two of us. Martin glowered on the fringe of the group.

Liz Raine flushed, and looked away. I was writing the list, and paid no particular attention. When no reply came, I looked up. She and Martin were looking at each other meaningfully.

'We hadn't intended to tell you today,' Martin said. 'But Liz and I are living together.'

'Living together?'

'We went on the boating holiday together, and then after the holiday I moved into Liz's flat,' Martin said. 'I haven't been home all summer.'

'I knew that,' I said.

'I came back last night to get things ready for the beginning of term,' Martin said.

'It's rather a lot to take in, all of a sudden and all at once,' I said.

'I'm sorry, Hilary,' Liz said. 'I'm particularly sorry that you had to know today. We really hadn't intended to tell you. We were going to leave it until you were better and out of hospital, and then tell you.'

'Tell me what, exactly?' I asked.

Martin looked apprehensive.

'I don't think we ought to discuss it any more this

afternoon,' he said. 'You ought to rest, and not disquiet yourself, Hilary. We can all discuss it again a bit later on.'

'Don't be silly,' I said sharply. 'Obviously there is more than you have said, and it's much more disquieting, as you put it, not to know what it is, and to imagine all kinds of things, than to know what it is you're holding back. What is it that you were going to wait to tell me until I was stronger? Not, surely, that you have been shacked up with your ex-psychiatrist for a couple of weeks? You must have known that I couldn't care less about that.'

'Be it on your own head,' Martin said. It always was one of his favourite expressions. 'Well, Liz and I want to get married.'

I struggled to grasp the ramifications of this.

'What about the school?' I asked.

There was a silence.

'You're not both proposing to run the school jointly, are you? I asked, 'You do realize that it's my family home, and I'm the beneficiary under the Trust my father set up.'

'Yes, I do realize that, Hilary,' Martin said. 'Maybe that's been the trouble all along, or part of it. No, we don't want to live there. I'll be leaving.'

'Leaving?' I said. 'But you're the Headmaster. I really can't take this in all at once. Are you giving notice? Do the Governors know?'

'I'm afraid that I am going to give notice,' Martin said, but the expression of regret was false, and his voice was tinged with triumph.

'Martin, could you just please tell me what it is exactly that you plan?'

Liz stepped in.

'I'm sorry to have to tell you today, Hilary. But perhaps you're right, since you know something, it's better to know everything. Martin and I want to get married.

We hope that you will agree to a divorce. Of course, he will leave the school, and find another post. He will stay there this coming term, to give you the opportunity to tell the parents, but he will be leaving at Christmas.'

'But he's the Headmaster, he runs the place!' I said.

'Yes, I've thought of that, and there's a very good Assistant Headmaster, Harrison,' Martin said. 'We can advertise the post if you like, and the Governors can interview candidates, but my recommendation would be that you appoint Harrison. He's a first class man, married with a young family, which always goes down well, and he'd do the job more than adequately.'

'I see,' I said. "You have got it all worked out, haven't you?' I saw too why Liz Raine had handed over the treatment of Martin to a colleague. Never sleep with a patient.

'You must feel very angry with me, Hilary,' Liz said.

'Angry with you?' I looked at her in surprise. 'No, I don't think so.'

'Didn't you guess anything?' Martin asked. They both harboured looks of secret triumph, I thought, like two cats who had eaten a bowl of cream.

'Not really. Oh, I suppose something crossed my mind, the first time that you referred to her as Liz, but I never had any serious suspicions,' I said.

'I wondered if your anonymous letter writer had told you about it?' Martin said.

'Helen Turner? No, she didn't.'

'Helen Turner . . .' Liz said.

'Do you know someone of that name?' I asked.

'No, I don't. Does she sign her full name, or just her initials?'

'Her full name, and gives her address, too, but it doesn't exist,' I said.

'Her initials are the same as yours,' Liz Raine said.

'Yes.' It was my turn to flush.

'How did she know about Martin?' Liz asked.

'I've no idea. But that's not all she knew,' I said.

'You mean you've had more letters? About me?' Martin said.

'No, not about you,' I said.

'Hilary, would you like to tell us anything about why you did what you did last night?' Liz asked. 'Was it anything to do with Martin?'

'No, it wasn't anything to do with Martin,' I said.

'What about the divorce?' Martin asked.

'What about it?'

'Are you going to agree to it?' he asked.

'I suppose so.' I looked from one to the other of them. Martin was standing by the window: angular, angry, pompous, irritating. Why on earth should Liz Raine want to spend the rest of her life with him? I could see what attracted him to her, however. She looked just like his mother.

'I hope you'll both be very happy,' I said.

She smiled at me.

'It's good of you to take it like that, Hilary,' she said. 'Would you like us to pop in again?'

'I don't think so, thanks,' I said, feeling suddenly hostile.

She was embarrassed.

'Well, if you give me the list of things you want, we'll get Martin's secretary to drop them in,' she said. 'And then perhaps we ought to be going, do you think Martin?'

I finished the list, and she took it from me. Martin gave me a brief, uncertain peck on the cheek.

'You won't do anything silly again, will you, Hilary?' he said.

'I shouldn't think so.' My voice was cold, my tone dismissive.

They were gone, and the room was empty. The sun went in, and I felt lonely again.

Chapter Twenty-two

THE NURSES OBVIOUSLY knew that it had not been an accident, and although they did not refer to it, I thought I detected an attitude in them, a lack of sympathy, an impatience, which contributed to my feeling of being unwanted and unloved. Fortunately they did not know that I was Hilary Toogood, as I had been admitted as Hilary Shipton.

The interview with the psychiatrist was not as bad as I had expected. He asked briefly why I had done it, and if I had ever done anything like that before. I managed to appear composed and contrite, and he said that he did not think I needed further treatment, but he'd be writing to my GP, and discharged me.

I had forgotten that I had no clothes to leave in. I had taken my blouse off when I had cut my wrist, and the ambulance-men had wrapped me in a blanket. Sister telephoned Martin, who came to collect me in the car, bringing some clothes.

I went back to Falconbridge and telephoned the office to say that I'd had a slight accident, but would be in in the afternoon. I was collecting up my things to take back to London, when Mother Shipton appeared at my door with a tray of tea.

'How are you feeling, dear?' she asked.

'My wrist still hurts, but I'm okay, thank you,' I said. 'When did you get back?'

'Martin telephoned me on Saturday morning, after he had taken you to hospital,' she said. 'I came back straight away.'

She stood irresolutely at the door of my room, obviously wanting something. I said, 'Do you want to come in?' and she came in, and sat on the sofa.

'What are you going to do?' she asked.

'Do?' I wasn't really attending.

'About the school, and everything.'

'Oh.' I realized then that of course she must be worried about her own future. Presumably she knew about Liz Raine. If Martin and I were divorced and he left the school, she could hardly stay on. We should need to find a new Matron as well as a new Headmaster.

I sat down and poured my tea.

'Are you going to have a cup?' I asked.

'I've just had some thank you, dear.'

'Do you know about Liz Raine?'

'Yes, I do.'

'They want to marry. Martin is leaving at Christmas.' She nodded. I said:

'I expect that the Governors will do as he suggests, and appoint Harrison. What will you do?'

'Well, I can't stay here dear, can I?'

I understood her bitterness. She had lived at Falconbridge for fifteen years, maybe more. I couldn't remember.

'Where will you go?'

'If Martin takes a job at another boarding school, I might apply to be a matron there. There's a terrible shortage, you know,' she said.

'What does Liz Raine think about that?' I asked. Liz and Martin might believe that it was my dominating and controlling ways that had blighted the marriage. I

213

thought the fact that Martin had never really been separated from his mother had something to do with it.

Mother Shipton said rather stiffly:

'I haven't discussed it with her. If it doesn't work out like that. I can always live with my sister in Southgate. We have always planned to spend our retirement together anyway. And I am seventy-one, you know.'

I didn't know, and I said so. I hadn't really thought about how old Mother Shipton was, but she looked to be in her sixties. She was remarkably spry.

'But what are *you* going to do, dear?' she persisted. 'Will you remarry?'

I felt disturbed and unhappy at the question. It reminded me of Toby.

I said, 'Oh no, I don't think so. I have no plans in that direction.'

'You're young, you must meet lots of men and have plenty of opportunities,' she said.

I shrugged dismissively.

'I haven't anyone in mind,' I said. 'Of course, in the future I might meet someone.'

I arrived back in London in the early afternoon. I went first to my flat, really to see if there were any letters from Toby. I kept hoping that there might be, although I didn't really think that there would. There weren't. I changed into a long-sleeved dress which covered most of the plaster on my wrist, and went into the office.

It was four o'clock when I got in. Ruth said:

'Oh, I am glad to see you. Mrs Carstairs is waiting. I thought that you would be in earlier, so I gave her an appointment for half past three. She's been waiting half an hour. She's in your office.'

'Blast,' I said. 'I was hoping just to clear up anything urgent, and make a quick getaway. What does she want?'

'I don't know,' Ruth said. 'She rang up this morning,

214

and asked if she could pop in. It was just after you'd telephoned, so I told her that you'd be late, and said that she could come in the afternoon.'

I sighed, and went into my office. Mrs C was sitting on my sofa, reading magazines. She got up as I entered, and bore down on me with a look of concern.

'My dear, you look so pale!' she said. 'I had a presentiment that something was not quite right, and I wanted to warn you. Were you badly hurt?'

How did she know that I had been hurt at all? Then I remembered, Ruth must have told her I was late because I'd had an accident.

'I'm fine,' I reassured her. 'I just slipped in the bathroom, and broke a bottle and accidentally cut my – my arm.'

Her eyes flickered over me, and took in the plaster which I could not entirely cover with my sleeve.

'My dear, such a nasty place to cut! So dangerous! You could have killed yourself,' she said.

I shivered.

'Are you cold, dear?' Mrs Carstairs said. 'You ought to be careful. It's a shock when something like that happens.'

'It's the air conditioning,' I said. 'It's too cold. What can I do for you, Mrs Carstairs?'

'It's not a good time for Librans,' she said. 'There's a lot of chaos and change, isn't there, dear? And a parting brings sorrow. But things will be better in the Spring.'

'In the Spring?' I said. 'Oh, I do hope they'll improve before that.'

'We mustn't give way, dear, must we?' Mrs C said. 'Best foot forward, soldier on. Every cloud has a silver lining. All's well that ends well.'

'It's an awfully long time till the Spring,' I said.

'Time flies,' Mrs Carstairs said. 'Look on the bright

side. Don't give way to self-pity. There are always others worse off, aren't there?'

I was furious. How dare she called me self-pitying? And I was even more angry because she was right. I had been feeling sorry for myself. And I had absolutely no business to. Any unhappiness was of my own making.

'I've annoyed you now, haven't I, dear?' Mrs Carstairs asked, with unfailing perception. 'But I'm right, aren't I?'

I must have stiffened. I relaxed and laughed.

'You are right, Mrs C,' I said. 'Do you want a cup of tea? I could do with some.'

I buzzed Ruth, and asked for tea.

'Now, what have you come for, Mrs C, dear?' I asked. 'Just to tell me that my life is the most godawful mess, which I know already, or is there something else?'

'I had the most splendid idea this morning,' Mrs Carstairs said, 'A real flash of inspiration. Heaven inspired, or heavens inspired, perhaps. I thought that we could try to find readers who had identical dates, times and places of birth, cast horoscopes for them, and see if their lives had run on similar lines.'

'That isn't a bad idea,' I said. 'Quite interesting, really. But how do we find readers who were born on the same dates and in the same place?'

'We could cheat a little, and go to Somerset House, or wherever it is now, and look up people born on the same day, and contact them,' she said.

I shook my head. 'It would take too long to trace them now,' I said. 'They'd be unlikely to be living in the houses in which they were born, twenty years or so on.'

'Well, how about putting a cod letter on the Letters Page from an imaginary reader who has the same birth-day as Princess Anne, asking if anyone else shares a birth-day with any member of the Royal Family?' she suggested.

'It's been done before, but it's always popular,' I said. 'Okay, let's do that, for a start, and see where we go from there.'

'You look quite exhausted, dear,' Mrs Carstairs said. 'When did you have this accident? You really ought to take a couple of days off, and rest a bit.'

'It happened on Friday night. I've been resting over the weekend, I'll be okay,' I said. 'Mrs C, can't you see any hope of things improving for Librans before the Spring?'

'It wouldn't be fair to mislead you, dear, but I think that things have got to get worse before they get better,' she said. 'Of course there's always hope, what would life be like without hope? This time scale is the most difficult thing of all for us astrologers to contend with. As I've said before, we know that something is going to happen, but can't be exactly sure when, not to within a week or even a month, sometimes.'

She drank her tea, and took herself off. Her remarks about self-pity had been wounding, but were really what I needed to make me look at myself and take a grip on the situation. I tried unsuccessfully to put Toby out of my mind for the time being. To a certain extent thoughts of him had been displaced by anxiety about impending separation from Martin, and the changes that were inevitable at the school. Although I did not love Martin (indeed I wondered if I had ever loved him) I had never dreamed that he would leave me and the school. Thinking about this occupied my attention. Adjusting to thinking of myself as a divorcee in the near future was strangely unpalatable. Why should I mind?

But I did mind. I didn't know why I felt so strongly about it, but the very word divorcee was hateful to me. It implied a woman alone, perhaps vulnerable. The façade of my marriage gave me a feeling of protection. Of course, I didn't have to divorce Martin, I could refuse.

But it seemed irrational to refuse, just on the grounds that I didn't want to be called a divorcee.

I started searching for other, more rational reasons for refusing a divorce. My career. Of course it wouldn't do that any good. My public image would be damaged. Would it really? The divorce action, if undefended, would be unlikely to attract any attention, and who on earth would care? Well, some people might.

I supposed that if I were going to backtrack on what I had agreed, I should, in fairness, tell Martin and Liz Raine as soon as possible. They certainly couldn't hold me to a promise made when I was in hospital, at my weakest, still suffering from shock. To spring on me the news of their relationship and bulldoze me into agreeing to a divorce on the spot had been unfair in the extreme.

I felt unusually indecisive and confused. I hated being in a state of indecision. It seemed almost worse than having made up my mind and feeling that I'd made the wrong decision. I decided that I would go back to Falconbridge shortly, within a week or so, and talk to Martin again about the whole thing.

The day after I arrived back at my flat in London, a letter with a French stamp fell through my letter box. I was surprised to see Dominic's writing on the envelope. I scrutinized the postmark. I could only distinguish 'VAR', which I knew meant Provence.

I drew out some airmail paper, and wondered what had made my son, usually a poor correspondent, write to me from France.

'*Chère Maman* (it began.)

'You'll never guess in a thousand years where I am, and who I'm staying with. I'm staying with my father at his country house here near Seillans.

'I never got to Greece. En route I stopped off in Paris, and rang up my Papa at his office. At first, of

218

course, he couldn't make out who it was. I kept telling him my name, and then I said that I thought he knew my mother many years ago, her name was Hilary. And he said *Ah, oui, Eeelarie*, and invited me out to lunch.

'At the beginning of the lunch he was very guarded, asked lots of questions about you, but wasn't giving anything away. Then towards the end, maybe he was convinced that it really was you that he'd known all those years ago, and that my phone call had been motivated by nothing more than a desire to meet him, and that I didn't want to blackmail him, or make any claims on him, or anything. I said that I'd just wanted to look him up, passing through on my way to Greece. Anyway, he said with a twinkle in his eye that he thought we were related. Perhaps he just hadn't been sure if I knew. I grinned back and said yes, I knew. And then he stopped being guarded, and said he'd often thought about me, and he was very pleased to see me, and why didn't I come down to stay with the family in the South of France, he was just about to leave Paris and go down there himself?

'So of course I decided to come. I thought if I didn't like it, I could make an excuse and leave, as they say in the *Sunday People*. But it's extraordinary, absolutely great. It's situated in the hills behind the coast, two and a half thousand hectares of vineyards and olive groves. It's a small château, really, with a tennis-court and a swimming-pool and a couple of Spanish servants.

'Best of all, I found that I had a brother – well, a half-brother, really. He's just seven months older than I am, and his name is Julien.

'His mother is dead. She died of cancer, a couple of years ago, and he still grieves for her, I think. Our father (who art in Var) has married again, and his second wife is an elegant lady in her forties. He has told her that I am his son, and she doesn't mind at all. Maybe if she'd had children by my father she'd have felt that they were displaced in some way by my sudden appearance, but they were both middle-aged when they married, she was a childless widow, and she accepts me absolutely, and is charming to me. I really like her.

'My father has also told my brother that we are brothers. Not immediately. At first, he introduced me as the son of an old friend. Then when I'd been staying here for about a week, he was lying by the swimming-pool with Julien one afternoon, and he told him the whole story. By that time Julien and I had already got to like each other, very much indeed, and Julien said that he was delighted, he had always felt the lack of a brother or sister, and I think he meant it. I said I'd always wanted a brother too, and we really do seem to hit it off exceptionally well. We play tennis, and swim, and cycle in the surrounding countryside.

'So they invited me to stay on, and I needed no persuading. I never got to Greece. Its been an idyllic time and what I'm writing for now is, to ask could Julien come back and spend next Easter with us at Falconbridge? I could have him stay in my flat at Oxford of course, but I think he'd enjoy Falconbridge more. I know you'd like him, and he wants to come.

'Please write and tell me, so if it's okay, I can get it all fixed up before I leave.

'I've been sitting writing this in the shade of a fig tree. Do you know why the ancient sculptors used fig leaves, incidentally? It's because the leaves were so big!

'My father has just walked past and asked me if I was writing to a girlfriend. I said no, to my mother. He asked me to give you his best wishes and to say that he has many happy souvenirs of you. I think he means memories! It was you who had the souvenir, wasn't it?

'Lots of love, Dominic.'

I read the letter through a couple of times with a kind of delighted astonishment. I was very pleased for Dominic, and surprised about his half-brother. It must have meant that Madame, Julien's mother, was pregnant when Pierre and I had our affair. No wonder Pierre had not wanted to know about my pregnancy. How extraordinary life was.

I was tempted to seize the telephone and ring Dominic, half-hoping that I might speak to Pierre as well. But it wasn't fair, and I resisted the temptation. I found a card, and wrote a brief message saying how delighted I would be to see Julien whenever he could come, and sending warmest wishes to them all.

Chapter Twenty-three

ON THE THURSDAY of that week, Helen Turner's last letter arrived.

This time, for the first time, she had marked it PERSONAL AND CONFIDENTIAL, so it lay unopened on top of the pile of mail which Ruth brought in. It was a cheap white envelope, and was postmarked London SW1. Even before I opened it, I guessed it was from her.

It was some time before I could bring myself to tear open the envelope. It lay on my desk like an unexploded bomb while I drank my coffee and braced myself to read it.

Finally, I asked Ruth to make sure that I was not disturbed and tore it open.

'Dear Hilary Toogood, (it said.)

'I feel that life is not worth living, and indeed a week or so ago I tried to end it all. I have led a worthless life full of deceit and lies and I do not feel that I deserve to go on living. I am no use to anybody, and nobody loves me or wants me. Can you tell me why I should not make away with myself?

'I tried to cut my wrists, but unfortunately I was found and taken to hospital. While I was recovering, my husband and his new girlfriend visited me, and he told me that he was leaving me.

'It would be better for them and for everybody else if I were dead. I think I shall end it all quite soon. 'Helen Turner.'

I felt numb. Perhaps my blood was literally running cold. Who was Helen Turner, that she knew so much about me, and so obviously wished me dead? She must be a witch. How could she know all that she knew? Was it Mrs Carstairs? Did she possess second sight?

My office was quiet. The only sound was that of pigeons making love noisily on the window-ledge outside. I hadn't got Toby to turn to, and I couldn't bear the thought of talking to Harry Ballsup again. I badly needed someone in whom to confide. My thoughts turned to the Snow Queen.

Quite why I should have wanted to go to her, I don't know. I hardly ever saw her. She was remote, distant, powerful, detached. Maybe she represented an omnipotent mother figure, and my need at that moment was to hide my face in someone's lap and weep. Maybe I thought she could help to ward off the forces of evil which Helen Turner had come to represent.

Anyway I picked up the telephone and asked Ruth to get me an appointment.

Ruth told me that the Snow Queen would see me in an hour. It surprised me. She was usually booked up for days ahead. I began to regret the impulse which had made me want to go and see her. But I couldn't back out now. So an hour later, I got into the lift, and went up to the penthouse where the Snow Queen inhabited her ivory tower.

Her office had no desk. There were a couple of low sofas with a coffee table between them. On it was a Swedish glass filled with roses. She sat on one sofa, immaculately dressed in a white suit, her grooming as impeccable as ever. I sat opposite her, feeling as always rather like a nervous schoolgirl.

She was cool and alert, but silent. She waited for me to say something, and when I could stand the silence no longer, I said:

'I'm sorry to take up your time, Shirley. I've been having some anonymous letters.'

She smiled encouragingly, but still did not speak.

I plunged on.

'Well, they're not exactly anonymous. They're signed 'Helen Turner'. Helen Turner doesn't exist. It's a fictitious name, and she gives a fictitious address.'

'How many have you had?'

Strangely, I wasn't sure.

'Six, I think. Maybe seven.'

'Are they threatening? Could it be a reader, or a reader's husband or wife, with a grudge? Someone who thinks you've been interfering, caused the break-up of a marriage, perhaps?'

'No, it's not like that,' I said. 'They're all about me. About things in my own private life. Things I thought that nobody knew, nobody at all.'

'What kind of things?' the Snow Queen asked. She asked in a completely neutral tone of voice, not curious, not condemning, just prepared to accept whatever I told her.

'Things about my marriage, about my life outside marriage. About my son, and my sister. She – the writer – knows details of things which I have never confided in anyone.'

'Are there blackmail demands? Do they threaten you with exposure?'

'No, there aren't any threats. That's what makes it so strange and difficult to deal with.'

'Have you talked to the lawyer, Harry Ballsup, about it?' she asked.

'Yes, I have.

'Useless, I suppose?'

'He suggested that I might have written them myself, because Helen Turner's initials were the same as mine.'

'Typical. How stupid.'

She sat thinking quietly, and I felt an enormous wave of relief sweep through me. She didn't think I was mad, anyway. She didn't believe that I had been writing letters to myself. It was immensely comforting and reassuring that this cool, collected logical lady was confident that I was sane, rational, and being persecuted for some reason which neither of us comprehended.

'You've no idea who is writing them, I suppose?' she asked.

I shook my head.

'Do you want to show them to me, or not?'

'I'd rather not. The last one –' I hesitated. 'I had another one today. It was a bit different somehow. It – you see, the writer describes things in her own life, only really they are things in mine. In this one, she said she had attempted suicide. She said she was going to try again, to kill herself, I mean. It was more sinister, more frightening.'

'I think you have to go to the police,' the Snow Queen said positively.

'Oh, I can't. I can't, really. You see some of the things . . . Well, in one of the earlier letters, she referred to something – not something I've done, but someone else, close to me – it's a criminal offence.' I trailed off into silence. I felt like an incoherent schoolgirl, but it was strangely comforting to be with this quiet but strong woman who seemed to have taken my burden and shouldered it herself.

'Did you try to kill yourself?' she asked.

'Yes.'

'When?'

'Last weekend.'

'Are you still unhappy?'

'Yes, but I wasn't planning to try again. Except – except she made me want to.'

'Maybe that was her intention.'

'Maybe,' I said.

'Well, you have two choices, don't you,' she said. 'Action or inaction. The action you can take includes going to the police, or hiring a private detective, to try to find out who is writing the letters and to put a stop to it. Or you can simply ignore them. Don't let her know that she is getting to you. After all, she doesn't even know that you have actually received them, does she?'

'I don't even know that it's a woman. It might be a man,' I said.

'I think it's a woman,' the Snow Queen said.

I studied her for a few moments. It couldn't be her, could it?

'Do you agree that those are the options open to you?' she asked.

I nodded. Somehow it made me feel better, this simplistic analysis of possible solutions. Or non-solutions.

'What are you going to do?' she asked pleasantly.

I sighed.

'I'm going to ignore them, and not let her know that she's getting to me.'

'Very well. Now, is there anything I can do to help you in any way?' she asked.

'No. Actually I think you have helped. You've helped reduce it to proper proportions. And you've helped re-assure me that I'm not mad, or disintegrating, or – or going to die.'

'Certainly not,' she said briskly. 'Come and talk to me again, whenever you feel like it. Oh – by the way, do you think she intends to try and do you any damage, with publicity in any way, I mean?'

'I don't know,' I said. 'But it's been going on for some

months. I guess if she were going to, she'd have done something before now.'

'Good. I mean, good that you don't think she's going to try to make anything public. And what about the depression, Hilary?'

'The depression?'

'The depression which made you want to kill yourself last weekend. You must have been depressed. It's a very angry thing to do.'

'Well, I haven't thrown it off, but I'm not going to try suicide again,' I said firmly.

'Do you think you need a holiday?'

'I need to go on working,' I said.

'Yes, it's the best antidote to depression, isn't it?' she said, surprising me again. I should have thought that depression would be a stranger to her.

She got up, and I got up too.

'I mean what I said, Hilary. Come and talk to me again if you want to.'

She dismissed me like a headmistress dismissing a fourth former, but –

'I'm very grateful,' I said. And I meant it.

The following afternoon, I went down to Falconbridge.

The Michaelmas daisies were out, straggling after the long, hot summer, and there was the smell of Autumn in the air. Cricket had given way to football, and muddy small boys raced round the back of the house, pursued by the under-matrons who were trying to chase them into the showers.

In my turret room there was a huge bowl of chrysanthemums, russet ones. I supposed that the cleaning lady had placed them there. Martin had gone out to dinner with Liz Raine, so I had the evening to myself. I took off my shoes and poured myself a whisky, and sat down in the rocking-chair to read my correspondence.

227

My heart leapt as I saw a letter in Toby's familiar hand-writing. I couldn't understand why he was writing to me at Falconbridge, but I felt an overflow of pleasure at hearing from him. There had been no word of any kind since the night we had had the horrible quarrel.

The envelope contained a single sheet of paper. There was no address at the top, merely the date, which was the previous Monday. The letter had been sitting at Falcon-bridge for nearly a week, waiting for me. Why hadn't it been forwarded?

The writing occupied one sheet only.

'My dear Hilary, (it said.)

'I hear on the grapevine that you've had an acci-dent, and been in hospital. Rumour has it that it wasn't entirely an accident. I tried to ring your office but you weren't in, so I assume you're convalescing down at Falconbridge.

'I felt it would be churlish not to send a note to say I hope you've now recovered. I've thought about you a lot, and wish you only well for the future. Things which have been said can't be unsaid, and I don't feel that we can ever return to the way things were before. But I wanted you to know that if there's ever anything that I can do for you as a friend, I hope you'll let me know. I want you to be happy. Try to be cheerful.

'Yours, Toby.'

I burst into tears. The horrid, formal stilted tone was not what I'd hoped for. How could he? 'It would be churlish not to send a note . . .' I sobbed bitterly for a few minutes.

Then I read it twice more, and read more into it.

'I've thought about you a lot . . . if there's ever any-thing I can do for you . . . I want you to be happy.' Did that really sound as though things were dead between us?

Was there a possibility that he might still care for me as he used to? Or was he just suffering from an attack of guilt?

On an impulse, I picked up the telephone, and dialled the Battersea flat. It was Friday evening, and normally he had left for Wales by now. But there was just a chance that he was still there.

Joy! Toby answered the phone himself.

'Toby! It's me. I've only just had your letter, just this minute. I didn't stay down at Falconbridge to convalesce, I went back to London last Monday, and they didn't forward your letter, so I've only just had it.' I knew that I was repeating myself, it was nervousness.

'Are you all right now?' he asked. His voice was nervous too, and carefully neutral, I thought.

'Yes, I'm fine.'

There was a pause.

'What happened?'

'I slipped in the bathroom. Oh, that's not true. I tried to cut my wrist, but Martin took me to hospital.'

'I'm sorry.'

'While I was recovering, he told me that he was leaving the school, and wanted a divorce. He's going to marry his psychiatrist.'

The instant I'd said it, I knew that it was a mistake. I suppose that I said it in a bid for sympathy, but I heard Toby's small, noncommittal 'Oh, I'm sorry to hear that,' and I knew that he would think that I was telling him that I was going to be free, that he would wonder what new demands I might make on him, that he would withdraw more from me, be more wary.

'I'm not sorry,' I said, making it worse. 'I mean, there's nothing left in the marriage, so why perpetuate it? I'm not sorry from that point of view, I mean. Not that I have any plans to do anything different myself. I shall just carry on as usual.'

'Well, I'm glad to know you're better, Hilary,' Toby said. 'It was good of you to ring and let me know. I'm just about to leave for Wales, actually, you just caught me before I went.'

'Maybe we could meet sometime,' I said desperately.

'I don't think that would be a good idea,' he said.

'Just to talk. There are things I want to say. I'm so dreadfully sorry for the appalling things I said that night.'

'Don't worry about it.'

'Can I see you sometime?'

'I don't think it's a good idea,' he said. 'I'm sorry, I've got to run now, Hilary.'

I was struggling with tears.

'Please, Toby . . .'

'Hilary, you're obviously still not yourself. Have you thought of asking your doctor for help? I'm frightfully sorry, but I've got to go, I'll miss my train.'

'Toby –'

But he had hung up. I sat holding the telephone, with tears streaming down my face.

And as I sat there, still holding the receiver to my ear, I heard a click.

And in that moment, I knew who Helen Turner was.

Chapter Twenty-four

SHE HAD NEVER wanted Martin to marry me, of course. She hadn't come out into the open with it, but I had been aware of her unspoken antipathy from the time that Martin and I started getting interested in each other.

I was certainly not the wife she would have chosen for him. She would have liked a daughter-in-law who was domesticated, dutiful, and who doted on her son as much as she did. One who would share her interest in Martin's health, and her concern over things like his constipation. She would have liked someone more malleable and less strong-willed than I. Someone with an unblemished past, unencumbered by another man's child. Someone who would provide her with grandchildren of her own, and seek her advice on their upbringing.

On the other hand, marrying me indubitably augured well for Martin's future. My father had always made it clear that I would one day inherit the school. It must have been obvious to both Martin and his mother from the start that if I married Martin he was likely to step into my father's shoes and become Headmaster eventually, although that had happened earlier than any of us had anticipated.

I remembered now the silence with which Mother Shipton first greeted the news of our engagement. It was brief, but telling. Then she recovered herself, and said she hoped that I'd be very happy, and kissed me, and could she help in any practical way over the arrangements for the wedding?

The wedding pictures tell a story. They always do. Dominic was off colour, and clung to me the entire day. He was sick in the middle of the reception, and the pictures of us cutting the cake have Dominic in the centre of them, as indeed do all the others. Mother Shipton is a disapproving spectre in the background. She is always disappearing off the edge of the photograph, as if she were wishing not to be present, or perhaps wishing the whole event were not taking place.

Maybe she was aware before I was that I didn't really love her son. Perhaps if I had loved Martin she would have forgiven me everything. Certainly we would have had a bond, which we lacked.

As it was, her antipathy generated antipathy in me. I resented her, and I resented her permanent presence in my home, and I didn't manage to hide my resentment and irritation very well, I'm afraid.

I suppose that it's just possible that without her, my marriage to Martin might have stood a chance. Although I'm not sure. I think we married each other for the wrong reasons, and were ill-matched, anyway.

I think, looking back, that Martin married me because of and not in spite of Dominic. Like many men who marry women with children, it was a mother for whom he was looking. But I was searching for nurturing too. My mother had left us when I was a small child.

Neither Martin nor I found what we wanted or expected.

Of course without Mother Shipton, Martin would have been a different person. He would have been stronger and more independent. He might have been able to give me what I needed, and might not have needed what I could not give him. But there had never been any question of being without her.

She moved away a little from him – from us – in the early days of our marriage, but not nearly far enough. She was given a new bedroom and sitting-room at Falconbridge, and Dominic and I moved into the self-contained flat which she had been sharing with Martin.

But her presence was everywhere. She walked in and out of the flat as though she still lived in it. If the place was untidy with Dominic's toys, as it frequently was, I felt guilty. She never said anything, but sometimes she started rather pointedly clearing them up.

It was difficult for us to be sexually free. Before we were married, in the year we were getting to know each other, Martin came secretly at night to my tower room. It was illicit and marvellously exciting. But after we were married, with little peace and no privacy, tensions set in and things rapidly went wrong.

I remember one evening a few weeks after the wedding. It was nearly midnight. Martin and I had been out. When we came back, everyone had gone to bed. Dominic was sleeping peacefully, and the house was quiet. We made ourselves tea and drank it in the sitting-room, sitting side by side on the sofa.

He had unbuttoned my blouse, and was lying with his head in my lap. We were engrossed in each other and did not hear her until she was standing just inside the room.

We sprang apart, suffused with embarrassment and guilt. The expression on her face was one of distaste. She didn't apologize, nor did she withdraw.

'If you want to do that sort of thing,' she said, 'the place for it is the bedroom. I wanted a word with Martin, but I'll speak to him in the morning instead.'

233

We slunk off to bed like children in disgrace, and it never occurred to me at the time to be angry at her intrusion. I was afraid that she would tell somebody what she had seen. I knew exactly how she would describe it.

'Behaving like a parlourmaid. Disgusting.'

I had heard her saying it when she caught one of the under-matrons kissing an assistant master behind the sports pavilion.

Martin and I went shamefaced to bed that night, and slept with our backs to each other.

But it was when she started irrationally dropping hints about a family that my hostility to her became almost unbearable.

'A pity for Dominic to be an only child,' she would remark. 'I was always sorry that Martin didn't have a little brother or sister. It was only on medical advice, of course. After I had him the doctor advised against having any more.'

When Dominic outgrew clothes or toys, she would suggest putting them away, 'just in case'.

'Only children can be lonely children,' she would say. 'My sister and I were such good friends. We still are. There's a big age difference between you and Jan, isn't there, dear? But then, the circumstances were very different indeed . . . I think it makes children less selfish to grow up in a family. A small family, of course. Two or three at the most.' Mother Shipton was of the generation for whom abstinence was the only reliable form of birth control, and which regarded more than two children as feckless, living evidence of an inability to control inadmissible appetites.

Anyway when I finally moved into a London flat, it was as much to free myself from her as from Martin. And yet the liberation itself was a source of resentment to me. It felt as though she had succeeded in driving me out of my family home, away from my security. She was left in possession. It was her territory more than mine, almost. She was the winner.

Why, then, this?

I sat in the rocking-chair in the gloaming, looking out over the lake and thinking it all over. There were many things I didn't understand, but I was nonetheless sure that I was right.

The sense of relief outweighed all other feelings.

Dusk fell, and I switched on my desk lamp. It made a soft pool of light in the darkening room. There was a storm brewing up, and there were rumblings of thunder in the distance.

There was a tap on the door.

I got up to open it, and Mother Shipton stood there with my supper tray.

'It was kind of you to bring it yourself,' I said. 'Won't you come in? I'd like to talk to you.'

I put the tray on my desk. She sat on the low sofa, and I sat in the rocking-chair, facing her.

'I think you've been writing me some letters,' I said.

She did not reply. She sat smoothing her skirt against her knee with her fingers.

'I know you have,' I said.

'How do you know?'

'You typed them on that typewriter there, on the desk, didn't you? It's always puzzled me that they looked strangely familiar in a way that I couldn't identify. It was when I heard you hang up the extension after listening to my last phone conversation that I realized. They were typed on my own typewriter. The 'e' is slightly out of alignment, and it's quite unmistakable.'

'What are you going to do?' she asked.

'How did you know all the things about which you wrote?'

She shrugged.

'It wasn't very difficult, living in this house.'

I suppose that it wasn't. It certainly explained the last letter. It explained knowing about Martin, and she must always have known about Dominic. She probably heard me talking to Martin about Jan. But Toby . . . how did she know about Toby? Listening to our phone calls on the extension, I suppose. And then there was Chris. She couldn't have known about Chris from eavesdropping: he had never rung me at Falconbridge when I was at home.

'What I don't understand is how you knew about Chris,' I said.

'He wrote to you here,' she said.

'I don't remember that.'

'Well, he did, if you think back.'

'I still don't see . . . oh, you steamed open the letter, did you? As well as listening in on the extension to my phone calls?'

She didn't reply.

'But there must have been someone else as well, helping you,' I said. 'Otherwise how did you get the letters posted in London?'

'There was no-one else,' she said.

'But they had London postmarks, there must have been.'

'I go to London frequently, to see my sister, or take boys to the dentist, or the school outfitters. It wasn't difficult.'

I sat watching her, feeling an angry knot of tension inside me. It had started raining heavily, and it was beating down on the roof and lashing at the windows.

'But why?' I said. 'Why did you do it? Did you want to drive me to kill myself? It wasn't the letters that made me try, you know.'

'No, it wasn't that. At least, not until the last one. Then I did wish . . . hope . . .'

'Did you choose a name with my initials deliberately?

236

Are you sure you weren't trying to drive me out of my mind?' I asked.

'You would never understand!' she burst out suddenly. 'Liz might, clever bitch that she is, with her claws in him now. But you couldn't.'

The mention of claws made me think of cats, and I thought she looked feline herself, arching her back and spitting at me. I shut my eyes to block out the sight, but the sound of her voice continued.

'Why should you have everything, have your cake and eat it, never a thought for others – oh no: self first, self second and self last. You had Martin and a job, a home and freedom, money of your own, plenty of friends, you always did exactly as you pleased. It wasn't fair!'

And then her anger seemed to abate, and I opened my eyes and looked at her. For the first time I recognized the frustration that had smouldered unnoticed in her for so many years, had found expression in the letters and had finally erupted in that frenzy of verbal accusation. She was jealous of me. Her life had been spent in depressing dependence on her father, her husband, her son. She had never had the opportunity or the strength of character to break away. Perhaps she longed for the kind of life I had. And maybe while she was sitting at my typewriter composing those hateful letters, for a few brief moments she actually was me.

I realized too that Liz was now the main enemy, the major threat to Mother Shipton's only source of fulfilment, the bond between herself and her son. At that moment, as she stood silently by the window, I felt almost sorry for her.

'What are you going to do?' she asked again, at last.

'Do? What can I do? You're leaving anyway, aren't you? If you hadn't intended to I'm sorry, but you are now. At Christmas.'

'I suppose that I brought it on myself,' she said.

237

'Yes. Literally. If it hadn't been for your letters bringing everything out into the open, Martin wouldn't have gone to a psychiatrist. He met Liz Raine because of Helen Turner.'

She sighed.

'Is there anything else you want?' she asked.

'What? What do you mean?'

She indicated the supper tray.

'Oh . . . no, thank you.'

'Well, I don't think there's anything more to be said,' she said.

And noiseless, catlike, she left the room.

The storm broke, and I sat listening to the thunder and watching the flashes of lightning over the lake, and the rain splashing down on the water in the moonlight. It felt cleansing.

Chapter Twenty-five

THAT WAS MORE than a year ago, now.

Mother Shipton and Martin left Falconbridge at Christmas, and she retired to her sister at Southgate.

The divorce went through in the Spring, and there was no publicity, but Martin hasn't married Liz Raine yet. He has a job at a tutorial college in West London.

The Governors appointed the Headmaster whom Martin had recommended, his wife took charge of the domestic arrangements, and the school continues to run smoothly.

My sister Jan left her girlfriend a couple of weeks after I visited them, and I last heard from her in Greece. Her Renault had broken down in Epidaurus, and she was living with a Greek shepherd.

Chris dropped out of University, and went to live with his girlfriend in the West Country. They grow marijuana and live on the dole.

I haven't seen Toby again at all, but there was a reference to him in *Private Eye* a couple of months ago. He left Jean after all, but not before she had managed to remove every penny from their joint bank account. He was in trouble over a restaurant bill.

And Dominic brought Julien back to Falconbridge last Easter, as he planned. When I saw Julien, it was just like seeing his father again, all those years ago. He looked exactly the same, with the same voice and the same mannerisms.

Julien brought me a note from Pierre, in which Pierre said that he hoped that I would look after his son.

'He has many things to learn, and I would so much like for him to learn them from you: you are accomplished to teach him.' I remembered that Frenchmen sometimes sent their sons to their mistresses for a sentimental education.

So I obligingly applied myself to the task. It is difficult to say who found it the most pleasurable, Julien or me. Of course for me it was an escape into a lost youth, but a delightful one, nonetheless. Julien is returning this summer to spend some more time with me at Falconbridge.

And all because of Helen Turner.

Last night, as I said, I dreamed of a village called Piscop, where once I was happy. It was June, and the poppies looked like splashes of blood in the hedgerows. It was June when it all began. I didn't know it at the time, but from that day onward, my life was destined to be different.